ISBN 978-1-330-74484-0
PIBN 10099824

1 MONTH OF
FREE
READING

at

www.ForgottenBooks.com

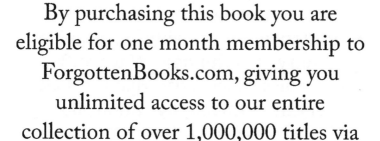

By purchasing this book you are eligible for one month membership to ForgottenBooks.com, giving you unlimited access to our entire collection of over 1,000,000 titles via our web site and mobile apps.

To claim your free month visit: www.forgottenbooks.com/free99824

English
Français
Deutsche
Italiano
Español
Português

www.forgottenbooks.com

Mythology Photography **Fiction**
Fishing Christianity **Art** Cooking
Essays Buddhism Freemasonry
Medicine **Biology** Music **Ancient
Egypt** Evolution Carpentry Physics
Dance Geology **Mathematics** Fitness
Shakespeare **Folklore** Yoga Marketing
Confidence Immortality Biographies
Poetry **Psychology** Witchcraft
Electronics Chemistry History **Law**
Accounting **Philosophy** Anthropology
Alchemy Drama Quantum Mechanics
Atheism Sexual Health **Ancient History**
Entrepreneurship Languages Sport
Paleontology Needlework Islam
Metaphysics Investment Archaeology
Parenting Statistics Criminology
Motivational

ROSE OF
THE WILDERNESS

OR

WASHINGTON'S FIRST LOVE

BY WALTER SCOTT BROWNE

AUTHOR OF ANDREW BENTLEY
Or How He Retrieved His Honor

Published by A. C. Graw, Camden, N. J.

THE ROSE OF
THE WILDERNESS

OR

WASHINGTON'S FIRST LOVE

TAKEN AND REVISED FROM AUTHENTIC SOURCES

BY WALTER SCOTT BROWNE

AUTHOR OF ANDREW BENTLEY
Or How He Retrieved His Honor

Published by A. C. Graw, Camden, N. J.

To one who has proven to be a wise counselor, a faithful and efficient physician, a true and steadfast friend in the hour of sore affliction.

DR. WALDO F. SAWYER

This volume

Is respectfully dedicated.

Vineland, N. J., January   1901.

CONTENTS

Contents

Illustrations

INTRODUCTORY.

The trend of fiction running in the line of works upon the early scenes in our country's history has probably been the incentive that has brought to light the pages of this book.

We have had no diary of by-gone days, but we have gleaned from musty records, out of print in the first half of the past century. Histories of the present day as well as those of early date, have lent their aid in securing data, and where such occurs we have given credit. They have also furnished us scenes and characters familiar to all readers of their pages.

The period through which our story extends antedates that of the Revolution by over a quarter of a century, although some of our characters figured conspicuously in that great struggle for freedom.

We desire to take our readers to that period known in history as "The Inter-colonial Period" when the muttering of a coming struggle might be heard, as the doughty Englishman disputed with the fire-eating Frenchman about boundary lines of a land that was yet the home and hunting-ground of the wily savage, who though ignorant and untutored, could not but draw his own conclusions, and, as history has recorded, well and fitly put forth the query, "If the English claim all on one side of the river, and the French all on the other, where does the Indian's land lie?"

That the character with which our story opens, was a bold, daring frontier settler, is a conceded fact, for the tract of land, at the junction of the waters of a stream known in Western Pennsylvania as Turtle Creek, with those of the Monongahela River, still bears his name.

As the reader progresses, much will be found graphically pictured which history has confined to a mere outline. We trust that in the perusal of these pages, the advancement made by civilization for a century and a half of years will fade from the mental vision of the reader and the scene be looked upon as it was at that time—an undeveloped wilderness, filled with savage beasts of the forest and a no less savage aborigine.   W. S. B.

THE ROSE OF THE WILDERNESS

OR

WASHINGTON'S FIRST LOVE

CHAPTER I.

SEEKING A FORTUNE IN THE "NEW WORLD"

GILBERT FRASIER entered this world near the beginning of the century in which he lived, and somewhere between the town of Colerain and Londonderry in the Emerald Isle where he first saw the light of day.

Whether his father or mother was cousin or forty-second cousin, or no cousin at all to some nobleman does not matter now, nor did it matter then to Gilbert, for he never thought anything about it.

The most important matter of recollection with him, was his marriage which took place on his twenty-first birthday to Nellie Laughlin, a pretty, rosy-checked, fair-skinned Irish lassie with dark

2

eyes and hair, who was a couple of years younger than himself, and whose heart although it was as light and tender as linnet's, had stood nearly a twelve-month siege before it surrendered to his attack.

When the surrender was made it was unconditional, and Gilbert ever afterward found it as fond and faithful as any ardent lover like himself could wish.

And now Gilbert wanted to make his dear Nellie a lady, but was unable from a cause quite prevalent among his countrymen from that day to this, namely, a want of funds.

The fulfillment of the desire nearest his heart put Gilbert into a serious train of thinking, and after much deliberation over the matter the most feasible thing that came into view, as his mental eye swept the horizon of his possibilities was a trip to America in order to make his fortune.

Not that he intended to leave his own country forever, for to the son of Erin there is no land with grass so green or sky so bright, as his own loved Ireland.

And so it was with Gilbert; though he was himself poor, and all the surroundings denoted the most abject poverty, yet to him it was a dear sweet country. He fostered the idea that a few years' sojourn in far-off America, of which he had heard seductive stories, might enable him to return to his native heath and live the remainder of his days like a gentleman.

What fine times it will be for Nellie, thought he, when dressed in silks and laces, she visits her poor cousins, the McLeans and the Finnegans, and gives each of them a handsome present on New Year Day.

So, it was decided that Gilbert should go to this far-off land of promise. But think not my reader that he proposed to go alone, that he be separated from his Nellie; far from it. He would as soon have thought of separating his head from his shoulders.

They

morning in April, 1723; and Gilbert felt as many an Irishman has since felt, on taking the last look upon his native land, that it required all his courage to prevent him from showing his sorrow.

For notwithstanding the expected prosperity that in his imagination awaited him in the Eldorado to which he was going, he felt he was purchasing it dearly by forsaking the land of his birth.

He looked at his wife, as she stood beside him

gazing at the fast receding promontory of Inis-howen, which was the last vestige of dear old Ire-land that she might ever see again.

He perceived that her eyes were red from weep-ing, and although his own heart was filled from the same cause, he thought it was his duty to comfort her; so making up a little doggerel he half whis-pered and half sung it into her ear as she leaned on the guard-rail and looked shoreward. ·

"We need not grieve our dear friends to leave,
For Erin's green fields again we shall see;
But first a fine lady in that land called Pennsylvania,
My dearest remember thou art sure to be."

Whether the promise of being a Pennsylvania lady had the consolatory effect upon his wife that Gilbert intended, we cannot say; but it is certain, that with the exception of a few weeks during which she, like many others on board, labored under the tortures of sea-sickness, she endured a boisterous passage of nearly three months with considerable liveliness and good humor.

At length land was sighted and after a pleasant sail up Delaware Bay and a portion of the river bearing the same name, one Sunday morning they hove to and landed upon the wharf of the then growing city of Philadelphia, and Gilbert with Nellie on his arm and twenty gold guineas in his pocket stepped proudly on shore.

We have no record that at that time he and his lady had to thread their way through the mazes of passing drays and heavily-laden wagons, or that it required the services of blue-coated policemen with an uplifted club to stay the busy throng long enough to allow the passengers from the vessel to reach what is still known as Market street.

The river was not crowded with ferry-boats going to and fro with their loads of humanity, nor the water churned into foam by the steam tugs rushing here and there as you see it now, but all was silent and still on that summer morning, excepting the usual noise and commotion incident to the landing of a vessel.

Gilbert was now in the Land of Promise, where his brightest dreams were about to be realized, where everything he should do would be richly remuncrated, where even the slightest disturbance of the soil would cause it to teem with richness, and the spreading of his hands toward heaven would bring down a shower of gold.

The expectation of Gilbert's may seem to be rather vivid, but it is not overdrawn; nor has Gilbert Frasier been the only immigrant that has landed upon our shores with a congested idea **of** the good fortune in store for him for the **mere** asking.

During the first week after their arrival, Gilbert was in ecstasy.   True, none of the expected riches had yet made their appearance, but he very reasonably ascribed this to his not having made any of the extra exertions necessary to attract them; for he was not a fool to suppose that wealth, ease and comfort would come even in this new land without some effort on his part.

But he felt he could make these extra efforts when they became necessary and, like a true Irishman, he considered his twenty guineas sufficient for all present purposes.

He therefore thought it could not be wrong to enjoy himself in a new country; and as Nellie, who was in a spirit of rejoicing to have her foot on terrafirma, was unusually cheerful and engaging, he could do no less than spend a week or two in showing the dear girl the novelties of the place.

At length his twenty guineas were reduced to ten, and Gilbert, who had a mixture of Scotch blood in him, began to think that he would soon be obliged to do something to prevent their further reduction.

He interviewed several of the citizens of the place, expressing a wish that they would acquaint him with the plan best adapted to the acquirement of wealth.

They greeted his verdancy with looks of surprise, but politely informed him that the only way they knew was to "go to work."

"Worruck!" ejaculated Gilbert, but in a tone so low his auditors did not hear him, for he had prudence enough to perceive that it would not do to affront these people by expressing audibly any feelings of disappointment he might have respecting their country.

"Worruck! an' was it for that, after a' that I left the toon of Maughrygowan, an' cam' owre the ocean, whan I thoucht I wad become a gentleman on me very landin'? Worruck! why what maur need I hae done at hame, than to hae labored for my daily bread?

"Dear me, Nellie, puir lass! is as little likely to become a 'lady in Pennsylvania' as I said in the song I used to sing, than she was in her ain country!"

However, Gilbert was not a man to be cast down by trifles, and as his eyes were now pretty well opened to the condition of things in the new country, and finding his funds every day diminishing, he seriously thought at last of betaking himself to work as he had been advised.

He was young, healthy and active, and really so far as he himself was concerned, he had no partienlar objection to a life of labor, other than that it was a slow way of bringing that affluence that had been the main object of his emigration.

His Nellie, however, was more affected at the thought of his being obliged to earn their living by the sweat of his brow, than Gilbert was.

She became homesick, and for several months inwardly pined after the oat-cakes, the hedge-rows, the green sward, the fairy haunts, and the rural sports of her native land. But her mind, naturally cheerful and elastic, soon recovered its tone, and becoming resigned to her situation, not only encouraged her husband in his industry, but assisted him by her own.

After a short time Gilbert's diligence and good conduct became noted among his neighbors, and several gentlemen of property were heard to speak in his commendation.

But, though resolute and determined to earn a comfortable and honest living, the income from his occupation, which was only that of a common laborer, was far from being sufficient to satisfy his wishes.

He was, also, all the more solicitous to change his employment for one more lucrative, owing to the fact that about this time he became the proud father of a fine son upon whom he bestowed the name of Patrick in honor of his tutelary saint.

Gilbert Frasier had been bred to no mechanical trade, and he had neither inclination nor talents for traffic.

The management of a farm was, therefore, what best suited him; and it was not long after the event just mentioned, that he agreed with a gentleman, who possessed land on the Juniata river a short distance above its junction with the Susquehanna, to remove thither, and cultivate for him a certain number of acres on the shares.

Gilbert resided upon this place about ten years, and by dint of energy and industry had prospered to such an extent, that he felt himself able to make its owner a proposal for the purchase of the land.

But an unforseen event occurred, which put an end to all his calculations of being a possessor of real estate in that locality.

A formidable party of Indians descending the river made an attack upon the white settlers in the valley, pillaged and despoiled their homes, destroying whatever came in their way, and carrying off as prisoners upwards of twenty families, and among them that of the unhappy Gilbert.

He was the father at his time of three children, two sons and a daughter, who, with their mother and himself, were carried rapidly for more than two hundred miles, over a pathless wilderness, covered in many places with a dense gloomy forest, corresponding in wildness to the savage prowlers on whose barbarous caprice their very existence was depending.

We will not elaborate upon the ills incident to a journey like this, to a helpless woman and children, subject to the cruelties of a heartless band of savages. The threats, the barbarities, the indignity heaped upon them by their cruel captors, the tears, lamentations, and actual sufferings of the captives, many of whom, during their rapid and cruel march, died of their wounds or ill treatment, can be as easily imagined as described.

The party at last arrived at an Indian town on the banks of the Allegheny river, called Catanyan, on the site of the now prosperous town of Kittanning.

Here a council of the chiefs and other great men

of the several tribes in the neighborhood met, in order to deliberate upon the fate of the prisoners.

Among this assemblage, Gilbert was surprised to observe five or six white men in military dress, but differing in style and decoration from any he had ever seen before. He was strongly inclined to believe them to be Europeans, the only thing which caused grave doubts about the matter, was their speaking neither English, Irish nor Dutch, the only European language of which he had any knowledge.

His doubts were, however, removed by one of his fellow-prisoners, whose knowledge was more extensive than his own, informing him that these military men were French officers, who were now exploring the country, and forming alliances with the Indian tribes.

His fellow-captive informed him that the presence of these men might be advantageous to the prisoners, as they would no doubt make exertions to save as many as they could, from that cruel fate, which in all probability would befall them if the Indians were permitted to exercise their own will and desire.

Accordingly it so happened, for cut of a party of about seventy unfortunates gathered in, there were only five selected to be burned at the stake, and twenty or more to run the gauntlet.

It was Gilbert's fate to be one of the latter; but he underwent the ordeal courageously, and being "brave and supple," as he himself phrased it, he reached the goal with the infliction of only a few bruises, which broke neither blood vessel nor bone.

A few days afterward the greater number of the prisoners were marched off, as Gilbert afterward learned, to Canada.

With regard to himself, he, together with his wife and children, was permitted to remain at the Catanyan town, even after all the other families were sent off, some of them being separated and sent far from each other in different directions.

This was a favor that puzzled him no little, but at the same time gave him all the greater joy as it was unexpected.

Nellie, whose mind had become greatly depressed on account of their misfortunes, soon began to recover her serenity, and especially so since she was permitted to enjoy the society of her husband and her children; she thought it ungrateful to repine at that Providence which had been so much kinder to her than to so many others of her companions in misfortune.

Gilbert's mind, also, took a pious turn on this occasion, so that both husband and wife felt, in their adversity, a disposition to religious exercises, to which, during the period of their prosperity, they had been strangers.

Although Gilbert and his family had been exempt from many of the severities which they saw inflicted upon many of their fellow-prisoners, their minds were still much disturbed with fears for their safety, for they knew not how soon capricious minds, like their captors possessed, would prompt them to torment and perhaps to destroy them.

But the same religious feelings which made them thankful to heaven for the reprieve they had already obtained, inspired them also with hope of continued protection and final deliverance.

Gilbert's mind was not so engrossed with his own concerns as to be forgetful of the sufferings and fate that had befallen his companions. He was at a loss to know why some, who to all appearance had been devout and more attentive to religious exercises than he had ever thought of being, were faring so much worse than himself.

"Ah, me, it is a wonderfu' thing," said he to Nellie, "to think how they were permitted to burn that holy man, Matthew Morrison, that they say never missed makin' family worship three times a day since he began hoose-keepin', yet to owrelook a neglictfu' member o' the kirk like me, an' no sa muckle as brak' a bane in my body!"

"Matthew Morrison was fit for heaven, an' the Lord took him," was Nellie's reply; "but He has gi'en ye time to repint."

In this manner did Gilbert and his wife frequently converse and encourage each other, and although their minds were much burdened with fears and doubts, they were still supported by the kindly influence of piety and hope.

It was not long, however, before Gilbert discovered the agent to whom, under Providence, he was indebted for the favorable consideration he had received from the Indians.

A French officer came one day to his tent, and to his great surprise addressed him in English.

"I have been the means," said he, "of preventing you and your family from being sent to Canada, and I wish a favor in return."

"A favor, your honor!" replied Gilbert, who instantly felt the workings of gratitude in his heart. "A favor-ay! that you shall have; only tell me how I maun do it, an' I'll rin the worl' owre, to oblige ye."

"I do not wish to send you quite so far," replied the officer, "but if you have no objection to part with your wife for a few weeks, it will please me much, for I have occasion to need her services in behalf of another."

At this Gilbert bent his head and looked somewhat glum, seeing which, the officer apparently changing his mind, remarked: "No, I will not separate you from her; I'll obtain permission for you and the children to accompany her and you will all be as secure there as here."

"An' where do you want us to gang? An' what do ye want wi' Nellie?" asked Gilbert in a half fearful tone.

The officer perceived the state of his feelings, and with a smile replied: "I shall answer your questions frankly. It is a lady, my own wife, who wishes at present for the society and attendance of a white woman. She is about to become a mother, and is unfortunately surrounded by Indians, and to the presence of her female Indian companions she has a pronounced aversion.

"When I perceived your wife among the prisoners, a married woman, the mother of children, and of decent and respectable demeanor, I at once conceived that she would make a suitable companion for my wife under present circumstances; and therefore I successfully exerted myself to prevent your being sent with the other prisoners.

"As to where I wish to send you.   My wife is at present under the protection of an Indian Queen, who resides on the banks of the Monongahela, a large river about forty miles distant."

During this statement the countenance of both Gilbert and his wife brightened, which evinced to the officer sufficient to satisfy him that they would comply with his wishes.

"We will attend ye, sir," replied Gilbert, instinctively reaching for his hat, of which the Indians had not deprived him, and which now lay on a short log, used inside the tent for a seat.

Nellie also assured him of the care and zeal with which she would serve his wife, in return for the kindness that had been shown them.

The next morning, therefore, the officer accompanied them to the residence of Queen Alliquippa, a short distance above the mouth of a stream called Turtle Creek, near the Monongahela River.

CHAPTER II.

FOUNDING A HOME IN THE WILDERNESS

QUEEN Alliquippa, whose blood is stated by the ancient chronicles, lately fished up from the bottom of the Monongahela, to have been as purely royal as a descent of upwards of forty generations could make it, received them with the true dignity of a queen, presenting each with a string of beads made of red berries, in token of her royal favor.

She was seated on a conveniently formed block of wood, covered with a neat mat, in the outer apartment of the wigwam, for this edifice, differing from most others of its kind, had two apartments instead of the usual one. The additional room had been constructed at the request of the French officer for the convenience of his wife.

But a word descriptive of this Indian queen: She was a widow, still young and considered handsome. Her manners united dignity with affability, and her personal attractions had lately induced several chiefs and great men to solicit her hand in marriage.

At the present time, her most encouraged lover was King Shingiss, a young warrior whose residence was on the south bank of the Ohio, about two miles below the confluence of the Allegheny and the Monongahela, and it was so confidently believed that he would be the favored one, that all the others had relinquished their suit.

Alliquippa was fond of admiration, but like many of her sex, among her pale-faced sisters, while she encouraged her suitors she managed to keep clear of a husband.

King Shingiss was much devoted to her, and she contrived to keep alive his hopes so long that he never sought any other for a wife, and after a courtship of many years, he died a bachelor.

Her tribe was called the Shannoahs, and was in complete and satisfied subjection to her authority, which she was resolved neither to depute nor divide with any one.

She was dressed, when Gilbert and his family were introduced to her, in a rather showy costume. A kind of diadem made of the red feathers of the flamingo plaited together, encircled her brow, and, in some places seemed to be fancifully enwreathed with her hair which was very abundant and of a glossy jet color.

A large, splendid crystal hung pendant from each ear; and from her neck, which was bare, hung a glittering chain of variegated beads.

A kind of gown or wrapper fabricated from a large silk shawl, which had been a present from the French officer's lady, covered her body from the breast downwards, being suspended from the shoulder by straps of beaver skin, so constructed as to have the fur on both sides.

This garment was also fastened around the waist by a beautiful fur belt of various colors secured with silver clasps; light colored moccasins of deer skin covered her feet, and completed an arrangement of dress of which Alliquippa was as proud as ever Queen Elizabeth was of her court-day robes.

The ceremony of introduction to her Shannoah majesty being over, she addressed the French officer as follows:

"My brother, I am glad you have come back so soon. My sister—your wife—was cast down in your absence.

"But I could not blame her, for I remember when Shanalow, my husband, went first to hunt, after our marriage, I was disconsolate and dreamed every night of evil until he returned.

"He is now gone to his fathers and shall never

more return, but he died of a breast-wound fighting the Ottawas, and our whole tribe has praised
him.

"Brother! you did well to bring these people;
your wife will be better pleased with a woman of
the east, than with my squaws. At another time
you may tell me why the rising sun gives a fairer
skin than the setting sun.

"Brother! I shall order provisions for your people, but your wife desires your presence. I hope
you will be free to tell me all your wants, and use
my wigwam and people as your own."

The officer made a courteous reply, bowed and
made haste to seek the side of his wife.

Nellie soon became attached to the officer's lady
who was, indeed, as sweet and lovely a woman as
ever the sun shone on. They had at first some difficulty in understanding each other's discourse, for
the lady who was a French woman, spoke but imperfect English; and with respect to Nellie's English, she scarce knew one word in ten.

But minds that are disposed to accommodate
each other soon overcome difficulties of this kind,
and it was not long before the French lady and
Nellie contrived to be both mutually intelligible
and agreeable to each other.

As to Gilbert, his habits of industry while he resided on the Juniata, rendered his present prospect of idleness irksome, but perceiving at the juncture of Turtle Creek with the Monongahela, a suitable place for building a log cabin, which he thought would be a more convenient and suitable residence for his family and the French lady, than the Indian wigwams, he accordingly proposed to the officer to erect one, declaring that with the aid of a few Indians with axes, he could erect within a week a far more comfortable edifice than any wigwam.

The officer gladly acceded to the proposal, and procured from Alliquippa, not only permission for Gilbert to build the house, but also a grant to him of several hundred acres of land lying in that locality.

Gilbert was delighted with the friendliness of the officer and the Indian queen, and at once commenced building his house, and as the queen directed a number of her Indians to assist him, it was completed in a shorter time, and more comfortable style, than the officer conceived to be possible.

His lady was conveyed into it; but in a few days, her husband's joy at finding her so comfortably lodged, was turned into grief and distraction by her death in giving life to another.

On the first intelligence of this event, he sank to the earth overpowered with anguish; but recovering his muscular energy he suddenly arose, hastened to the side of his beloved, and pressed her cold form to his bosom in an agony of sorrow.

Tears gushed from his eyes, while to all appearance he became more calm. He asked to see his child, which Nellie brought forward. He kissed it with convulsive fervor, and again burst into tears.

Turning to Gilbert he said, "This has been a dreadful blow to me, and the loss of my lovely wife is more than I can bear. I need not now recount her virtues, her loveliness, her tenderness.

"The world has nothing for me now! But what will become of this tender plant? Oh! Mrs. Frasier! I beseech you, will you not be a mother to it, for it now has none?

"And you, my friend!" and here he caught Gilbert by the hand, "take the place of its unhappy father, who is now unfit to look after it." With this he ran to one of his wife's trunks, and returning said, "Here, take this," and he cast upon the table a purse filled with gold. "And whatever else these trunks contain, use it to support my child; bury my wife decently. Oh, my Father! her grave will be here in the lonely wilderness, but her soul is with thee in heaven." He again sought the side of his dead wife and embraced her inanimate form tenderly, saying, "Farewell! farewell!" Then he hastened from the house and was soon lost in the forest.

Alliquippa, who was much distressed by this occurrence, herself attended, and ordered a number of her tribe to assist at the funeral of her deceased friend, which they readily did; so that Gilbert had the satisfaction to see the remains of this unfortunate lady deposited in the earth in as decent and respectable a manner as the circumstances of time and place would permit.

As for the infant whom Providence had thus thrown upon his care, he was resolved to do for it as a father, and cherish for it a father's affection and care. Consulting his wife, he found her not only ready to approve, but solicitous to perform every benevolent wish he had conceived in its favor.

They named the little orphan Marie, this being the name of its dead mother, and Gilbert and Nellie resolved that they would esteem and care for it as their own offspring.

It was now a matter of much deliberation with Gilbert and his wife, whether they would remain where they were, or endeavor to obtain permission from the Indians to return to their former home on the Juniata.

"I canna weel tell, Nellie," said he, "what's best to be done.   Gin we stay here, we may ne'er see the face o' a gospel Christian again, unless it may be some blackguard trader, drappin' ance or twice a year doon the river, to cheat the Indians o' their furs.   I ne'er liked them traders; it's their cheating that mak's the Indians sae wicked against the white people."

"An what's the warst o' it," remarked Nellie, "if we stay here, we'll no see a worshippin' congregation in a hale lifetime."

"But we can worship as the Bible directs in oor ain family," replied her husband, "for Joshua said, that he an' his hoose should serve the Lord, an' ye remember what oor minister at the Juniata has aften said, that if we seek the Lord sincerely at oor ain fireside, he will be foon' there as readily as in a temple.

"Besides, I fear muckle whether the savages will gie us leave to gang back; an' ye ken it's an unco road."

"Ah! I weel ken that," said she, "it's na road ava.   In Ireland we had better through the peat bogs."

"Ah, dinna talk of Ireland," replied Gilbert, heaving a sigh; "it makes my heart sair ilka time it's named," and there was perceptible moisture in his blue eye.

After some moments of silence he again broke forth, "An' I have been a thinkin', Nellie, it were better to bide here a bit, as we may hae a chance to hear frae, or may be see, oor wee helpless Marie's father, gin he be in the lan' o' the leevin'."

"Ye're quite richt, Gilbert; puir wee Marie!" Here Nellie lifted the object of her condolence in her arms and kissed it.

"Gilbert, I think it wad be wrang to gang aff. The gentleman may coom again, an' he may want his dochter, an' wadna' ken where to find her if she were gane."

"It's a' true," replied her husband; "an' ye ken the place on the Juniata was nae oor ain either, an' the place has been a ruined, so, on the puir bairn's account, I think we had as good content oorsels.

"I'll e'en try to fence awee, an' chap wood, an' put sime things in order to mak' us leevin-like through the winter; an' wi' the blessing of God, we'll try to be content an' thankfu'."

It was now that Gilbert set about to establish a permanent home in the wilds of Western Pennsylvania ; and his persevering industry, in a short time, created the smiling fields of a productive farm around him, which in a few years attached him so much to the place, that he abandoned all thoughts of ever leaving it.

Alliquippa and her Indians continued friendly to him, and occasionally assisted him in the heavier exertions which his improvements required.

But they never seemed to care to imitate by making comfortable homes for themselves.

They were now almost entirely occupied in planning and executing predatory and ofttimes bloody attacks upon the frontier settlements of the British colonists, who with wonderful hardihood were every year encroaching more and more beyond that mountainous region, which formed the barrier that seemed to exist between the eastern and western portions of the continent, and to which the Indians seemed resolved if possible to confine the white settlers.

History informs us that the French, who at this time claimed the whole of Western America, from Quebec to New Orleans, were now very industrious in urging upon the Indians to restrain the rapid progress the British settlements were making in that direction.

The savage warriors had, besides this, other inducements to urge them in lifting the hatchet against the adventurous frontier settlers.

These settlers, instead of attempting to soothe and conciliate the red man whose heritage they were gradually appropriating to themselves, treated the Indian, ofttimes unnecessarily, as an enemy, and always repaid blood with blood, and outrage with outrage.

But while there were exceptional cases where the feeling between the settler and his dusky neighbor was a friendly one, in which the Indian respected the rights of his white brother, the general feeling existing between the two races was that of enmity and hatred.

CHAPTER III.

DEVELOPMENT OF BEAUTY IN THE WILDERNESS

LTHOUGH separated from the Christian world, as Gilbert Frasier conceived himself to be, he possessed many comforts, for which he was truly thankful.

His farm had advanced yearly in improvement, and increased in productiveness, and being for years the only cultivator of the soil for many miles around him, and living convenient to a navigable river, which was even at that early date a considerable thoroughfare to those adventurous spirits who traded with the Indians, he could always find, without any difficulty, ready purchasers for his surplus produce.

With respect to security of both life and property, he felt quite at ease.

He knew that Alliquippa and her lover Shingiss were both his friends and declared protectors; beside his own inoffensive conduct, and his useful industry and occupation, from which, at one time or other, all classes of the neighboring Indians had derived some benefit, had interested them in his prosperity, and created a feeling of attachment that would have led them to resent any injustice done him by any of the neighboring tribes.

In regard to his children, his family increased in years, but did not in numbers, save the addition of the infant Marie, who was looked upon with strong affection by the entire family.

His eldest son, Patrick, was soon able to be of some assistance in the farming to which he applied himself industriously until he reached the age of eighteen, when, being of a restless disposition, and far more shrewd and daring than his father, he manifested love for traffic rather than labor; and, contrary to his father's wishes, spent much of his time in rambling over the country, and dealing with both Indians and white people, as chance gave him opportunity.

By this time, however, his younger brother, who was called Dennis, but more often by the endearing name of Denny, was able to fill his place on the farm, so the father's industry suffered but little inconvenience from the defection of his first-born.

His daughter, whose name was Leonora, was the youngest of his three children, and but one year older than the little orphan, Marie, whom Providence, as we have seen, had thrown upon his care and affection.

Leonora grew up to be a handsome young lady, the picture of health and good humor. She was a frank, honest girl, with no conception of the busy outside world, which she would have been well adapted to enjoy, had this been her prerogative, but in blissful ignorance of what lay beyond the confines of her humble home, she roamed the woods in safety without fear of a betrayer and in the full enjoyment of a true child of the forest.

Such was the companion from infancy of the heroine of our story, lovely Marie Frasier, for such we must for the present call the little orphan, who had been taught to look upon our friends, Gilbert and his wife, Nellie, as her only parents, upon whom she always bestowed the endearing name of father and mother.

Although in their persons both these young women were highly attractive, their attractions differed both in kind and degree. Miss Leonora was of the Saxon type, fair-haired and blue-eyed, with a regularity of features. She was, perhaps, rather robust and stout in her appearance to suit the general idea of symmetrical beauty; yet, to many tastes, her plumpness and vigor were more pleasing than otherwise. Her manners might be considered by the exacting as being forward, but this was fully atoned for by her innocence, archness and vivacity.

As for her companion, Marie, she was in her bearing and manner, modesty without coldness, delicacy without affectation, and affability without obtrusiveness.

Her person was more inclined to that slender form of nymph-like beauty, always admired, yet possessing that solidity and roundness indicative of a healthy and sound constitution.

Her motions and gestures were natural and graceful. As to the charms of her countenance, it was as full of magical attraction at the age of seventeen as liquid black eyes, shaded by thick silken eye-lashes, surmounted by a white polished forehead, with the damask bloom of her cheeks, and the coral of her lips, all combined could effect; and to this were added the dark ringlets profusely flowing around her fair temples and falling upon a snowy, swan-like neck, which impressed those who beheld her with that "inexpressible somewhat" which no iciness of heart could resist, and made her the delight, as well as the admiration of all who beheld this "Rose of the Wilderness."

Such as we have described, were the two flowers that had grown into beautiful bloom in the home of Gilbert Frasier.

But they also differed in their natural aptitude and relish for acquiring knowledge.

To Leonora the labor of study was an irksome task, while her sister Marie ever courted it as her chief delight.

It will be naturally supposed that this inclination for learning must necessarily have been greatly restricted; but a means had been furnished by Providence to a greater extent than could have been expected in so dense a wilderness.

A singular old man, named Tonnawingo, whom the Indians regarded as a prophet, frequently made his residence with Queen Alliquippa's people for several months at a time, and as this was in the vicinity of the home of the Frasier's, he took great delight in teaching Gilbert's children, and especially seemed interested in giving instruction to Marie, for he saw the child was so anxious to receive it.

Gilbert, upon their first acquaintance, expressed his astonishment that such a variety and extent of information was in the possession of an Indian; but he was informed by the old prophet, that he had in

his early youth imbibed a great thirst for knowledge; in consequence of which, he had run away
from his tribe, who had opposed his desires for
study, and he had traveled for several years through
the towns of New England, where he studied the
English language, and became acquainted with
various sciences.

"From thence," said he, "I visited Canada to
learn what I might be able of French. There I
learned to speak the French language. The Governor at his own expense placed me at a seminary,
with the intention of qualifying me to act as an
emissary among the Indian tribes whom he wished
to secure as allies to the interests of his country.

"My friends received me kindly upon my return
and forgave my leaving them, as they said it was
the promptings of the Great Spirit that I might ac-
quire knowledge to direct them in their affairs with
the white people.

"But strange they will not permit me to teach
any of their young people the sciences I have
learned, saying, 'If it were useful for their young
men and young women to know these things, the
Great Spirit would communicate it first to them as
their fathers.'

"However, they give me credit for my knowledge, and most all the tribes consult me in all their undertakings and generally follow my directions.

"But I do not wish my knowledge to be useless; I wish to communicate it, and since the children of my own people will not hear my lessons, I am glad that yours will."

The reader may wish to know how the old prophet came to learn of Gilbert's interesting family.

It happened about two years after Gilbert's settlement upon the Monongahela, and under the following circumstances.

His son Patrick, or Paddy as he was usually called, who was then about twelve years of age, had gone one day into a deep glen or defile, about a mile from home, in search of some cows that had been missing, and not finding them, he amused himself by climbing up the precipitous rocks, which formed the sides of the glen, when happening to make a misstep, he fell from a considerable height and broke one of his legs.

His cries brought to his side the old Indian, who was in the forest nearby, who immediately placed the unfortunate boy upon his shoulders, and carried him home, where with great dexterity of skill he proceeded to set the limb and place the boy in as comfortable a condition as possible.

Gilbert had of late heard of this Tonnawingo, and on one occasion, a few weeks before, had seen him, but had never spoken to him.

Grateful now for the services he had rendered his son, he invited him to frequent his house, and enjoy his hospitality, whenever he should visit the neighborhood.

"We'll maybe no' treat you in your ain way, wi' roasted venison, an' sic loike, although we kill a deer noo an' then; for we ha' leev'd unco muckle in the Indian fashion, this twa year back; but homsumever, come an' see us, my freen, an' we'll aye mak' ye welcome to a share o' what's gaun."

"My brother," said Tonnawingo, "whenever I have occasion, I will accept your kind offer, but I want you to know I do not accept it as pay for carrying home and attending your injured son.

"A virtuous Indian will receive no return from men for an act like this. If he did, the Great Spirit might refuse to give him that reward which he expects when he dies; for He rewards everyone who is not rewarded here, a hundred fold better than either Indian or white man can.

"My brother, hearken to me. I will take you as my friend, I will eat at your table, for I have been taught to use the instruments employed in eating
b the nations of th as

"I will take pleasure in attending to the wants of your son, for the great Maralooma has imparted to me some skill in bone-setting."

He was faithful to his promise, and waited daily upon his patient for several weeks until a cure was perfectly accomplished.

It was during these visits that this Indian sage became attached to Gilbert's little girls, and that he resolved to act as their tutor.

He also extended his instruction to the boys; but the chief object of his labors in that direction was little Marie, who, although the youngest, soon showed herself the most capable and willing to profit by his instruction; and thus a bond of friendship was cemented.

There was another copious source of information within Marie's reach, of which the instruction of her friendly perceptor enabled her to avail herself.

This was a small but well selected collection of books of both English and French literature, found in one of the trunks belonging to her mother, which the reader will remember her father mentioned to our friend Gilbert on the sad day of the death of the child's mother.

She was soon taught to read and understand French authors, almost as easily as the English.

She valued the books all the more, as the prophet Tonnawingo, whom she esteemed as a second father, was often called away on business of the tribes with whom he was connected.

On such occasions he was obliged to be absent for many months at a time, during which she generally felt as much solicitude for his safety as if he had been some near and dear relative.

Next to Tonnawingo, and the members of her own family, Marie's greatest favorite and most agreeable associate was Queen Alliquippa.

This Indian lady had always manifested for her a strong affection, to which no doubt the melancholy circumstances connected with her birth gave rise, but which the maiden's own endearing sweetness, loveliness, and good nature, strengthened as the years went by, and which finally became a sincere and permanent attachment. In consequence of this intimacy with Queen Alliquippa, Marie obtained a considerable knowledge of the language spoken by the Indians of her tribe.

Thus, notwithstanding this young lady was reared in the heart of a vast and trackless forest amid the savage tribes, yet Providence had not only

protected her childhood from injury, but had, almost miraculously, afforded her such means of cultivation of mind, as in a great measure supplied the
wants of a more regular and finished education.

Thus we find this young lady approaching wo-
manhood with all the endowment of mind, and
charm of person, like unto a richly developed rose
of rare perfume which eminently qualified her to
adorn and delight the most polished society in civilized life.

CHAPTER IV.

A REVELATION

THUS until about her seventeenth year, did the life of Marie Frasier pass along in an unruffled and undisturbed stream of content and satisfaction.

No misfortune had occurred to herself or friends of such importance as to occasion any lasting impression of grief upon her mind.

She had about reached this age, when the first unpleasant experience of a lasting nature came upon her.

Of the history of her birth she had hitherto been kept in ignorance, and had never entertained the least suspicion that Gilbert and his wife (who had always treated her with the most affectionate indulgence), were not her parents.

Alliquippa's attachment to her was the cause of her now becoming acquainted with the truth. This Indian princess, who was advancing in years, was childless, and had for some time past, unknown to Marie, cherished a strong desire to adopt her for a daughter.

She had once or twice expressed her wish to Gilbert, but could not procure his consent. She thought, however, that her favorite was now sufficiently old enough to act for herself.

She, therefore, one day as they conversed together in her wigwam, unexpectedly addressed Marie as follows:

"My daughter, hear me! and think seriously on what I am going to say.

"Nature has not made me thy mother, but affection for you has long ago told me that it would have been well had she done so; for had you been of my own blood, I could not have loved you more strongly than I do, or felt more interested in your welfare.

"Daughter, our customs enable me, in this case to correct nature. You are already the child of my heart.

"I wish to make you the child of my adoption. If you consent I shall call the heads of my tribe together, that they may confirm my purpose."

This unexpected proposal both astonished and confused Marie so much that she could not at once reply.

Alliquippa therefore continued: "My child listen again! I see you are perplexed. Perhaps you do not love me so much as I thought, or, perhaps you may be unwilling to live in this wigwam, after my manner.

"My child, listen to me! If you become my daughter, you will be honored by our tribe. Kings and Sachems will desire you in marriage; you will, if you choose, have the privilege of rejecting them, and yet keep them in subjection as I did. Or, as Shannalow, the eagle of his tribe, gained me in marriage, so may some great warrior gain you, and make you happy in his love, and joyful in his renown.

"You have heard me, my child! Will you become my daughter?"

Marie was still much perplexed for a reply. She was resolved to refuse, but she feared to offend.

She felt she must say something; and she endeavored to express her refusal in terms as little offensive as possible.

"Mother," said she, for thus she always addressed her, "I have heard your proposal which is the result of kindness to me.

"It excites gratitude in my heart, and although I cannot become your daughter, for I have parents to whom I owe a child's affection and duty, yet I love you as much as though I were your own daughter."

"My child, hear me! I believe you love me, but hearken to a truth. It is right you should hear it.

"What parents have you in the world nearer to you than I am? None! Or is there one that loves you better? None. Gilbert Frasier is not your father, nor is his wife your mother, as you have supposed.

"Alas! she who bore you, died in giving you birth. What! my child! Be not surprised. Oh, do not tremble so! I did not wish to give you pain. Oh! Spirit of Maneto! save my child!"

Here Alliquippa sprang forward and caught Marie, who appeared to be in a faint and falling from her seat.

Her countenance had turned deathly pale, and sensation for a moment forsook her. She, however, recovered gradually, but it was several minutes before she could collect her senses sufficiently to speak distinctly concerning the strange news she had received.

When she could control her voice she addressed Alliquippa. "My mother, I have indeed heard that which distresses me.

"I will not ask you to tell me the whole story.

I will ask it of my father. But, no, I think you said I had no father. Ah! was I dreaming? Or am I really an orphan?"

"My child," replied the queen, "Alliquippa never told a lie. What I said was the truth. The great Father is your only parent, but he is a good one; and he has given you many friends who love you.

"Hearken further. I wish you to be my daughter, because I have no child, and you have no parent, and because I love you, and I believe you love me.

"But my brother, Gilbert Frasier, and my sister, his wife, love you also, and have been good to you.

"They are of your own race, and you may not wish to leave them for a mother of a red color. But, child, I wish to speak plainly; follow your own inclinations.

"If you become my daughter, I shall be glad. If not, you can still be my friend, and I shall be satisfied."

For these generous sentiments, Marie felt, and expressed a sincere gratitude to the Indian queen, and bidding her an affectionate farewell, returned home, with a mind more disturbed and oppressed by melancholy reflection than she had ever before experienced.

Upon her return, her agitation was so apparent that it was observed by the affectionate Nellie, who felt for her all the anxious solicitude of a real parent.

"What ails you, Marie?" said she. "I doot something's wrang; my bairn, are you no weel?"

"No, my kind mother," she replied, "I am not well; but it is my heart alone that is sick. Alas, that heart feels a debt of gratitude which it will never be able to repay."

"Why, my child," said Nellie, surprised at such a remark, "what's come owre ye? That's strange talk indeed! I doot some o' these books ye're aye readin' hae put ye crazy. I often tauld ye it was wrang to study sae muckle.

"Tak' mair divarsion, an' sport yoursel', like Leonora, for it vexes your puir mother to see you sae."

"My mother, do you say?" cried Marie, almost unconsciously. "Ah, would to heaven you were my mother, then you would not see me now so unhappy."

"Would I were your mother?" repeated the alarmed Nellie. "Did ony body ever hear the like o' that?

"Why ye ken, I hae aye been your mother, yes

an' I aye will be your mother, for ye hae aye been a gude bairn to me. Dinna cry noo, my bonny jewel, dinna cry sae. Some yen foul o' tongue hae told ye some ill story to vex you. But dinna mind them, my bairn, ye hae aye been my ain, an' aye ye will be my ain."

So saying, she kissed Marie, who was weeping bitterly, and with her handkerchief wiped the tears from the sorrowing girl's eyes, while at the same time the moisture was breaking from her own.

"Tell me, my bonnie lamb, what vexes ye sae, for I canna bear to see ye cryin' this way."

Marie grasped her hand; she looked into her countenance and saw that her heart was full, and she could not increase its sorrow by disclaiming that tender relationship she had hitherto believed to exist.

Impulsively she cried, "Yes, I feel that you are my mother, and the best of mothers, and shall still be so, though I have been told you were not."

"An' wha was sae hard-hearted as to tell you sae, my puir bairn? Shame fa' their ill tongues; could they no' hae been better employed than to blab oot what can noo do naebody gude to hear?"

"Ah, then what I have heard is true, my mother!

Oh, I must still call you so, though I fear I have no right."

"Nae richt, Marie, my ain, so lang my ain wean? Who dare tak' the richt frae ye to ca' me mother? Sair day it will be to me when ye cease to do sae."

"Yes, you have been the tender protector of my infancy, and the affectionate supporter of my childhood, and I never can, and never shall, think of you in any other light than that of a parent."

They now embraced, and felt a confidence and comfort, springing up in their hearts that soon restored them to tranquillity and cheerfulness.

Marie then informed her mother of Queen Alliquippa's proposal to adopt her as her daughter, and of the account she had given her of the loss of her parents.

Nellie, in return, acquainted her with all the circumstances connected with her birth, of which the reader is already informed.

She ended her narrative by remarking: "Your father an' I would hae tauld you this lang syne, but we feared it wad be an unco trial, an' ye micht hae thought we did it frae unkindness. But ye canna say so noo.

"The trial's owre; an' I am glad o't, an' I hope

in God the Great Parent o' us a' that he'll keep us a' happy for a lang time tigether."

Her perceptor, Tonnawingo, had been for several months absent at the time Marie received the intelligence of her state of orphanage; and her tranquillity of mind had been considered restored before his return.

His acute penetration, however, soon discovered that something had taken place since he last saw her, to disturb that cheerfulness and vivacity of disposition which she had always displayed, and which he knew was her natural disposition.

He mentioned his suspicion, and without hesitation she told him the truth.

"My daughter,' said he, "you do wrong to grieve for conditions which you cannot change or recall, and which no fault of your own has produced.

"You say you have no kindred, but you only mean such kindred as have been called so, by the customs of the world. These it may sometimes be a comfort to have, but it is not always a misfortune to want; for the faults of a man's kindred often reflect upon him their evil consequences, when he himself is blameless.

"But, daughter, you have kindred. The Father of the world has given us all a common origin.

"We have all sprung from Himself, and every one you see is, therefore, your relative, whether white man or Indian. Such is the unchangeable law of nature, and so long as you act justly and uprightly towards these, your relatives, they are in duty bound by that same unchangeable law, to honor, respect, and protect you.

"And now, my daughter, I would say to you, be satisfied with your lot. God has given you kind and loving protectors, in my brother Frasier and his wife; and have I not been to you the father of instruction, and can you think me less than a father in affection, or that I shall ever see you in misfortune and not step forth to relieve you?

"Daughter, be of good cheer. Your blessings are many; you have health, understanding and knowledge, loving friends on earth, and a kind and loving Father in heaven."

CHAPTER V.

ABOUT two years after Marie Frasier had learned of her state of orphanage, an event took place, which had an important influence upon her destiny.

Shortly after the treaty of Aix--la-Chapelle, at the close of the war known in history as King George's War, in which the boundary lines of the British and French domains in America were still left undecided, the British Government claiming an unlimited extent of territory in the west, granted a large tract of land, situated about the head-waters of the Ohio river, to a number of noblemen and wealthy merchants, who associated themselves together under the title of "The Ohio Company."

This company, which was formed somewhere about the year 1750, contemplated territorial as well as commercial advantages, and employed several adventurous individuals to explore the country with a view to its settlement.

They soon learned that the French, who also

5

made pretensions of a claim to this part of the country, would resist any British settlement that should be attempted.

But "The Ohio Company," nothing daunted, and persistent in their designs of forming a settlement, in the year 1752, resolved to send out a party and take formal possession, and erect a fort on the southwest side of the Ohio near Chartier's creek, about three miles below the present site of Pittsburg.

Thomas Addison, Esq., a wealthy merchant of Philadelphia, and a director of the company, was one of the chief promoters of this enterprise.

He was a native of Ireland, and of the same neighborhood as our friend Gilbert Frasier. This gentleman had an only son named Charles, born shortly after his arrival in Philadelphia, which was in 1730.

Being very solicitous about this young man's education, he had, when the boy was about fifteen years of age, sent him to Europe where he studied for five years at Trinity College, Dublin, and spent another year in traveling over the British Islands, and several parts of the European continent.

After an absence of six years, he returned to Philadelphia, only a few months previous to the fitting out of the aforementioned expedition to the Ohio.

Being a young man of an enterprising disposition and inquiring mind, he felt a strong desire to explore the western wilderness, and learn the language and customs of the Indian tribes.

He communicated his wishes to his father, and requested permission to avail himself of the favorable opportunity offered to him of gratifying them, by joining the intended expedition.

His father perceiving that an expedition of this kind would add to his son's stock of already valuable knowledge, granted his request, and as Charles' education, talents and courage, were well known, he had no difficulty in getting him placed at the head of the expedition.

At the time Charles Addison undertook the management of this enterprise, which was one, in those days, not only novel, but full of daring and danger, he was in his twenty-second year, and as accomplished, active, and handsome a young man as any lady would wish to behold.

His stature wanted but one inch of six feet.   His features were well formed and expressive, glowing with benevolence, and animated with good nature.

His eyes were dark, intelligent and penetrating.

His hair black and inclined to curl, while his complexion had the ruddy hue of an Irishman. He was brave, courageous and strong, and in every way eminently qualified to command the expedition.

A journey from Philadelphia to the Ohio river, at the period of which we are writing, was quite a different thing from what it is now.

At the present day there is nothing to obstruct the traveler in making a trip so speedily that it is not entirely robbed of pleasure, except it might be the annoyance of a badly supplied purse or the extremes of heat or cold.

At the time Charles Addison and his party set out, for more than two-thirds of the way there was not a path nor a track to direct them onward.

The party started about the latter end of August. It consisted of twenty persons. They had about two dozen pack horses laden with luggage, consisting of provisions, ammunition, laborer's tools and merchandise for barter with the Indians.

They were all hardy, courageous, able-bodied men, regardless alike of fatigue, hardship or hazard.

The majority were men accustomed to work, such as laborers, masons, and carpenters; and they were all able and willing to assist in case of need, in the performance of any duty.

Addison, and a half-pay military captain, who had fought against the Indians in New England, and understood several of their languages, also an engineer and a surgeon who was not only employed as such but as secretary to the expedition, constituted the only individuals not professionally workmen; unless we exclude from this class, Addison's body-servant, Peter McFall, who had followed his dear master from the sweet city of Dublin—"Och, long life to it—over all England, Scotland and Germany, Italy and France, and now to America; and was ready besides to follow him all the world over, and Ireland into the bargain, if he should ever go back to it."

Every man of this stout-hearted, stout-bodied party was well armed, and well prepared to encounter either the natural obstacles of the way or the attacks of an enemy, should they meet with any, whether French or Indian.

They left Philadelphia laden with the prayers and good wishes of the citizens, and the fourth day afterward crossed the Susquehanna on a flat-boat amid the cheers of those residing on its banks.

As they proceeded, the obstacles to their progress increased; but we will not go into a detailed account of each day's travel.   Suffice it to say that, by persistent effort, they accomplished the herculean task of climbing the almost insurmountable mountains, and hewing their way through dense thickets that bedecked the western slope, bridging over ravines and morasses, resting for days at a time.   It was six weeks from the date of their setting out before they reached Shannapins, a small Indian village at the headwaters of the Ohio where later Fort Duquesne was built, and where the busy city of Pittsburg now fills the air with the scream of its steam whistles, and the whirr and hum of the wheels of industry.

They remained here several days, trafficking with the Indians, from whom they had not as yet met with any molestation.

Instead, several of their chief men, who visited them, seemed to be friendly disposed.

Among others, Alliquippa's lover, Shingiss, King of the Delawares, treated them with great attention, and ordered his people to furnish them with provisions and furs in exchange for their goods, whenever they wanted them.

His residence being near the place where they had instructions to erect their fort, Addison took care to secure his acquiescence, and assistance in the undertaking, by a liberal present of rings, pen-knives, small looking-glasses, tobacco boxes, glass beads and other trinkets.

In managing these matters the half-pay captain aforementioned, whose name was Ridgely, acted as interpreter; and the whole affair was settled so much to the satisfaction of all concerned, that a few days after their arrival at Shannapins, Addison thought proper to remove the party to Chartier's creek and take formal possession of the ground he intended to fortify.

He soon marked out the place best adapted for a fortification. It was on a high bank near a creek on the south side of the Ohio river, commanding its channel, but sloping towards the land, so as to afford an oportunity of making a strong resistance against any attempt to approach from that direc-tion.

Here he resolved to at once throw up a small en-trenchment, and erect a block-house for tempor-ary defense, for he was informed that the French commander at Fort Le-Boeuf, about twenty miles distant, had expressed great displeasure at the re-port of this attempt to establish a post, and it was highly probable he would resort to violence in order to drive him off.

Addison thought it would be hardly probable that force would be used for such a purpose, as it was then a time of peace between France and England; but, at all events he conceived it prudent to erect some sort of defense, for if the French commandant should not openly attack him, he might secretly spur on some of the Indian tribes to attempt to force him away.

His men were immediately set to work; some in preparing timber for the block-house, and some in digging the trench.

They had been two or three days employed in this business, when Peter McFall, who had been hewing timber at some distance from the rest, perceiving a deer, threw down his axe, and seized his gun (for, to guard against a surprise, each man was ordered to have his gun by him while at work), he proceeded to follow the deer for a short distance.

It had stopped, and Peter in a crouching position was silently and slowly endeavoring to approach it, threading his way through some thick undergrowth, when, all at once, he heard the sound of human voices, as if talking together.

He thought no more of the deer, for he was altogether attracted by the sound, which did not seem unfamiliar to him.

He drew nearer with as much silence as possible and soon discovered the words to be French, a language of which he had acquired some knowledge while attending his master upon his European travels.

He cautiously approached nearer, until he obtained a stolen view of the speakers.

They were white men, and although they were not in uniform, still by their appearance and talk he had reason to believe that they were French. Each of them wore a plain round hat, a short gray colored hunting coat and gray pantaloons.

They were standing leaning upon their guns, beneath a brush covered bank that over-looked a small stream, and concealed, only four or five steps away. Peter was enabled to hear their conversation quite readily.

After listening to their discourse for fifteen or twenty minutes, he became quite impatient to communicate to his master the information he possessed, for he doubted not from its nature that there was mischief soon to be expected.

Withdrawing. rather incautiously he attracted

the attention of the two men who, espying him, immediately fired at him.

One of their balls passed through his hat, and another through the skirt of his coat, without injuring him. He speedily returned their fire, and saw one of them fall, but he did not wait to learn whether killed or only wounded.

He hastened through the woods with the swiftness of a deer, and soon stood panting and exhausted before his master.

"Oh! holy Bridget! Master!" cried he in a great flurry, "I am wounded both in the head and the tail!"

"Wounded! How?" exclaimed Addison. "Why, what has happened, Peter?"

"Och, nothing, your honor," replied Peter, somewhat recovering his breath; "but, be dad, I shot a Frenchman as nate, your honor, as nate, yes, as nate as a pigeon."

"Then, Peter, I dare say it is the Frenchman, and not you that is wounded."

"Och! now, master, sure didn't I tell you the truth? Look at the ball they shot through my head; I heard it whistling like a pipe-staple. You'll see it there in both sides of my hat, your honor. Be dad, it flew like the wind through a barn door."

"But it has not cracked your skull for you, I hope; let me see. Why, you blunder pate, there is not so much as a scratch here."

"Och, your honor, let Peter alone for that. The devil niver yet made the bullet that broke my head, although he sent one through my tail, too.

"By my soul, it was tight going, to be shot through at both ends at one time master?"

"True enough," replied Addison; "but tell me how this affair has happened. Where saw you the Frenchman, and what was he about?"

"By my soul, sir, it wasn't one, but two of them I saw skulking, like thieves from a copper with a black thorn in his fist.

"It was just, your honor, under the brow of the big ditch yonder where the little river runs, that I spied the black-guards; they were speakin' French, when I listened like a lark and heard every word of it."

"What was said Peter; what conversation did they hold? Did you hear it distinctly?"

"Ay, faith, I did hear it. Why, my own mother never heard me squalling plainer."

"But what did they say, Peter? Tell me,

quick." "Why, they just said they would take every soul of us prisoners, if them Indians, the—the —hang their name."

"Go on, sir! What about them? Never mind their name."

"The Ch-Chipys—I think they called them. When they would come on, they said they could take us all at our work."

"Did they say, Peter, when they expected these Chippeways, as I suppose was their name?"

"By the holy St. Patrick! but you're right, your honor. How did you hear them? You know the whole matter better than I do. Och! what it is to be learned now!"

"Peace, Peter! and tell me if you heard when these Indians are expected?"

"Faith, your honor, I believe they expect them already, for they cursed them for not having come yet."

"Haste, Peter! Sound the bugle and call the men immediately."

Peter did as was directed and in a few minutes the whole party was assembled.

Addison communicated to them Peter's account of the danger that threatened them, and desired them to keep a good look out and not to separate till further orders were given. He then conferred privately with Captain Ridgely on the best measures to be adopted.

It was agreed that the men be at once employed in constructing a hasty parapet for immediate defense, of such materials as they had prepared, so that if attacked they might have some shelter from the enemy. At the same time a messenger was sent to King Shingiss, acquainting him with the state of affairs, and requesting his assistance as an ally in repelling any attack.

Shingiss with five or six warriors, soon waited upon Addison, and addressed him in the following manner:

"Brother, I will speak freely. Your people and the French people dislike each other, and many of us dislike you both.

"Your two nations disagree about this country, which belongs to neither of you. It is a hundred generations since the Great Spirit, who made it, first gave it to our fathers, and to their sons for a hunting ground.

"The Indian has possessed it ever since. Is it not strange that you white nations should quarrel more fiercely about that which is ours than we do ourselves?

"Brother, I will speak the truth and you shall hear. We have no objections to your lodging among us, and trading with us, so long as you trade fairly, and dwell peaceably, making no attempt to engross our land.

"Brother, hear me! I gave you permission to build here, because I know you cannot as we do, live in wigwams, and I wanted you to be comfortable, that you might have no cause for complaint, and that you might longer trade with us.

"Brother, let me now say, that you have not yet displeased me, but the French have; and if my warriors were at home I would now help you, for you have my permission to live here and the French have no right to forbid you. I will call upon the Shannoahs.

"Their warriors will come when they hear my story, and with those of my own tribe that are with me, I will come to you; but there will be a whole day before we can assemble."

Shingiss now took his leave; and it was scarcely an hour later, when two warriors of his tribe came running toward the tent occupied by Addison.

While yet at some distance they were heard to imitate the screeching of an owl, the signal by which they informed each other that a foe is approaching.

When they reached Addison, they informed him that there was a large party of the Chippeways within a short distance to attack him, and that their king was very sorry he had no force at hand to assist in repelling them.

They had hardly delivered their message when the terrific war-whoop was heard to rise from different quarters of the wood at once; and Addison had hardly time to form his men into a posture of defense, ere a continued peal of musketry began to rattle all around, and a shower of bullets sent by foes, yet invisible, came humming through the interstices of the half-finished breast-work they had in their haste attempted to throw up.

He did all in his power to encourage his men, and they, indeed, fought gallantly, but their situation was extremely disheartening.

They knew not the exact strength of the enemy, but they had reason to believe it was superior to theirs. Nor did they know to what point to direct their efforts, for every part of the surrounding forest seemed to contain a concealed foe, who poured a destructive fire upon them.

At length the savages becoming bolder, drew

near, and thus exposing themselves to the **fire of** the English, a number of them were killed.

But they continued to approach, sheltering themselves as much as possible behind trees, until Addison, perceiving there was no chance of keeping them off much longer, determined to make a charge upon them with the bayonet, in order, if possible, to cut a passage through them, by which means he hoped that at least a remnant of his men might escape.

He gave orders to this effect, and led the way himself, armed with a brace of pistols, and a large broad-sword.

His men followed unflinchingly, and soon drove off all the savages that were before them. But they were suddenly closed upon by a host from behind, and every man was seized by five or six Indians, and either killed or taken prisoner, and securely bound upon the spot.

Addison, placing his back to a large tree, defended himself for a considerable time, even after he saw that all was lost; for he determined to die fighting, and make his death so costly to his assailants that he would not be taken prisoner, and thus he would escape the tortures to which he knew as a prisoner he would be subjected.

He had used his pistols with deadly effect, but now nothing remained but his broad-sword, which he wielded with such skill as to make his enemies wary of approaching him.

He had laid several of them bleeding at his feet with mortal wounds, when he perceived one of more than ordinary strength, valor and fierceness, approaching with the utmost fury in his countenance.

When within a few rods of Addison he stopped, and called in a loud commanding voice to those who were fighting with him, to cease.

They immediately did so and withdrew to a distance. Addison stood firm and collected, waiting the attack of this formidable savage.

The warrior, having observed the kind of weapon possessed by the white man, and disdaining to use a weapon which he supposed would give him an advantage over his opponent—whom he wished to fight only on equal terms—threw away his battle-axe, with which he had often turned the tide of victory away from his enemies, he occupied a moment in snatching, from the dying grasp of Captain Ridgeley—who had fallen near him—his sword, which was nearly of the same size and formation as that of his antagonist.

At this instant, Addison paid a tacit, but high compliment to the magnanimity of his opponent, by relinquishing his station at the tree, and coming forward to meet him in the open space; for he instinctively felt that the followers of a brave man, although they should be savage, would not dare to disgrace both him and themselves by using unfair means, in the moment of combat, to secure him the victory.

The combatants now met, and fierce and terrible was the encounter. For, although they respected each other's bravery, each was determined to destroy or die.

The Indian managed his unusual weapon with wonderful address; and it required all the skill Addison possessed (and he was an educated swordsman), to ward off the fiery and rapid thrusts, strokes, and movements of his antagonist; and when at the beginning of the conflict he tried on his part to strike, or thrust, he was always baffled by some unexpected and unaccountable turn of his opponent's weapon or bodily position.

The savage, however, could make no impression upon him. He was too well acquainted with every manoeuvre for that.

Both were beginning to be wearied and pro-voked at such an unavailing contest.

Addison reflected that should he in the end be the conqueror, there was no possibility of escaping the terrible tortures destined to one captured by such foes, hundreds of whom stood around, ready to seize and carry him bound to a death of torment, the moment his victory should be declared.

This thought rendered him desperate, and al-most careless of results. He made a sudden spring upon the Indian, the blade of whose sword he caught firmly in his left hand, and thrusting it aside with uncontrollable force, he dashed his own into his opponent's heart.

The Indian fell, and expired without a groan, a fate which the victor, at that instant, ardently wished had been his own; for as many savage hands as could lay hold on him, had now seized him and he was carried away bound along with eleven of his company, who were also prisoners (the remainder having been killed on the field), to the Chippeway encampment, to undergo the investigation and judgment of the victorious chiefs.

All the way to the encampment, which was on the north side of the Ohio, about two miles from the field of battle, the Indians continued shouting and dancing, and singing songs of triumph in a manner so wild and frantic, that to their unfortunate prisoners their conduct seemed tainted with actual madness.

The evening was nigh at hand when they arrived at the camp, which was composed of a number of rude and hastily erected tents and wigwams, in one of which the chiefs assembled, and having approved of an appropriate song of victory, ordered two of their best singers to chant it in the hearing of all the warriors, many of whom joined in the chorus.

We would like to give our readers this song, but the attempt on the part of the white prisoners to understand the Indian tongue was a failure, besides their minds were burdened with thoughts of their impending fate to the exclusion of everything else.

After this song the whole savage party spent the evening in feasting, and dancing, and every species of exhibition they could contrive to display their feelings of triumph and exultation.

The prisoners were exposed to view during the whole of these revels, in order to stimulate the joy of the revelers, by keeping in their minds a recollection of their victory, as well as to mortify their enemies.

At length the hour for repose arrived, and the wretched prisoners were huddled together in a wigwam, and left to endure the agony of their own reflections until morning.

They were all securely tied, both arms and legs, and a sufficient guard of Indians placed around the wigwam to render their escape impossible.

CHAPTER VI.

DETERMINING THE FATE OF THE CAPTIVES

ITH the rising sun, the victorious Indians started from their repose, and
the noise and bustle of life again animated the camp, and broke in upon
that monotonous dullness which had been so op-
pressive to Addison during the night.

Two Indians soon entered the wigwam, and, as-
certaining that none of the prisoners had escaped,
distributed refreshments among them, although
the despondent feelings of the captives prevented
them from partaking to any extent.

Shortly after that, a council of the chiefs met to
deliberate concerning the prisoners, who were ordered to be present, that they might receive their
doom.

This consultation took place in the open air, in a
small glade that skirted the banks of a rivulet, or
run, as such small streams are usually called.

Here the prisoners, tied in pairs to each other,
were seated on the ground, near the centre of a cir-

cle formed by all the warriors, armed with guns in
their hands and axes and tomahawks in their belts.

Beneath a large chestnut tree near the centre of
the circle, sat seven chiefs and three Frenchmen,
upon logs apparently placed there for their comfort
and accommodation.

To these seven chiefs had been entrusted the de-
termination of the fate of the prisoners.

When they commenced their deliberations they
spoke separately, each, when he had anything to
say, rising in true parliamentary style and addressing himself to an elderly warrior, who appeared to
be their principal sachem or King.

What each man said, was communicated to the
French by an interpreter, by which means Addison
became acquainted with their various feelings regarding a disposal of the prisoners.

The first proposal made was to sacrifice half of
the prisoners according to their custom, and to
give the others to the French; the division to be
made by lot.

To this the French refused to agree, and one of
them standing up, addressed them as follows:

"Brothers! you say it is to please your departed
warriors, that you would sacrifice these men?
Where are those warriors now?

"Are they not in heaven?   Are they not happy, having done their duty, and having died bravely?

"If they are now already happy, will the torture of these men make them more so?

"Will they not rather be angry with you, seeing these prisoners fought bravely, and heroes always esteem brave men, and wish them well?

"Do you think that the English will never take any of your people prisoners?   And think you that, if you now destroy these, their brethren, they will not destroy your people in return, when any of them fall into their hands?   Think of this, brothers; they are a warlike nation, and have you not heard of them gaining victories in other wars?"

One of the chiefs arose and made reply. "Brother! hear my answer to your speech.   Our departed braves we know to be happy, nor do we think it will make them more happy to burn these prisoners on their account.   But it will show them our affection for them, and they will say to each other, our brothers loved us so much that they cannot endure the people by whom we fell, but consume them from the earth.

"Brother! if the English do not burn us when they make us their prisoners, it is not because they love us, but because it is not their custom, and the reason why we burn them, is because we revere the ways of our fathers and walk in them.

"Brother! let the English adopt our custom if they wish; it will not dissatisfy or alarm us.

"Our people have often been burned by our enemies; it was their fate and we submitted.

"But, brother, I wish to please you, for your people are our allies and friends. I will propose, therefore, that of the six prisoners that belong to us, we shall save one-half from burning, by adopting them as our sons; with the other half we shall support the customs of our fathers, and sacrifice them to the memory of our slain brothers."

The French still remained unsatisfied, but they almost despaired of making any better terms with their savage allies.

They were about to give up the attempt to save the unfortunates, when one of the three, who had, by examining the prisoners, found that there were four who were so badly wounded that they were not likely to survive many hours, conversed a few minutes with his companions, and then addressed the chiefs of the council as follows:

"Brothers! our nation and yours are warm friends; we have been often useful to each other.

"No seeds of strife or discord shall be sown by us. If you grant us one thing, we will therefore, oppose you no further.

"We wish you to choose now those you will adopt as sons, and then permit us this evening when the sun goes down, to select the number that falls to our share. The others will be those you will offer according to your customs."

By this plan the French hoped to spare from a cruel death, those of the party who were yet in possession of all of their physical vigor.

To this proposal the council appeared willing to accede, with one exception, an aged chief, who alone had not yet expressed his assent.

This warrior, during the entire proceedings said nothing, but had manifested great interest and attention to all that had passed.

His countenance was grave and mournful and his entire demeanor expressive of sorrow.

He now arose in considerable agitation, and addressed the council as follows.

"Warriors! Behold me! I stand alone like an old oak that has its branches cut from around it. ·

"Brothers! I know you grieve for me. It was but yesterday that I was sheltered by a sapling that grew from my own roots, stronger and more comely than myself.

"That noble sapling, the pride of the whole of our tribe, has been stricken down by a white man, and I look upon that white man now—mine eyes pierce his soul"—and here he fixed his gaze upon Addison with a look in his eyes of intense fierceness and hatred.

"Brothers! I disagree with the proposal made by our French brother, unless you will except from the number to be saved, the slayer of my son.

"You all knew Carrawissa; were you not proud of him? Was he not an example to your warriors? An ornament in peace and a thunderbolt in war?

"Brothers! Give heed to me! Do you not grieve for him? I look into your faces and they tell me that you do grieve from your hearts.

"Then let me ask, how can you save his destroyer? But, hear me, if you can consent to it, I cannot. I request that you deliver him, who bereaved you of a hero, and me of a son, into my hands that he be made an offering to the memory of that departed hero, and that he may satisfy the vengeance of the father who lost so noble a son.

"The man that slew Carrawissa must be destroyed or my sorrows will never cease.   I will **not** yield to the proposal of our French brother, because it might deprive me of my victim.

"Brothers and warriors! Carrawoona has spoken! You have heard me."

The entire council seemed much affected by his address, and remained in silence for some time after the speaker sat down.

At length one of the council arose and addressed the assembly.

"I have heard Carrawoona and I am affected, for what he has said is true. His son was a hero, greater than his fellows, as the noble eagle is greater than the buzzard or the hawk.

"We were proud of him for he was a true Chippeway, and no other tribe could show his equal.   It was but yesterday we said: 'Now we will gain the victory, for Carrawissa leads us.' But when shall we say so again?   Never!

"Warriors! Carrawoona has asked what is right; he has asked that we honor his son, by sacrificing a foe to his memory.   And who so fit and acceptable a sacrifice as he who slew him?   Can **we** refuse so just a demand?

"Can we say, 'Carrawoona, we grieve for your son's death, but we will not avenge it?'

"We admired him, but we will not honor him; we loved him, but we will let his memory pass from our minds as the shade vanishes when the sun shines.

"A hero is dead; we were proud of that hero. Our foes have often fled before him; but he has fallen in his youth, in the midst of his glory, when he had before him many years of usefulness.

"His destroyer is in our hands, and shall we spare him? Our brothers, the French, will not ask it; but to please our allies, I will propose that all the prisoners except the slayer of our hero be theirs.

"Let them save them if they wish it, but the slayer of Carrawissa must be given to Carrawoona. Brothers, you have my proposition."

This was accepted by the whole of the seven chiefs and, after several unavailing attempts on the part of the French to procure its reversal, they had at length to yield.

Addison was then sentenced to the flames; and his execution was ordered to take place under the direction of Carrawoona, before the sun should hide behind the western hills.

When the chief sachem had finished his decree,

the prisoners were all given over to the French, with the exception of the ill-fated Addison.

The council was about to dissolve when some straggling Indians, at a distance, were heard to give a peculiar shout, denoting both joy and admiration, which was indicative of the approach of some distinguished and respected visitor.

The cry of "Tonnawingo! Tonnawingo!" was soon heard from numbers of the assembly; and Addison perceived a man rapidly descending a rising slope of ground which bounded on the northward the low glade where the council was held.

He stopped a few yards from the warriors, when the braves, all rising in a body, saluted him in the Indian tongue with the words: "Welcome, thou messenger of the Great Spirit!" after which the chief sachem invited him to come forward.

The new comer was grave, venerable and majestic in his appearance, and in his manner there was something awe-inspiring.

His head was bare, for when he stopped, he had taken off his cap of bear skin, which he now held in his left hand, while he lifted his right hand and his eyes toward heaven in the attitude of devotion.

His bearing indicated an unusual degree of fervor, dignity and intelligence.   His nose was of the aquiline form, and his cheek-bones rather prominent; his forehead was high and round, rising backwards into a broad, smooth, and shining crown, altogether bald, but from the sides of which, and also from behind, an abundance of long black hair, mixed with gray, streamed down upon his shoulders, and was arranged so as to cover part of his cheeks, and hang on each side down upon his breast.

From his dark, piercing eyes there issued an expression of authority, convincing to the beholder, while at the same time it excited a feeling of reverential awe.

His dress was simple, consisting of a long woolen garment, like unto a shirt, the skirts of which reached below the knees.

Above this, a mantle of tanned bison skin rested on his shoulder and hung loosely down his back in the manner of a mantle. His moccasins and leggins of half-tanned deer-skin were of the usual construction, and completed his dress with the exception of the leathern belt around his waist, to which was attached a deer-skin pouch, containing, as the Indians declared, some mystical books, in which were recorded the communications he received from the Great Spirit, whose prophet they believed him to be.

In his right hand he held a long rod, around which were entwined a variety of feathers taken from birds of different plumage, and this rod was looked upon by the Indians as being sacred, and to which they gave the name of the "Prophet's wand."

When he approached the council, he stretched out his wand toward the chief sachem, and addressed him as follows:

"My brother, I am sent to talk with you. The Great Spirit, whom you worship knows all things. He knows what you have decided upon to-day. It was he who sent me.

"Then hearken to me, and let all these warriors hearken, for my words are dictated from above. I was not of your council. No one saw me here.

"But Maneto has sent me a good Spirit, who has declared to me your proceedings.

"I will, therefore, speak freely. You have offended the Great Spirit this day, by your sentence against that prisoner (pointing towards Addison), and, if you execute it, you will offend him still more.

"Maneto loves you; he has given you a great

victory; he has cast down your enemies before you, and he now warns you, lest you sin too much against him, and provoke him to consume you more than he has consumed them.

"Take warning therefore and sin not!

"Hearken to my voice! Maneto wishes you to spare this young warrior. He has a service for this young man to perform, which he communicated to me. He, therefore, calls upon you to spare him, and give him into my possession.

"Brothers, and counselors, you have heard! Will you obey the voice of the Great Spirit, and preserve his love, or will you disobey him, and provoke his vengeance?

"Brothers, let your chief say what is your choice."

The chief-sachem arose and replied: "Prophet! I will give my own opinion. The Great Spirit should be obeyed. We are the workmanship of his hands, and he has a right to our submission.

"What are we without him? Were it not for him, we would have neither deer, nor buffalo, nor bear's flesh to eat, nor air to breathe, nor water to drink, nor weapons with which to destroy our enemies.

"Prophet! you say he has use for this prisoner,

whom we were going to burn, in order to please the spirit of Carrawissa, which yesterday left its body; but it is better that we should please the Great Spirit who has existed forever, and can easily recompense Carrawissa if we do him an injury.

"Brothers and warriors! I think none of you will refuse to give our prisoner to the prophet, Tonnawingo, as the Great Spirit commands us.

"If any one refuses, we will hear him; if none speak, I shall order the prisoner to be loosened and given to the prophet."

Here he paused for some one to reply, but, all continuing silent, he was about to command the prisoner to be given up, when Carrawoona arose in great agitation.

"What, brothers! Have you so soon forgotten my son? Will no one speak in his behalf? Has he no friend here who will ask justice for him?

"I cannot believe the story of Tonnawingo, for prophets have sometimes spoken falsely, or they may have mistaken dreams for the orders of the Great Spirit.

"Listen to me. The Great Spirit loved Carrawissa, and made him a hero; think ye then, that he would thus command us to defraud his memory of the accustomed sacrifice?

"I, for one, cannot think of it. I, for óne will not consent to spare the prisoner. If Carrawissa has a friend in this council, let him now speak."

When he sat down, the same chief that had so warmly espoused his cause in the former part of the deliberations, now arose and addressed him.

"Brother! I am the friend of your son's memory; but I am a worshiper of the Great Spirit, and desire to obey him, far more than to please any friend.

"I spoke sincerely for your son to-day but I did not then know the will of Maneto.

"He wishes for the victim we intended for your son. We cannot refuse him, and your son cannot be offended. Brothers and warriors, we must give up the prisoner."

Carrawoona arose again, and in a hasty and impassioned manner exclaimed:

"Brothers, hear me again! I am but one among hundreds, and my voice is nothing. But were I only one among thousands, I would let you hear it.

"I say, the man who slew my son shall die. I will hunt him over the earth till he be sacrificed. My heart must have revenge; Maneto could never forbid it; I do not believe what the prophet says.

"He says that Maneto wants the white man;

what can he want with him?   Are there not plenty
of Indians to perform his errands and to worship
him?

"If it be true that Maneto wants some one,
would he not prefer an Indian?   If the service he
wishes to be done requires honesty, are not Indians
more honest than the whites?

"Hear me, brothers! I will not believe that for
any purpose, the Great Spirit would prefer a white
man to an Indian.

"Has Tonnawingo said what Maneto wants with
the prisoner?   If Maneto wanted him he would
have told for what purpose.   But he has not, or we
would have heard it, if Tonnawingo be his prophet.

"Brothers, you perceive there is something
wrong in the matter; be not like children, ready to
believe every story.   Act wisely; comply with the
customs of your fathers, and refrain from them
only when you have sufficient reason. Carrawoona only asks justice for his son, and the Great
Spirit never yet opposed justice."

He sat down, and Tonnawingo again advanced.
He pointed his sacred wand—the very motion of
which had power to strike awe into the minds of
the savages—three times toward heaven, and three
times toward each member of the council.

He then raised it, and stretching his arms upward and with his eyes directed to heaven, exclaimed:

"Oh, Great Spirit! what is man, that he should question thy will? Didst thou not make him? Dost thou not sustain him? And he dares to ask for what purpose thou layest claim to thine own.

"Happy is it for him that thou art not like him, but merciful, or thou wouldst consume him for his presumption."

Then, turning abruptly he waved his wand over the assemblage of braves, with such energy as to cause the hardy savages to tremble.

"Brother," said he, turning to the chief sachem, "I claim that prisoner in the name of the Great Spirit; I claim him as successor to my gifts; order him to be unbound."

The chief sachem instantly complied. Addison was released from his thongs, and Tonnawingo advancing toward him said:

"Follow me, my son! We go to worship our Great Father!"

He followed his conductor, who, with his eyes steadily fixed upon heaven, in an attitude of deep and solemn devotion, walked slowly from amidst the assembly towards the east, leaving every individual who beheld him, not excepting Carrawoona, awe-struck, and fixed immovably to his place, as if by the effects of enchantment.

It was several minutes before any of the Indians recovered from the spell that was over them sufficiently to speak.

Carrawoona was the first to recover from the enchantment, which the appearance, attitude, and energy of the old prophet had seemingly cast upon the council.

With a piercing war-whoop, he started up, all the wildness of ungovernable rage contorting his features, as he addressed the assemblage.

"Warriors, hear me! I am bereaved; I am defrauded.

"Did my son deserve such treatment? Would Carrawissa have acted so to the memory of any one here?

"Warriors, what have you done? Think of it. You have permitted the destroyer of a Chippeway and a hero, to walk free from his bonds, and to escape that fire through which his soul should have been sent as a grief-offering to comfort the spirit of my departed son.

"Chippeways, it is useless now to argue; it is useless to complain. I will act; is there any man here who will act with me? I will have my vengeance. Has Carrawissa here any friend who will assist me?

"You condemned the white man, and by your sentence he was mine. You could not take him from me, and I will yet have him, and execute your sentence.

"Warriors! I again ask, is there one who will assist me?" He sat down, and no one offering to reply, the chief sachem addressed him.

"Brother! we love you, but your madness grieves us. If you fight against Maneto we must resist you, for in contending against the Great Spirit you are led into wickedness and must be overcome."

Carrawoona started to his feet, and in a tone of rage, bordering upon absolute frenzy, he exclaimed:

"Chippeways! have I no friends, then? Am I alone in my wish for justice? Do you want to frighten me from my purpose? You should have known long ere this that Carrawoona cannot be frightened.

"My revenge you call madness, but I call it justice; you advise me to desist from seeking it, but I will not listen to you. I will talk no more, but will pursue the destroyer of my son. My weapon shall find his heart, even if it be through the heart of Tonnawingo; nay, the bosom of Maneto will not protect him.

"Maneto will protect no one from justice, but should his lightning shrivel me on the instant, if I only obtain vengeance on my enemy, I shall be satisfied."

He here gave a sudden yell, and made a leap to the eastward, as if he intended immediately to pursue the object of his resentment.

The chief sachem ordered him to be stopped, when a warrior rising, called out:

"Brother! let Carrawoona take his way. We have nothing more to do with the business. We have given up the prisoner as the Great Spirit ordered.

"He has not ordered us to restrain Carrawoona's madness. We should not take the protection of the white man out of the hands of Maneto. Let Carrawoona go, we have done our duty."

The furious and untractable savage was accordingly allowed to pursue whatever course he pleased and the assembly broke up.

CHAPTER VII.

JOURNEY TO THE FORT

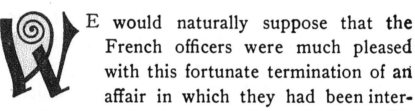

E would naturally suppose that the French officers were much pleased with this fortunate termination of an affair in which they had been interested so much. During the time that their feelings alone influenced them they did heartily rejoice; but when they reflected on the political consequences that might arise from the escape of any of the English prisoners, especially the leader of the enterprise, they began to feel uneasy, and heartily to wish Charles Addison in perdition, rather than that he get back to Philadelphia, or any other place where he might inform the world of what they had done.

They felt a strong repugnance to have any human being sacrificed in the cruel manner in which the Indians often sacrificed their captives; but, they, at the same time, dreaded the results which they had a good right to suppose must take place if the government of Great Britain should hear of the

part they had taken in the attack upon their subjects in the time of peace.

As men, they rejoiced in the safety of Charles Addison, but as politicians, and servants of a European
power, which might not in the end, sanction and
defend their conduct, they feared the evils that
would result from the arrival of Addison among his
friends, when he would likely make public to the
political world the part they had played in provoking the assault made by the Indians on the whites.

The more, however, they considered the matter,
the influence of the political consideration increased; and rather than be brought to an account
for their conduct, by their own government, or be
the occasion of a European War, of which they
could not foresee the consequences, they became
the more heartily inclined to wish that the prisoner,
for whom they pleaded so strenuously, had been,
by some means or other, put out of the way, for it
was from his information alone that they believed
they had anything to fear.

Had Addison, like the other prisoners, been in
their custody, then everything would have been to
their satisfaction, since they could hold them for an
indefinite time, and liberate them only when other
national concerns had occurred to render what they

had done of too little importance to occasion an inquiry. Possibly under the influence of these considerations, and perhaps with a view to save the life of Addison, one of the French officers offered Carrawoona a large reward if he would bring Charles Addison, a living prisoner to them, to the fort at Le-Boeuf, within six months from that time. To this offer the chief replied:

"Brother! what do you mean? Do you think I will give up my son's right for a hire? Will I let him remain unavenged for the sake of presents? No; I will pursue this white warrior from no such motive. I would not move my finger to injure him for the paltry object of gain; and listen to me, had I him now in my possession, all the wealth of your great king would not save him from being sacrificed to the spirit of my departed son.

"Brother! I leave you to pursue our released prisoner, but it is to destroy him, for he who killed my son must not walk abroad upon the earth."

So saying, he left the Frenchman with a look of high disdain, and set off on his revengeful errand.

The day after the council was held, the French proceeded with their prisoners for Fort Le-Boeuf, which was situated on French Creek, near where the present town of Waterford now stands.

It was the commander of this fort who, in conformity both to his official instructions, and to the general policy of his government to prevent any English settlement from being made west of the Allegheny mountains, had excited the Chippeways to attack our hero's party, and thereby laid the foundation of that memorable war which, although it began disastrously for the British arms, yet resulted under the auspices of the energetic Pitt, in the total expulsion of the French authority from this entire territory.

It was during the disastrous period of this war, that the celebrated but unfortunate expedition of Braddock to this region of country, took place, and we believe had more influence in drawing the attention of mankind towards these remote regions, and their savage inhabitants, than any other transaction recorded in history.

This noted expedition, which is still referred to as an epoch in the annals of the French and Indian War, will—on account of the influence it had upon the fortunes of the characters in our story—again come under our notice during the progress of this narrative, when we hope to be able to give the reader a more detailed account of this battle so dis-

astrous to the British arms, than can be procured
from any history extant.

We may here observe, however, that it is not our
intention to dwell more minutely upon these matters that are already known to the world, than will
be necessary to afford a clear and satisfactory view
of their connection with the individuals in whose affairs we are more immediately interested.

The French officers who, as we have seen, were
both glad and sorry at the escape of Charles Addison, finding that they could not make a better of it,
cast care aside, like all true Frenchmen usually do,
and with their share of the prisoners, set out the
next day for Fort Le-Boeuf, in order to have them
there secured, as soon as possible, from any accident, whether through escape or Indian violence.

The prisoners were now only seven in number,
four having died of their wounds the preceding
night. Of those who survived three were slightly
wounded, among whom was our acquaintance,
Peter McFall, whose left arm had been broken by
the stroke of an Indian battle-axe, before he submitted to be bound.

Thus, of those twenty gallant fellows who had
so lately crossed the Allegheny mountains, only
eight were now living; and but five had escaped

from their savage foes without personal injury, their leader, Charles Addison being of the number.

The French were assisted by a dozen Chippeway warriors in escorting the prisoners to their destination, the remainder of the savages having decided to continue their excursion into the Virginia settlement, for the sake of additional plunder and scalps.

When the escort with the prisoners had proceeded about five miles on their way, they came to a small tent, situated at the foot of a hill close by a purling brook at which they halted.

In this tent were three squaws, and two Frenchmen, one of whom was lying on a fairly comfortable bed made of buffalo skins and some blankets spread upon dry leaves, which, as it was now well advanced in the fall were scattered in great abundance all through the woods.

This man was suffering from a severe wound he had received in the groin, made by a musket ball which still remained there.

His appearance, as well as that of his companion, immediately suggested to Peter McFall that these were the men he had overheard conversing previous to the attack of the Indians, one of whom he knew he had wounded. He heard this man moan once or twice from the pain he endured, and his heart smote him from a consciousness of having been its cause.

He went forward to the patient and taking him by the hand, said: "Now, honey, did ye never see me before?"

The man looked at him and answered, "No." "By my soul, then," he continued, "but your eyes were not so good as mine.   And it is lucky for my head that they were not, or else a bullet might now have been lying as snug in my brain as in your kidney, my jewel!"

The man stared at him, when McFall, as if struck with a happy thought, broke forth: "Arrah now! I have it as nate as my nail.   Be aisy now, you'll be cured as stout as a young buck in a jiffy, my dear.   I'll have the doctor at you at once, and with his tongs and pincers, he'll soon whisk out into your fist the fellow that now tazes you."

Here he called out to the young Philadelphia surgeon we have before mentioned, whose name was Killbreath.

"By my sowl, doctor! here's one of the natest jobs for you, you ever did in your life.   Och, now! if Doctor McFadden was only here, he wouldn't be after asking the second bidding to do it; but the

Lord bless you, doctor, you are able to do it, for didn't you splice my arm as firm as a whip-handle."

The surgeon approached, and offered his services in extracting the ball which tormented the sufferer, and the French having taken possession of the instruments he had brought with him from Philadelphia, they were soon produced and the operation at once performed.

When Peter got the bullet in his hand, he examined it closely, then he commenced flinging it in the air and catching it again, exclaiming as he continued the operation: "By Saint Patrick, I have ye once more, my honey, but when I again send you scampering after a Frenchman, don't stick in his hips, me love, to torment him, but blow his brains out at once, or don't touch him at all, my darlint."

Peter was here interrupted in his apostrophe to the bullet, by one of the Frenchmen accosting him rather abruptly, in an unintelligible mixture of French and English, which for us to repeat verbatim would be as difficult as the reading of it would be uninteresting.

They attempted to converse with one another, but it was a miserable failure, although Peter did not doubt that the Frenchman was trying to charge him with the misfortune that had befallen his comrade.

The wounded man understanding the charges made by his countryman explained to him that Peter was not wholly in the blame, and that they both had been aggressors on account of acting in the character of spies.

Peter, finding the patient had exculpated him, seized his hand, and cried out: "Arrah! long life to you, an' 'tis yourself that is a gintleman an' sorra the day it was that I sent me bullet to nestle in your kidney; but the doctor will fix you up in a week, as sound as a church bell!"

Here the surgeon interrupted Peter, desiring him to leave the patient, so that he might enjoy that quietness and repose so necessary after the operation he had undergone.

Peter complied, observing, "Sure, doctor, you know better than I do."

The performing of this operation, and the enjoyment of a plentiful repast, consisting of venison, wild fowl, Indian-corn bread, and various other luxuries supplied from the French stores and which the squaws, with the assistance of the Frenchmen had prepared for the party, consumed so much of the time, that it was proposed to pitch

8

a few more tents and spend the remainder of the day as well as the night.

This agreeable proposal was relished by the entire company; and the French during the evening got into such good humor with the prisoners, that they permitted them to join in the revels, ordering the Indians, however, to keep a good lookout, lest any of them should escape.

As to the surgeon, whose manners, education, and good sense, proclaimed him to be a gentleman, soon after the operation was performed upon the suffering Frenchman, obtained upon his parole and promise not to leave them until their arrival at the fort, the indulgence of being master of his own actions, and the command of a rifle, for the purpose of hunting.

There are no people in the world better qualified to enjoy the passing moment than the French. They have the happy faculty of dismissing care whenever it becomes troublesome to their feelings or unnecessary for their purposes; and on this evening they exerted that faculty in a masterful manner.

True they had brought themselves into a predicament calculated to make a most serious impression upon their minds, yet when filled with sub-

stantial fare and their hearts warmed by a stimu-
lating potion of whisky grog, they for the present,
bade adieu to all unpleasant reflections and passed
the hours in mirth and enjoyment.

If the French are noted for unthinking frivolity
the Irish are no less so for a fervency of feeling, by
which they are enabled to suppress the suggestions
of care, as effectually as the French can dismiss
them.

Hence, when opportunity presents, they are ever
ready to yield with their whole heart and soul to
the full tide of enjoyment, and swim away on its
stream, regardless of consequences.

On this occasion, there was none who entered
into the humors of the evening with more spirit
than our Irish friend, Peter McFall.

Grief, vengeance, and every other uncomfortable feeling, were banished as unwelcomed guests;
while good humor, sprightliness, cordiality and
joy were invited to be present by the merry strains
of a Frenchman's flute, and the jolly sounds of an
Irishman's voice; for, in the intervals of the flute
player's performance, Peter with great spirit, industriously exerted himself to prevent the company
from wanting for music, by singing the merry dit-
ties of his native country.

At the commencement of the sport the Indians entertained the party by giving the various dances of their nation. The war dance, the hunting dance, the courtship dance, the marriage dance, and the birth dance, had each its characteristic gesture and manoeuvres—some of which were to the eyes of the Europeans so grotesque, wild and ludicrous, that they were kept in an almost continuous roar of laughter.

Peter was particularly tickled with the romping and capering of the squaws, who were tolerably handsome women, and were nothing loth to exhibit their personal attractions in the various attitudes of their native dances.

"By the holy St. Patrick! But it's yourselves can do it in style, my girls!" exclaimed Peter, while he snapped his fingers and beat time with his feet, in high glee and admiration at their extraordinary and laughable performance.

His fancy was particularly taken with the gracefulness and agility of the youngest of the squaws, who really made an interesting figure among the group, and at every remarkable bound she gave, snap went Peter's fingers in the air, dash went his heel upon the ground, and loud rose his vociferous cheers of applause.

"Well done, by the powers of O'Leary! Och! kape it up, you swate little sowl."

He thus kept vociferating, while the company kept laughing, almost as much at his extravagancies, as at the singularities of the dances.

At length his heels itched so much to bear a part in the boisterous amusement, that he could keep his seat no longer, but springing up, and with his sound arm, hooked in with the squaw who pleased him so much, he leaped, and bowed, and capered among the Indians with all his might, imitating as well as he could their gestures and movements, to the great admiration and delight of all present.

When the Indians and Peter had finished, the French took up the exhilarating pastime and the sport was continued until all had grown weary. After resting a short while, they partook of some food, and again resumed their merry-making.

This time was spent in the singing of some jovial songs, of which only one has come into our possession, which was sung by the light-hearted Peter, and without the need of translation, which we would be obliged to give had it been the Frenchman's song, we now present it to the reader.

PETER McFALL'S SONG

In Ireland so frisky
With sweet girls and whisky,
We managed to keep care and sorrow aloof;
Our whirl-i-gig revels
Would make the blue devils
Crawl out with the smoke
Through a hole in the roof.

To seek for promotion
I crossed the wide ocean,
Was ship-wrecked and murdered,
And sold for a slave;
O'er mountains and rivers
Was pelted to slivers,
And met on dry land.
With a watery grave.

Again safe in ould Ireland,
On that happy island;
With beauty and whisky
To make my heart glad,
By the sweet flowing Liffy,
I'm off in a jiffy,
With a whoop for ould Ireland
And Baling-McFad.

The next morning the party commenced their journey to Fort Le-Boeuf, leaving the wounded Frenchman, who was unable to bear a removal, in the care of one of his countrymen and two squaws.

They arrived at the fort on the fourth day of their journey, without meeting with any accident worth recording. Here the escort of Indians received presents for the services they had performed and were dismissed.

The prisoners were all safely confined within the ramparts, except the surgeon, who was occasionally permitted on parole, to recreate himself in the surrounding country.

Our friend Peter had it in his power, very shortly after his arrival, on account of his understanding a little French, to exchange the situation of a prisoner, for that of a servant to one of the officers, but he promptly refused to do so, from a mental resolution he had made, to not serve any one in a menial capacity except Charles Addison, at whose side the desire to be, had become the ruling passion of his mind.

He was treated fairly well as a prisoner, and the gay, sprightly manners of the garrison were quite congenial to his disposition; but still he was a prisoner, and under control of certain regulations which he did not relish; and what was worse, he was absent from his beloved master who might be so situated as to require his services very much. He, therefore, jolly, gay and thoughtless, as his disposition was, felt his situation as a prisoner.

CHAPTER VIII.

ADDISON ACCOMPANIES THE PROPHET

ALTHOUGH Tonnawingo and his protege had retired in a slow and deliberate manner, as long as they were in view of the Indians, yet they were no sooner removed from their observation, than the prophet, who was aware of Carrawoona's implacable hatred and fiery temper, thought it best to hasten onward with greater speed.

He also conceived it prudent to change his direction, so that if the revengeful savage should pursue them, he might be thrown off the proper track. He accordingly turned toward the northward, in which direction he kept for about two miles, then turning toward the east, in about two hours after he left the savages he reached the Allegheny river, nearly six miles above the Shanapin's town.

Here they entered the wigwam of an Indian, who received them with great reverence and respect. Tonnawingo desired this man to prepare some refreshments, and while this was being done he beckoned to Addison, to whom he had not spoken a single word, since their leaving the Chippeways, to follow him.

He led the way into a narrow dell or dingle, a short distance from the wigwam, and to the great surprise of the young man, addressed him in English. "My son," said he, "let us here worship the Great Father of all, and thank him for thy deliverance."

They fell on their knees, and the prophet lifting his eyes, and spreading his hands to heaven, addressed the Supreme Author of all things as follows:

"Almighty Spirit! We kneel here to adore thee and to thank thee. Thy greatness fills us with wonder, thy power with awe, and thy purity with admiration. Thy goodness inspires our love, thy readiness to forgive, our hope, and thy forbearance to punish, our gratitude.

"Thou great and good Spirit! We humbly adore and thank thee, at this time in particular, for the manifestation of thy goodness in delivering this youth, as thou hast this day done, from the hands of an unpitying and cruel enemy who had determined to destroy him.

"He thanks thee because thou hast, in this man-

ner, assured him of thy friendship; and I thank
thee, both because thou hast saved him, and in doing so, hast made me thy humble instrument. We
entreat thee to be our protector from evil, our deliverer from distress, and our director and conductor through all the snares and intricacies of life,
so that we may act well pleasing to thee, and be
worthy to be called thy children, and deserving of
thy favor.

"Almighty Spirit! we have done, and we hope
thou hast been graciously attentive to what we
have said.   Amen."

When they arose, Addison caught the Prophet
by the hand.   "Father," said he, "permit me to ask
who art thou, whom that holy God we have been
worshiping, has made the instrument of rescuing
me from a cruel death?"

"My son," replied Tonnawingo, "I am a man
like thyself; I have borne trials, perhaps more severe than thou hast, and yet survived them; for the
Great Father has been good to me. He has sustained me, and, thanks be to his goodness, he has
not left me without some comfort in the world.   I
wish to serve him in that way which is most pleasing to him, by doing good to his creatures.

"I make it my business to go from tribe to tribe,

endeavoring to reconcile them when they quarrel, or, if they will fight and destroy each other, I do all in my power to mitigate their unnatural ferocity.

"When I cannot do that, I try to disappoint them if possible in the execution of their barbarous designs."

"I may have other cares and employment on hand, but my son, I wish you to inquire no further concerning me. Tonnawingo cannot now tell all he knows to the world, and I should not wish inquiries to be made, that I must refuse to answer.

"My son, you are now in a vast wilderness, far from the habitation of your people, without friends or resources. Something must be done for you, and as our common Father has thrown you upon my protecting care, I shall do all I can, but let me first ask, what would best suit your desires?"

Addison now stated to him the name and residence of his father, and gave him a concise account of the expedition he had commanded, and which had ended so disastrously. He concluded by remarking, that he now saw nothing left for him but to make his way back to Philadelphia as speedily as he could.

"My son," said the Prophet, "you speak wisely; to return to your friends is the most prudent thing you can do.   But the journey is long; and considering the state of the country, to a single individual, and especially a white man, it is impracticable.

"You will find no provisions on the way, and there is no path to guide you, for more than two hundred miles of the journey.

"I shall do all I can to assist you, for in this country you are not safe.   My brothers of the different tribes will distrust you, for they have reason to both distrust and dislike white people; but from Carrawoona your greatest peril will arise.   Beware of him, for I know he is implacable and will seek your destruction.

"My son, until we can prepare matters for your return to the East, I will tell you where to reside, and where I hope Carrawoona will not find you, About fifteen miles from us, on the bank of the Monongahela, lives the only man of your nation in this country.

"His name is Frasier; he is my friend and will entertain you till I meet you there, which will not be many days.   I would go with you now, but I must watch the motions of the Chippeways, and especially of Carrawoona, that I may frustrate, if possible, any attempt against you.

"My son, we will now partake of refreshments

prepared for us in the wigwam; its owner will supply you with arms for your protection, for he is my friend; but as the day is now advanced, you had better lodge with him to-night, and in the morning you will proceed to the house of my white brother, Frasier, where you will remain till I see you."

They returned to the wigwam, and together partook of a well prepared repast of wild fowl, and a preparation of Indian corn called "Hominy," after which Tonnawingo departed, having first given Addison particular directions how to find the way to Gilbert Frasier's residence.

It is needless to repeat the expressions of gratitude poured out by the youth to his deliverer when they separated, but the Prophet bade him to look alone to the Great Father, as his deliverance came alone from that source, and that he was only an humble instrument to bring about a desired end.

There is no feeling so conducive to sound repose as the impression of being in the favor and under the protection of a Supreme Providence.

The wonderful deliverance which Addison had, from an awful and apparently inevitable fate, produced upon his mind the impression that he was under the care of a Divine Providence, and with this feeling, he laid himself down upon the bed of dry leaves, and buffalo skins prepared for him in one corner of the wigwam by its friendly owner, and enjoyed a sound and refreshing sleep, which continued unbroken till the morning.

When he arose, his friendly host supplied him with a gun and a war-axe; and with the former upon his shoulder, and the latter together with some ammunition and provisions girt to his side, he set forward on his journey to Gilbert Frasier's.

The reader would not look upon it as a journey at the present time, but only a delightful trolley ride of a few hours, but it must be understood that where now stand thickly populated suburban towns with paved streets, that by the use of the electric light know not the shadows of night, at the time when our hero was making his way to the home of the friend to whom he was directed, all was an almost impenetrable wilderness.

The directions which Charles had received from the Prophet, were plain, and he set forward fearing nothing, although it was the first time he had been altogether alone in the woods. But this very circumstance, instead of making a disagreeable impression, threw over his journey a peculiar charm of novelty and romance, which to his youthful mind was more attractive than repellant.

The distance was only fifteen miles, but he consumed the greater part of the day before he reached the Monongahela.   At this stage of his journey he felt uncertain, from not seeing the marks referred to in his directions, whether Gilbert Frasier's house was, in respect to the river, above or below him.

In this state of uncertainty respecting his course, he rested himself beneath a large maple tree that grew upon the bank, amidst a thicket of sassafras, elders and hazels, that he might reflect a little in order to determine which way to proceed.

Prominent among other subjects that then came to his mind was that of how, and why, a white man was enjoying a permanent and unmolested residence in such a country, and amid such inhabitants.   What could induce a single individual of European origin to settle among such a people, and in such a wild region, he could not understand; and if it had not been that he considered it almost profane to doubt the word of Tonnawingo, he should have considered the story of a white man being located in that region as altogether fictitious. He was resolved, however, to believe it, since his deliverer had said it, but he concluded that this man must be some adopted son of a savage, perhaps married to a squaw, and in point of manners

and habits but little superior to the wild brothers
of the forest.

Having come to this charitable estimate of Gilbert Frasier's character, he arose and began to
pursue his course up the river, almost careless
whether or not it should bring him to the residence
of one of whom he had formed so indifferent an
opinion.

The only desire that prompted him to make an
effort to find the place was that Tonnawingo had
agreed to meet him there.   Again, the place would
no doubt afford him a comfortable shelter at least.
With these thoughts in his mind he was advancing
from the thicket, when to his utter astonishment,
he perceived two decently attired white females approaching him down the bank of the river.

He suddenly drew back into his concealment, not
with fear, but struck with awe; for he could not suppose it possible that civilized white women would
be found apparently unprotected in such a place;
for at his first glance he saw that they were not
squaws.   He for an instant concluded them to be
nothing else but supernatural beings, sent for some
divine purpose.   His calmer judgment convinced
him that this was not the case; yet he thought it fit
to remain concealed for a few minutes, until he had.

discovered something more satisfactory concerning the creatures that had struck his excited fancy as being almost too lovely to be earthly.

When they drew near enough to be more minutely distinguished, he became satisfied that they were real flesh and blood like himself; and he was delighted to hear them converse in the English language, for not perceiving him, their discourse was not interrupted as they passed.

"It was indeed a noble act on the part of Tonnawingo, whose whole pleasure seems to be in doing good," said she, whom he perceived to be by far the more handsome of the two, and whose loveliness had completely riveted his attention, so much as to make him almost overlook her companion, who replied:

"And Paddy says that the prisoner was one of the finest looking men he had ever seen; I do hope Carrawoona will not find him."

"A good Providence will protect him!" said the first. "That God who afforded him such a timely rescue is able, and I trust will still be willing, to extend over him his shield of safety."

Addison, who at once knew himself to be the subject of this conversation, experienced something inexpressibly sweet in the tones of that voice which had uttered this wish for his safety; and he was only prevented from rushing forward to express his gratitude, by that profound feeling of awe he had experienced at the first appearance of the young ladies.

He came forth gradually, out of his concealment, as they moved from him. At length descending into a little valley they were hidden from his sight.

"I will follow them," thought he, "although it be not the course I intended. Such lovely creatures can lead nowhere but to safety and to happiness."

He accordingly hastened after them; but, on coming to the point at which they had disappeared, he was surprised to behold, in a romantic valley beneath him, through which a rivulet meandered, making at a short distance a union with the Monongahela, a neat and prosperous looking farm, with its worm fence, its orchard, its meadow-ground, and its fields of Indian corn and stacks of grain, surrounding a large, substantial log dwelling house, of comfortable appearance, while not far away was a log barn, with cow-house and hog pen attached.

He paused for a moment at the unexpected sight. He felt something congenial to his very being in the appearance of the sheep, cows and horses that were grazing in the meadow.

The fair object which had attracted him hither had been concealed from view by the intervention of some trees; but he now again perceived her, with her companion, advancing along a short lane towards the dwelling house.

He hastened after them, when through an opening in the wood to his left, he suddenly perceived two men digging potatoes in a field, which here spread itself to view between him and the river. He at once made his way toward them.

CHAPTER IX.

A FRONTIER WELCOME

THE two men whom we left Charles Addison in the act of approaching, were Gilbert Frasier and his son Denny. They were so busily employed in hoeing out their potatoes, that they did not observe him until he had advanced almost to them when Denny called out:

"Father, look! There is a white man comin'!"

Gilbert turned around, and with a feeling of both surprise and respect lifted his hat, and then standing stock still with his hoe in hand, gazed intently at the stranger until he spoke.

"My good friend," said the stranger, "I am an unfortunate wanderer in this wilderness, where I am both surprised and delighted with the sight of a white man. May I ask a few nights' lodging from your kindness?"

"Lodgin'! Yes, wi' a' my heart—a white man! an' a gintleman!—wi' a' my heart! But, may I ask your name, sir?"

"My name is Addison."

"Addison, Addison! You ca' wi' the Ohio settlers; I doot na', sir, ye hae been unfortunate.

"But we'll gang to the hoose, sir. Ye'll be needin' somethin' to eat an' drink, na doot—for there's no muckle to be had that's guid for ony thing in this woods."

So saying, he moved forward a few steps—then suddenly muttered—"Wha kens! wha kens!—it may be sae"—and, turning around he asked:

"Addison, ye say they ca' ye?"

"Yes."

"An' canna ye mind to hae ever heard o' yen Thomas Addison, wha, when I leev'd on the Juniata I was tauld had come frae Ireland to Philadelphia?

"That Thomas Addison is my father."

"Thomas Addison! your father! My auld frien'!" Here he threw away the hoe which he had till now retained in his hand, using it as a walking stick, and catching Charles eagerly by both hands he continued his exclamations. "Why! why! the sin o' my auld frien' frae Maughrygowan! come to ask lodgin' frae me—ay that ye'll hae, the best that I can gi' ye—the best bed, the best meat, the best drink, the best o' everything that Gilbert Frasier can gie you. The sin o' my auld frien' frae Maughrygowan—Denny! Denny! rin fast, my braw lad! rin fast, and tell your mother that the sin o' my auld frien' the sin o' Thomas Addison o' Maughrygowan, is come to see us.

"An' haste ye, Denny! get the white-faced calf killed—it's the fattest—an' be na langsome, noo—that' a braw lad!"

"An' the sin o' my auld frien' Thomas! (Here he again eagerly shook both of Charles' hands.) The sin of Thomas Addison has cam' a' the way awre the Chestnut Ridge, to ask lodgin' frae me. Guid bless ye, man! ye'll hae lodgin' and leevin' frae me baith, as lang as ye like.

"But come in, come into the house. Nellie, puir Nellie! hoo glad she'll be to see the sin o' her auld acquaintance! Ye were na born in Maughrygowan, were ye?"

"No," replied Charles, "Philadelphia is my birth-place."

"Ah! weel, it's na difference—ye're the sin, an the gran'-sin o' Maughrygowan men—an' na doot a true Irishman in your heart."

Charles assured him, evidently very much to his satisfaction, that he had a great partiality for that country; for not only being the land of his fathers, he had there received the chief part of his education, and spent the happiest portion of his life.

"Then ye hae been in Ireland, sir?"

"Yes, within these last six months I sailed from Londonderry."

"Frae Derry! frae Derry! An' hoo did the auld country an' the auld city look? An' were ye at Maughrygowan too, dootless?"

"Yes, I spent part of last winter there."

"An' was everything the same? Ah! I doot na, there are mony changes there syne I saw it."

They had by this time arrived at the door of Gilbert's dwelling, where Nellie, in consequence of Denny's information, was waiting in a state of great impatience to meet them. Recollecting Maughrygowan, and the days of her youth, she had just taken time to make herself presentable by putting on a clean cap and shawl.

"Nellie! Nellie!" exclaimed Gilbert, as they approached where she stood in the door; "here, here is the sin o' young Squire Addison, oor auld acquaintance, an' the gran'-sin o' the auld squire, just came frae Derry owre the sea, an' a' the way owre the Allegheny Mountains, an' the Laurel Hill, an' the Chestnut Ridge, to ask lodgin' frae us! Did you ever think o' seein' sich a day?"

Nellie made a curtsey and, Charles holding out his hand, she caught it, and while tears were welling up in her eyes, she bade him welcome, adding:

"Ah, sir! indeed ye pit me in min' o' auld times, ye hae sae muckle o' the braw looks o' your father. Glad I am truly, to hae you frae the place un'er my roof. I kenned your father weel in Maughrygowan; ye hae muckle o' his looks!

"But coom in; we maun get something ready to mak' ye comfortable, for ye maun hae had a hard time in the woods. I wonder in the wide warl hoo ye could guide yousel' among them."

As they entered the house, the fair creature whom Charles had looked upon from his concealment in the thicket, as she passed by with her companion, came forward to meet him. She was introduced to him as Gilbert's youngest daughter; and Nora, who had been in another apartment at that instant appearing, she was introduced as the eldest.

The manner in which these two buds of the forest received Addison, was considerably different. From Denny's report to his mother, they knew that some extraordinary visitor, and a white man, was approaching them. When they received this report they were both in a plain every day garment, but with this Nora was not content. She hastily retired to improve her appearance and exhorted Marie to do the same, but this she declined.

When Marie first saw Charles Addison, a feeling undefinable, such as she never before experienced, seized upon her mind, which caused her in a certain degree, to repent not having followed Nora's advice; and his name suggesting to her that this must be the same interesting person, so lately rescued from the savages by her revered Tonnawingo, she more than ever regretted that, while it was in her power to do so, she had not made a better appearance in his presence.

The reception she gave him was therefore rather shy and timid. On the other hand, Nora, prepared for the occasion, with all her rural grandeur on her, addressed him with an ease, gayety, and self-possession savoring somewhat of familiarity, which Charles would have felt rather disagreeable and unbecoming but for the apparent candor and innocency of the maiden.

On the other hand, the intelligent and enlightened Marie exhibited the bashfulness, diffidence and confusion of the rural maid.

But strange to tell, Charles Addison gave unhesitatingly his preference to the manner of his reception by Marie. In her he either saw, or fancied he saw, the effects of artless nature, genuine modesty, and refined sensibility.

"Thir twa lassies o' mine," said Gilbert, after all were seated, "hae been brocht up like deer among the woods here, an' it maun be a treat for them to see ony thing like a civilized white man. Lassies, hauld up your heeds, an' dinna be shy. Mr. Addison is a gintleman born, the sin o' my auld acquaintance, young Squire Addison of Maughrygowan.

"But, sir, Paddy tells us ye hae had an unco escape frae them wicked Indians, the Chippeways, but Tonnawingo can manage them when naebody else can—he's a wonnerfu' man that."

Charles now informed him that it was by Tonnawingo's directions that he had obtruded himself upon his hospitality.

"Obtrude, sir!" interrupted Gilbert. "Obtrude! I'm no' very muckle learned, sir, but I think that word means comin' to whar' yea's no' welcome. Noo, sir, gin ye were na as welcome here as in your father's parlor this house should na belong to Gilbert Frasier."

"I appreciate your hospitality," replied Charles, "and may have to ask the privilege of enjoying it for several days."

"I'm glad o't it. Ye'll no think o' ganging hame this six months, at ony rate. The winter's sae near at han', it wadna be possible."

Charles replied that his duty required that he should carry or send speedy intelligence of his late disaster to Philadelphia; but as regarding what measures he should adopt concerning his return, he would be governed entirely by the advice of Tonnawingo.

"Ye're richt, my frien'," said Gilbert; "Tonnawingo kens everything aboot this country, an' will na direct ye wrang."

At this juncture Nellie, who had some time before excused herself, now entered the room and announced that supper was ready.

CHAPTER X.

ADDISON MEETS HIS FATE

WHEN Charles saw the plentiful, and even luxurious table that was spread before him, and the good-hearted and contented family, whose own industry, under the blessings of Providence, had thus procured it for them in a wilderness, his heart was filled with a sensation of pride for his race.

Impressed with this feeling and his surroundings, his heart was in a fit state to join fervently and thankfully in the simple but sincere address which Gilbert made to the Giver of all good before commencing the meal.

Many a more splendid supper has been given and described than this repast, furnished by the good house wife of Gilbert Frasier. I will therefore be excused from entering into any tedious particulars concerning it. Suffice it to say that an elegant roast joint of the fatted calf which Denny had speedily sacrificed for this joyful occasion was placed in front of our hero's plate, and by special request Charles was asked to do the honors of carving, which he accomplished gracefully.

Mrs. Frasier had under her jurisdiction a fine fowl, stuffed with the most delicious ingredients the good hostess could command.

Gilbert himself had charge of a large dish of mealy potatoes, which he said were as good as any he ever raised here, yet they were nothing like the kind he raised in Maughrygowan.

After a time Marie and Nora distributed to the company enticing slices of pie and custard. Then after the disappearance of these Gilbert returned thanks, the cloth was removed, and from a corner in the cupboard near by a bottle of brandy was produced, and soon the fragrant odor of the punch bowl arose, as in a social way the coming of their guest was celebrated.

On this occasion the social bowl did not frighten away the ladies, as it mostly does within many circles of society, but in Gilbert Frasier's family there had never been any excess in the use of spirituous liquors, and the presence of the cheering cup was not looked upon as an evil. The ladies, rather for the sake of sociability, did not hesitate to pledge, in a draught, their good wishes for their visitor's health and prosperity.

Neither did the gentlemen indulge too heartily in the use of the fascinating liquor. They drank moderately, and while so doing indulged in pleasant social converse.

Gilbert related to Addison the history of his life, from the leaving of his native country up to the present time, however excepting that relating to the birth and adoption of Marie.

In return, Addison gave him the history of the expedition he had lately commanded, its unfortunate fate, and his own adventure and providential deliverance from the Indians.

Marie listened to his recital with great interest, and seemed much moved when he related his hairbreadth escape. She fervently exclaimed at the close of his narration, "Grand and glorious Tonnawingo, who has had it in his power to do so much good!"

"Heaven bless ye, my bairn," said Gilbert, "for that gude-hearted sayin.' Gin Tonnawingo could only teach the Indians humanity to their prisoners, I think he would be amaist as great an' usefu' a man as Moses, wha taucht the Jews the sixth commandment; gin the savages only knew that commandment, and feared to break it, I'm thinkin' I micht soon hae white neighbors plenty roon me, and may be some Irish families, an' 'tis no' likely that Nellie an' I wad then break our hearts sae muckle about Maughrygowan."

"Alas!" cried his wife, "bonny Maughrygowan will ne'er be oot o' my head gin a' the Irish in America were to settle beside us.

"It's bonny green meadows, an' it's hawthorn hedges, wi' their sweet smelling blossoms, an' the larks an' the thrushes, an' the lads an' the lassies, an' the sports of a simmer evening, an' the jokes an' mirth o' a lang winter's nicht. Ah, I canna think o' them without a sair heart, for—for—I'll ne'er see them again!"

Here Nellie's heart filled, and she wiped away a tear. The conversation here reverted to old Ireland, which aroused in the breast of the good dame such tender recollections that she retired to the privacy of her room to find relief in weeping. Her daughters withdrew also, and as Charles arose to bid them good-night, he was irresistibly impelled to say to Marie:

"This has been my happiest night. I shall never forget it!" He then checked himself as if he felt he had taken too much freedom, and resumed his seat considerably embarrassed, although his eyes were fixed steadily upon the door through which she had passed.

His meditations were soon interrupted by Gilbert addressing him: "Ye hae na seen my Paddy yet. I christened him for oor auld Irish saint; he's a thorough-gaun chap, winna min' the farm. He is a bit owre fond o' the chase by times. Ye hae na seen him yet, Mr. Addison?"

"No," replied Charles, who had by this time thrown off his reverie; "no, but I have understood that you had a son by that name."

"Ay, but he's a quite different chap frae Denny. He's a smart fellow, sir, an' a wee bit crafty in his disposition, when he's dealin' wi' the Indians. I'm no pleased at it, for I dinna like them cunning tricks, it's so much like cheatery.

"He palms on them shells, an' beads, an' brass rings, an' ither things, no' worth a button, for whilk they sometimes gie him back, loads o' skin o' musk-rat, an' beaver, an' buffalo, that he sells to the traders comin' doon the river for fifty times as muckle as they cost him. I canna think it a' tegither fair. I canna see the gude o' him tradin' this way. I'm sure that a' the skins an' trumpery he has gathered tegither, this six years past, would-

na get us a comfortable dinner in thir woods. I
kenna what they're gude for here, but to look at."

"Father," remarked Denny, who had just come
in from caring for the cattle for the night, as his
father commenced his uncomplimentary picture of
his brother's character and employment, "Father,
I maun say you speak owre hard o' Paddy. He
dinna cheat the Indians half so muckle as some o'
the ither traders; they say he deals fair, though he
makes hard bargains. The gentleman maunna
think Paddy sae bad as ye ca' him."

"I perceive," said Charles, "that it is not with
your approbation that your son has devoted himself to traffic rather than agriculture."

Before Gilbert had time to make reply, they
were interrupted by the door opening without ceremony, and the object of their conversation entered.

The father arose with a show of pleasure in his
face and saluted him. "An' there ye are, my lad.
We were just talking o' ye, an' I was telling this
frien' o' mine—Paddy, ye maun ken that's a frien'
o' mine, a sin o' my auld acquaintance, Thomas
Addison, the young squire o' Maughrygowan. Ye
dinna kin the squire, Paddy, but your mither
kenned them a' weel; an' her heart was filled this·

yera nicht wi' joy to see the sin o' her auld frien'
un'er her roof in this wild wilderness."

Paddy had by this time approached Charles, and
cordially taken him by the hand, expressing great
pleasure to see him in his father's house and safe
from the savages.

This young man was rather below the medium
size, and of a slender, but very firm build, indicating agility and endurance of fatigue, rather than
muscular strength.

His countenance was expressive more of ingen-
uity and cunning, rather than deep thought and
caution.   He was so much sun-burnt as to be almost of that Indian hue which he sometimes affected when he wished to flatter the native tribes.

He also often dressed in their fashion, and as he
had learned several of their languages, and spoke
them fluently, he could not easily be distinguished
from many of his red brethren.

He had been present as a spectator at the Chippeway council which had so nearly sacrificed Addison, clad in his Indian attire.   He was now dressed
in the usual garb of a frontier's man.

When he first entered the room he had a musket
in his hand and a long knife of the dagger form,
for bleeding any animal he might shoot on his ex-

cursions, which was placed in a leathern sheath suspended from a belt at his left side.

He hastily deposited his gun in one corner of the
room, then joining his father and Addison, entered
into the conversation, addressing their guest:

"Mr. Addison, I know of your miraculous deliv-
ery from what seemed to be a cruel death, but you
have gained one friend by your experience, for
whom it was indeed worth while to endure something. I mean Tonnawingo, the prophet, although I confess I should be very loath to undergo
what you did.

"You will have reason to keep a sharp look-out
for Carrawoona, for he is a revengeful and vindic-
tive enemy. He has vowed to sacrifice himself
or you, and is at this present time ranging the
woods, like a wild and infuriated animal, in search
of you.

"You are safe here for the present and in the
meantime I trust the Prophet will take steps to
send the intractable savage off in another direction."

"I fear," said Addison, "that Tonnawingo will
incur the enmity of this man, that he may suffer in
consequence—and perhaps lose his life—and that
would be a greater loss than mine."

"You have nothing to fear on that line," returned Paddy; "Carrawoona, with all his ferocity, will not dare to harm the Prophet, for if he did he would be held in abhorrence by every Indian man, woman and child, as the destroyer of Maneto, their chief deity."

"For myself, then," said Addison, "I will fear nothing; let the savage do his worst."

"By heavens! sir, I like your spirit," said Paddy, "and I shall keep an eye on Carrawoona myself if he pursues you to this neighborhood, where I know every foot of the country, a thousand times better than either he or anyone of his tribe."

Addison thanked him for his friendly intentions, remarking that with such protectors he would feel safe, yet would keep a vigil, that he might not fall into the hands of Carrawoona unawares.

Paddy observed that the night was pretty far advanced, and proposed retiring. His father yielded to the proposal, although he said he would "hae been glad to hae cracked an 'oor or twa langer wi' his Maughrygowan frien'," but he comforted himself with observing that "it wadna be the last nicht he should share a bowl of punch wi' him."

.. Although young Addison's body was sadly in need of repose, his mind had too many objects of contemplation to dwell upon, after he had retired for the night, to permit him soon to enjoy slumber.

He had, of late, experienced so many changes of an eventful nature, that his finding himself in safety within the home of a friendly white man, and in the enjoyment of more feminine loveliness than he had ever dreamed of meeting in this unsettled region, was sufficient to drive away all thoughts of slumber, and truly the charms of this "Rose of the Wilderness" he had met in this humble home of a daring settler, had made such an impression upon him that within there was the prompting of a passion stronger than that of mere friendship.

With such a lovely creature for a companion, he felt that his life would indeed be one of happiness; but without her, alas! it would be one of misery.

He felt he could brave any difficulty that might arise in his way to prevent him from claiming her as his own. He realized that he had various points to make secure before he could even claim her hand. First of these was the fair maid's affection and her consent to be his; next was the consent of his father, as he might object to an alliance of this kind. He might even strenuously forbid, while the maiden herself might decline.

These thoughts frequently came into his mind to

torment him, but being of a sanguine temperament he dismissed them.

He wished that Tonnawingo was only present. He would tell him how he felt and he believed that the advice of the Prophet would be a safe monitor.

With his resolution fixed, Charles at last resigned himself to sleep, in which there were no doubt, beautiful visions of lovely and bewitching maidens.

Some, who may peruse this page, may wonder in what condition was the mind of the fair Marie.

No doubt the thoughts then passing through her mind were of a character favorable toward the young man.

The whole of the following day was spent by Charles Addison in a manner most delightful to a youthful lover, in looking upon and listening to the mistress of his heart.

In beholding and conversing with Marie, the world and all its concerns were forgotten. If during the preceding evening the chains of love were thrown around his heart, they were now riveted there, never to be severed; and so delighted was he with these chains that he would not have exchanged them for King George's crown.

He was afraid of arousing her displeasure by a premature disclosure of his desires, therefore he resolved to first consult Tonnawingo, whom he knew to be her friend, although during the day there were several occasions when he could hardly resist the temptation to reveal the true state of his feelings.

Towards the after part of the following day as he walked along the bank of the river in company with his beloved and her sister, his feelings so plainly betrayed themselves as to leave Marie no room to doubt concerning them.

It was a beautiful afternoon, in that most delightful of all seasons on the American continent, characteristically called "Indian Summer." The atmosphere was enjoyable, equally free from summer's heat and winter's cold.

The trees of the forest were in the season of decay and shedding their wasted verdure profusely around them. The trio indulged in pleasant converse, both of the girls enjoying greatly the description Addison gave of his travels in Europe. Quite often as his eyes looked into those of Marie, there must have been a tell-tale expression in them, as something caused her cheeks to glow with a rich crimson.

The presence of her sister, Nora, rendered his making a declaration to the lovely girl at his side rather embarrassing, but still he could not refrain from expressing the happiness he enjoyed from being in their company. They had continued their walk some distance along the river bank before either of the three realized how far they were from their starting.

The proposal to return was made by Nora who, recalling to mind some household duty she had yet to perform, declared it would neither be wise nor prudent for them to continue farther.

They accordingly began to retrace their steps, but had not proceeded far upon their return, when Nora, observing some cattle a short distance in the woods, which she wished to drive homewards, ran after them, and left Charles alone with Marie, thus affording him the much desired opportunity to relieve his heart and mind.

"Alas! Marie," said he, as soon as their companion was out of hearing, "I have expressed my feeling of happiness here, but the true cause of my happiness—Oh! would to heaven that you knew it and approved of it!"

"Mr. Addison," she replied, in a tone and manner which had become suddenly serious and embarrassed, "what good would my knowledge of that circumstance do you? If it will do you good, pray let me hear it, for I will rejoice to serve you. But if you are happy, as you say, is it not enough? Be content and continue so; my knowledge of your concerns, or my interference with them, can surely do you no good, for my power is exceedingly limited."

"Ah! my dear friend," he cried impulsively, "you alone, of all the world, have the greatest influence over my future, you alone have—"

"Sir," said she, interrupting him, "this is mysterious language. How I can in any manner control your future, I do not understand, nor do I wish at present to be informed. Mysteries and secrets have never been pleasing to me; a knowledge of your secret might possibly do me harm. Now when I think of it properly, I desire you to let me remain in ignorance concerning your affairs."

"Ah! Marie," said he, "why put this cruel injunction upon me? But it is your wish, and I shall obey."

They then walked on for some time in silence, during which our hero's manner betrayed great agitation. Marie, afraid that this might continue after their arrival at the house, and be observed by some of the family, stopped in their walk and said:

"Mr. Addison, I trust that what has occurred between us this evening may not be allowed to change our bearing towards each other, nor interrupt whatever degree of friendship may have existed between us.

"I assure you I have not changed my opinion of you, nor will I unless a change becomes perceptible on your part."

"Marie! Marie!" said Charles, looking seriously and with feeling at her, while he laid his hand upon his heart, "I here solemnly promise, that whatever may be your wishes, only let me know them, and I shall obey them—for obedience to you is, and ever shall be, my chief happiness."

Marie blushed deeply, for she could not now avoid comprehending his meaning, but she said nothing, and continuing their walk, they soon arrived at the house.

CHAPTER XI.

ADVICE OF THE PROPHET

IT was not many days before the Prophet visited the Frasier cabin. Addison was delighted to see him, and during a short conversation held together, Tonnawingo informed him of the unsuccessful attempts Carrawoona had made with the neighboring tribes to secure their assistance in pursuing him.

"But," said he, "my son, although it is not likely he will find any one to assist him in this locality, you are still in constant danger, for his implacable hatred of you, as the slayer of his son, will impel him onward, and he will never weary in searching for you.

"You know not how soon from some unsuspected ambush he may hurl a missile of destruction upon you. I would suggest that for your own safety, you fix an early day for your return to your friends in the East. Our brother Frasier will furnish you with a horse and provisions, and I will procure you a guide. My son, I desire your safety with your people, for I fear for it here."

"My father and my deliverer," said Addison, "I know you wish your son to be happy.   Ah! if you wish him to be so, do not so soon bid him leave this place.   When I last saw you, I wished for nothing more ardently than to get out of this wilderness. Now, I am most loath to leave it; for in leaving it under the present circumstances I shall separate myself from happiness, and perhaps bid adieu to it forever."

Here he explained to the Prophet the condition of his mind and heart toward the fair Marie.   The old Indian listened with interest, when, at the close, he quietly asked the question: "My son, may I ask if the maiden knows that you love her?"

"Alas! father," replied the youth, "she has not permitted me to make a declaration.   But I believe she suspects—Ah! she cannot but suspect how I feel."

"Hear me, my son," said Tonnawingo; "the maiden you love is the child of my instruction, and as dear to me as if she were my own off-spring.   Her peace of mind and her prosperity, therefore, are as much the object of my solicitude as yours can be. I shall try by close study of her, to learn the true state of her feelings toward you.

"If I find her averse to your attentions I shall

then require you, for her sake, to relinquish all pretensions to her, for I will not sanction any measure
that may serve to interrupt the tranquillity of her
life."

"Father," interposed Addison, "by what you
have said you have bidden me despair. I hoped
for your interference in my behalf, but, alas! I now
expect none. You will not befriend me—nay,
you will oppose my efforts to gain her favor, unless
you discover that I already enjoy it. Father, you
may save yourself the trouble of making the inquiry, for I know I do not enjoy it. She has forbidden me to speak to her the feelings of my heart.
Oh! if I had only permission to plead my cause, to
tell her how much I adore her, I know she would
pity me, for she has a kind heart."

They conversed in this strain for some time.
Addison in the impetuosity of his youth and the ar-
deney of his passion, beseeching Tonnawingo to
use his powerful influence with the fair maid of the
forest, to induce her to look upon his suit favorably.

To all this, the Prophet answered in his grave
but kindly manner, bidding him to be patient, but
to first secure himself from the impending danger
of an attack from Carrawoona.

After some reflection over the matter, the young
man decided it were more advisable for him to proceed to the East, that he might the easier return if
possible to win the hand of this "Rose of the Wilderness," that had already so firm a hold upon his
heart.

He therefore declared to Tonnawingo, that as
soon as the necessary preparation for his journey
could be made he would, for a time, bid farewell to
scenes, in which for the space of only a few weeks
he had felt more the extremes of joy and sorrow,
than ever during the whole course of his previous
existence.

The effect of his conversation with the Prophet
was visible upon him the entire day, and Marie
could not help but observe it.   Indeed her own
spirits were not in the most lively mood, for she
had noticed that preparations were being made for
the departure of their guest, Tonnawingo having
decided that it would be best that Addison should
only remain another day with them.

She truly experienced a sense of disappointment
in realizing that this interesting young man was so
soon to leave them.   With her keen perception,
she had divined what he had attempted to declare
to her; but would it be prudent on her part to en-

-courage his partiality for her, when fortune would compel them to occupy such different spheres? She did not realize that this strange feeling within her, aroused by the contemplated departure of one who had so lately come within her circle of acquaintance was the first germ of a love that was springing up in her own heart for this brave, manly young person who was at best but little more than a stranger to her.

There was not so much the desire to crush these kindlings of affection, as to suppress any external manifestation that might lead the others to suspect the true condition of her heart.

During the whole of the evening she kept up her spirits very successfully; and so well did she control herself, that when Tonnawingo, with the design of discovering how she was affected toward their guest, talked pointedly to her about his leaving them, professing great admiration for the manliness, and general excellence of his character, and his great regret that necessity compelled him to take his departure, she completely succeeded in deceiving him with regard to the state of her affections.

She acknowledged that he was a very fine and accomplished young man, but she spoke in such a careless manner, that Tonnawingo supposed she conceived it of no importance whether he was or not.

She pitied his misfortunes, and wished him at a safe distance from Carrawoona's vengeance, but expressed it in so calm and even a tone that the Prophet was led to believe she felt for Addison only the natural interest due a friend and acquaintance.

When the morning came of the day which was to be the last that he would abide with them, she felt agitated, so much so, that she feared if she stayed at home, she might betray herself. She thought it prudent that she spend the day at a distance.

Therefore after breakfast, she accordingly set off on a visit to Queen Alliquippa, so that the lover, very much to his mortification, felt himself compelled to pass the last day of his stay at the Frasier abode alone, without the satisfaction of seeing the adored of his heart.

His chagrin at her absence was all the greater owing to the rest of the family paying him more than usual attention, and frequently expressing regret that it did not suit him to remain longer with them.

He felt depressed in spirit, for he could not help but see that she was avoiding him, and he reasoned in his mind, that certainly she would know that he would desire her presence on this the last day of his sojourn with them.

The day was well advanced into the afternoon when unable longer to bear her absence, especially as he was not sure whether she would return at all before his departure, he resolved to set out for Alliquippa's and solicit at least a parting interview.

He accordingly, without acquainting any one of his intention, set off in that direction. Fortune sometimes favors lovers even in their most desponding moments and, on this occasion, she favored Addison, so far as to permit him, when but a little more than half way to Alliquippa's residence, to meet his Marie returning homeward alone in the forest.

His heart leaped with joy as he beheld her continuing to advance; for he was afraid when he first saw her, that in order to avoid him she might return back to the queen's residence.

But it were best to inform the reader of what Addison himself was at that time ignorant. That a feeling similar to his own had actuated the return of Marie. She had thought that she might perhaps be carrying her caution too far with respect to her lover (for she well knew that Addison was such) and that it would be acting with too much harshness, to both his and her own feelings (for Marie felt in her heart a something else for Charles Addison than the sentiment of mere friendship) and she felt that it would be unkind to him to deny him an opportunity of saying a farewell, which in all probability might be the first and last.

"I will, at least see him once more before he departs," she said to herself; "there can be no harm in that, since we shall say good bye, likely never to meet again."

Their feeling upon meeting was mutual, although the impulsiveness of Addison gave evidence of the greater delight. Seeing she manifested no thought of turning from her course, he hastened to meet her, holding out his hand by way of salutation as he greeted her: "Oh, Marie!" said he, "how glad I am to meet you; I really feared I was to be deprived of taking a long, but I trust not a last, farewell."

Marie could not conceal her blushes and confusion as she took his proferred hand; but in as light a tone as she could command, she replied: "Your not seeing me, Mr. Addison, would I trust have

been no great disadvantage to you, and I trust
it would not have added one particle to either the
length, wildness, or difficulty of your journey
homewards."

The sensitive nature of the young man felt the
irony in her words, but, controlling his feelings, he
calmly replied: "It would have dispirited and en-
feebled me. I should have felt that you wilfully
avoided me from some personal dislike, and I
would be far less capable of enduring the difficulties of the journey than if I commenced it with a
consciousness of possessing your esteem and good
wishes."

"My esteem, or good wishes either, can be of
but little importance to any one," she replied; "but
such as they are, I have no hesitation in sincerely
saying that they are yours, in welcome, wherever
you go, and if no harm befalls you until I wish it,
you will always be in safety and comfort."

"Oh! dare I ask nothing but esteem from you?
Is there no warmer feeling of your heart to which
I may lay claim? Will it be presumption—"

"Sir!" she said, interrupting him, "I wish to hear
nothing at present upon that subject to which I see
you wish to bring the conversation.

"We are soon to part, and may perhaps never

meet again.   To cherish more than sincere esteem might be detrimental to the peace and happiness of us both.   Let us, therefore, look upon each other only as—"

Here they were both startled by the report of a musket, the ball of which struck Addison in the right arm, breaking it.   This was immediately followed by a blood-curdling war-whoop of a fierce and powerful savage, who leaped with ferocity upon him, now unable to defend himself, and throwing him upon his back, held him firmly down with one knee upon his breast; with his left hand he grasped his victim by the throat, forcibly pressing him to the earth, while with his right hand he brandished his tomahawk, exclaiming:

"Destroyer of my son, where liest thou now? In his father's grasp.   Yes, smile, thou spirit of Carrawissa!   This is thy victim; I sacrifice thy enemy to thee in despite of Tonnawingo.

"Thy blood shall appease my passion, thy scalp shall gratify my pride, and thy soul I shall devote as an offering to Carrawissa.   No prophet of Maneto shall save thee now."

So saying, he collected his whole strength, and the fatal blow was in the act of descending, when the clear, sharp crack of a rifle was heard in the forest, and at the same instant the savage fell lifeless by his victim's side, a bullet having penetrated his brain.

Addison being thus unexpectedly freed from the grasp of his terrible foe, sprang to his feet, and hastened to the side of Marie who had fallen in a faint from the effects of such a terrifying scene.

At that instant Paddy Frasier came hurrying to his side, but first directing his attention to Carrawoona, whom the reader has already recognized in the Indian making the attack upon Marie's companion.

. Paddy examined the prostrate savage, and upon perceiving the ragged hole made by his bullet in the temple of the now defunct warrior, he shouted: "By heavens! it is what he deserved. It was a very good hit, too, at such a distance. I took the very spot I aimed at; I could get no nearer, but never yet, since I was a boy, have I missed at a hundred yards. It has done the business neatly and killed him snugly, thank Providence."

Marie's senses were now returning, and the first words she distinctly heard were the awful ones, "and killed him!" which, in the present scattered state of her senses she supposed were applied to Charles Addison, whom she did not at first perceive beside her supporting her head with his sound arm, while his wounded one hung bleeding by his side.

"Ah! my Charles!" she exclaimed in a frenzied manner, "has he killed thee? Has the monster killed my beloved? Oh! let me see him! Is he dead? Oh, that I could die with him! Why did he not kill us both?" Here her senses had returned so far that she began to discover the truth, when her face which had been deathly pale, now crimsoned with blushes and she stammered "I—I —I Oh! what—"

Addison now spoke in a soothing tone, "My dear girl be calm; neither of us is killed."

"The God of Heaven be praised," she repeated; "but Charles, how is this? Was not that shot mortal? And surely I saw you fall beneath the grasp of that dreadful savage."

"That was all true enough, my dear," replied Addison, "but I have had a Providential deliverance; my enemy, Carrawoona, has breathed his last, thanks to the accuracy of your brother Paddy's aim."

"Oh! Charles how thankful we should be!" Then checking herself, as if she realized she had expressed her feelings too warmly, she said: "Indeed, Mr. Addison, you have singular reason to be thankful for the protection of heaven, which has now twice so miraculously rescued you from impending fate."

"I am thankful, Marie," said he, "not for my deliverance only, but also for my danger, for it has been the means of letting me see that the heart, whose affections I would rather possess than anything else in the wide world, is not indifferent to my fate. Oh, Marie, there has been sweet consolation afforded me this evening. Tonnawingo will now not ask me to leave thee so soon."

"Mr. Addison," said she, "you have, I doubt not, discovered the weakness I wish to conceal; but let us talk at present no more about it."

"Ah!" she exclaimed, noticing the condition of his right arm, "I fear you are wounded, perhaps dangerously so. Oh, Charles! the worst may not yet be over!"

"The worst is over my dear," said he, in a low voice, so that Paddy could not hear him. "I think this injury nothing, when I consider the sweet confession I have gained from lips of, to me, the loveliest woman in the land."

"Oh! let us hasten home," said she, "that your arm may be bound up, Charles. You surely have suffered in the short time you have been in this wilderness; but let us hasten.   Your wound must indeed be very painful," and as she said this she beamed upon him a look of tenderness and affection that caused Addison to almost forget the pain of his injured arm.

"Yes," said Paddy, turning from an examination of Carrawoona's skull which gave evidence of his skill as a marksman, and addressing the lovers; "Yes, Mr. Addison must be taken care of.   This savage, thanks to the goodness of my rifle, will require no more care."

"The goodness of your eye, Paddy, I believe also deserves credit for this result," said Addison.

"No matter about my eye," replied Paddy; "the worst is your broken arm, which needs attention. Marie, lend me that shawl; I will sling it to his breast till we get home, and then Tonnawingo will fix it as neatly as he did my broken leg long ago." Marie hastily loosened her shawl, and tremblingly assisted Paddy in fixing the fractured arm with it, so that the motion of walking might not give him pain until he reached the house, which was accomplished without accident.

CHAPTER XII.

ADDISON DECIDES TO RETURN EAST

W E can only imagine the mixture of alarm and joy, produced upon the arrival of Addison at the Frasier cabin. The joy was soon in the ascendency when Tonnawingo, after deftly binding up the arm, declared that the hurt was not dangerous, and that a few weeks of care and good nursing would be all that would be required.

Paddy came in for a share of attention, and he was joyfully thanked and loudly praised for his keen eye and steady aim on this occasion.

As for Charles, the assurance he now had of being beloved by the mistress of his heart, and the kind attentions which, in this time of his affliction, she unhesitatingly paid him, gave him such a delightful flow of spirits that he appeared all cheerfulness and animation.

Tonnawingo, who did not know that he had discovered the state of Marie's feelings, naturally ascribed his good humor to his having so providentially escaped from his persecutor, together with the prospect he now had of enjoying a longer stay with the woman he loved.

The Prophet took opportunity to have a talk with Addison, and from him learned the existing state of affairs between him and Marie. Tonnawingo was pleased to learn that this child of his tutorage reciprocated the passion of the young man whom he had learned to love in their short period of companionship. "My son," said he, "if you have her affections, you have indeed a valuable prize, which I trust you will ever possess wisdom enough to appreciate justly, and honor enough to cherish fondly."

"My son, I go off to-morrow to the Northward. 'An Indian council requires my presence in a few days. It will be three weeks before I return here. You will by that time have likely recovered, and I expect will soon be ready to proceed to Philadelphia, where you may meet your father and smooth the way for the attainment of your future hopes."

During Tonnawingo's absence, Addison, who had exchanged an almost broken heart for a broken arm, improved rapidly, and this home in the wilderness increased in its attraction day by day, for was not the only being he deemed necessary to his happiness—Marie Frasier—domiciled under the same roof?

The matter dearest to his heart being thus providentially placed upon the most favorable footing, he began to reflect upon the propriety of his returning home, that he might not only acquaint the Ohio Company of the misfortune that had befallen their expedition, but also arrange matters for a speedy return to the wilderness with the necessary means to make Marie his wife.

Paddy Frasier, to whom gratitude now closely bound him, was desirous of accompanying him on his journey, for the purpose of carrying his furs and paltry wares to Philadelphia, to exchange them there for such merchandise as suited the Indians.

This was very agreeable to Addison, because he would not only prove a pleasant companion as well as useful on the way, and then upon their arrival at Philadelphia an opportunity would be offered him to reward Paddy, by a present of merchandise, for the great service he had been to him, in the murderous attack of his enemy, Carrawoona, in the forest.

Gilbert Frasier himself was pleased at the prospect of his son making a journey to the East, and the father anxiously hoped he might fall in with some good Christian woman on the journey whom he might bring back with his other eastern goods, and this he intimated to Paddy, who was then assorting, cleaning, and packing up his wares.

At length our hero's arm was sufficiently strong to permit him to undertake the journey, and the day drew near when he was to bid farewell to his beloved.

Tonnawingo had returned from the Indian council, and the guide whom he had some time before provided for Addison was in readiness.

This man, whose name was Manluff, was much in awe of Tonnawingo. He was, at the same time, well acquainted with the whole of the mountainous district of Pennsylvania, from the Chestnut Ridge to the South Mountain. He was one of the best qualified persons our travelers could have procured, to conduct them through the intricate wilderness.

Although fully equipped and ready for the journey, Addison was loath to commence the journey, and succeeded in delaying the date of departure, much to the chagrin of Paddy, who was anxious to be off.

At length it was decided that the next rising sun should see them on their way. He had just en-

joyed what he considered would be his last private
interview, at this time, with Marie, and in the evening was wandering alone in one of Gilbert's fields,
indulging in a train of reflection, when he was
startled by a person springing over the fence near
which he was meditating, and suddenly to his great
astonishment, who should stand before him but the
well known form of Peter McFall, who eagerly
caught his hand and exclaimed:

"Och, Master! now I have found you at last.
Just put your hand here, and feel how Peter's heart
beats, for I'm all out of breath with joy, and with
running to see you alive. By the powers of Killarney! but I thought the old prophet had taken
you to heaven with him and I feared I should never
see you again."

"Then you are pleased," observed his master,
"that I must fret and fight a little longer with this
troublesome world."

Before Peter could make reply they were joined
by Doctor Killbreath who had been traveling with
Peter, but who had been left behind in Peter's great
delight to greet his beloved master. The doctor
was greeted warmly by Charles. "My dear
friends, I am glad you have both come at this criti-

cal moment, for I was about setting off to-morrow for Philadelphia.

"Now we can all go together. What say you, doctor? My good friend, Frasier, who lives here, can have you both equipped for the journey in a single day."

"There is nothing I wish for more sincerely," replied the doctor; "the sooner we get out of these wilds, the better. I am happy that we got here so opportunely. I have indeed reason to thank Peter for it."

"No, by my soul!" said Peter; "you may thank master there, for I would not have thought of leaving the French yet, if the old prophet hadn't told me how master lived here with a dacint Christian and an Irishman, heaven bless him! But I must see him and shake his ould hand for him on account of the ould sod."

"Come along then, friends; old Gilbert will be glad to see you," replied Addison. "Yonder comes his daughter, Nora. Doctor, you must take care of your heart, for she's a pretty girl—and I know it is tempting to meet a pretty girl in the wilderness."

"I suppose you have found it so, Mr. Addison," replied the doctor.

"I cannot say much about it, doctor, but I know you are no woman-hater, and Nora, as you will soon see, is really handsome."

"I acknowledge," returned the doctor, "that in this region I should consider the sight of a handsome young woman a real treat."

"Well, take care of your heart my good friend," said Addison, "for here comes real temptation."

At this juncture Nora, who had been in the woods on some errand, and was now returning home, turned off in another direction, as if to avoid them.

Addison called upon her to stop, which she did, and the party approached her.

"Why do you run away from me, Nora?" said he. "Here are some of my old Philadelphia companions, just escaped from Fort Le-Boeuf, and one of them is a countryman of your father."

"My father will be glad to see them, no doubt," said Nora.

"And won't you also make them welcome?" asked Addison. "Here is Doctor Killbreath, whom I hope you will find a pleasant acquaintance?"

Nora, who had taken a sly look at the doctor, and observing his eyes fixed upon her with a mean-

ing she did not exactly understand, but which she
thought did not denote anything uncivil coyly
made reply:

"Sir," said she, "I will do my best to make your
friends comfortable, for I doubt not they deserve
our kindness."

The doctor bowed, and advancing a step offered
the rustic maiden his hand, which she clasped with
true rural simplicity.

Peter observing this, burst forth: "Arrah! let the
lassie alone, for good manners! The pretty creatures always know good manners; God bless their
kind hearts, for sure my mother was one of them."

"And have you never seen any of them you loved
better than your mother?" said Addison.

"Well, the Divil take me, master, but I have,"
replied Peter. "But it was in swate Dublin, your
Honor. Arrah, master, just think how it pleased
me to sit beside her and look into her beautiful
eyes and hear her swate bird-like voice. Alas! poor
Molly McNickel, dear lass, she may never see Peter
again."

The party had now arrived at the house, and a
hearty shake of Gilbert's Irish fist soon dispelled
from Peter's volatile heart the melancholy feeling

which the remembrance of the happiness he once enjoyed with Molly McNickel had aroused.

Their host showed them true Irish hospitality, and while they are entering into the enjoyment of it we will relate very briefly how the doctor and his companions severed their relations with their French captors at the fort.   The doctor, as has been stated, was in the enjoyment of a parole, and spent much of his time with his rifle in the woods. On one of these excursions he was fired at by an Indian whose aim not being accurate, the doctor luckily escaped.   Not so with his adversary, however, for the doctor returned the fire with such correctness of aim that the career of the murderous savage was quickly brought to a close.

He proved to be a brave of the Ottawa tribe, and ere long, the knowledge of how he came by his death being learned by his tribe, great was the clamor and demand made of the commandant of the fort that the white man be handed over to be a sacrifice to appease the spirit of their departed brother.

The matter was finally left to a council of twelve, six being Indians and six being Frenchmen. The Indians labored long and earnestly to induce the white men to surrender the unfortunate doctor to·

be committed to the flames, to appease their wrath. Their demand was so urgent that the Frenchmen were upon the point of surrendering their victim to them, when the coming of Tonnawingo, the Prophet, was heralded.

The Council paused in their deliberations as the old Indian approached. He entered their council circle with majestic tread, waving his wand in the air; as he reached the centre of the circle he paused, and waved his wand three times above his head, then spoke, addressing the Ottawas:

"My brothers of the Ottawas! Ye seem not at this time to know the will of Maneto. He has sent me here to reveal it. This white man, whom you would sacrifice, has killed one of our brothers.

"But I must tell you the Great Father said he should die by the hand of this white man, for our slain brother excited the act.

"Do not then bring down the vengeance of Maneto by destroying this prisoner. You have heard what I was sent to say; I hope, my brothers, you will attend to it."

One of the Indian counselors, named Palaro, replied:

"Prophet! to obey the directions .of Maneto, who governs all things, is our duty. You say that

Maneto requires us to let a white man who has killed an Ottawa go free. Is it not fair, in order that our tribe may be convinced that pardoning our prisoner was right, to ask what sign you can give of your words being the words of the Great Spirit?"

Tonnawingo now lifted his eyes towards heaven, and continued in this attitude with his countenance expressive of great supplication. This he did for several minutes, then spoke earnestly. "Ottawa brothers, hear me! You have desired a proof that Maneto does not desire the sacrifice of this man. Listen to me, brothers.

"There is a high rock on the shore of Lake Erie, the top of which was rent last summer by the hand of Maneto. You, Palaro, know the place, for you had your wigwam in the shadow of this rock at that time, and was miraculously preserved.

"Brothers, on the third day from this, let three of your warriors proceed to this rock. A living eagle will be found there, fixed in the breach made by the thunder. Seize him—he will be a sacrifice to the memory of your dead brother, and a more acceptable one to his spirit than this prisoner."

The council determined to send in search of the eagle, and accept it as a substitute for the prisoner who was given over to the charge of the French, on condition that if no eagle was found, he should without delay be put to death in any manner the Indians desired.

It was now that Peter McFall, who had by accident met Tonnawingo, and learned from him of the whereabouts of his beloved master, aroused by the great desire to see him and knowing the impending fate hanging over his companion, the doctor, set about planning an escape.

Fort Le-Boeuf was situated upon the bank of the western branch of French creek. It occupied a small cleared space of ground surrounded by a stockade made of strong piles driven close to each other into the earth, sharpened at the top, and more than twelve feet high, with port holes for cannon and loop holes for small arms cut through them.

The garrison at this time consisted of about two hundred men.

How to make an escape for himself and his friend was what now agitated the mind of Peter no little. He had discovered a small sewer, commencing in the yard of a wash house which was occupied by a number of squaws in the service of the garrison.

This sewer had been made for the purpose of carrying off to the creek the waste water used in washing. It was through this passage that Peter reckoned that he and the doctor might be able to escape.

While he was arranging his plans, the company who had been sent to procure the eagle as represented by Tonnawingo, returned, having in their possession a large, live, gray eagle, which was regarded with wonder and surprise by both the French and Indians assembled at the fort.

The eagle was at once bound to the stake and blazing faggots heaped around it; and while the sacrifice was being made the Indians chanted forth with great fervency the glory of Maneto, the praises of Tonnawingo, and the valor of their deceased warrior.

During the scene of excitment, Peter McFall. and his companion, the doctor, were busily making their exit from the fort by way of the sewer, which, while it was not a very desirable route, proved adequate and they emerged from it close to the creek, whose waters served them in performing their ablutions and cleaning their clothes from the filth of passage through which they had gained their liberty.

They did not tarry long, but boldly pushed forward into the forest, and when daylight arrived were quite a distance from the fort.

After three days wandering through the dense undergrowth they arrived on the banks of the Allegheny river, which they followed for some distance.

Finally, after nine days from leaving Fort LeBoeuf, they reached the vicinity of the Frasier home, and met with Addison as stated.

CHAPTER XIII.

GOVERNOR DINWIDDIE DESIRES AN EMBASSY

THE separation of dear friends has always been accompanied with regret and sorrow, and in the case of Charles Addison's parting with Marie, it was not different from similar cases before and since, but they both bore the grief philosophically.

The party who commenced their journey three days after the coming of the two friends alluded to in the previous chapter, were Dr. Killbreath, Paddy Frasier, Peter McFall, Manluff, the Indian guide, and Charles Addison.   Besides the horses on which they rode, they had along with them three others, two of which were laden with Paddy's merchandise, and the third with provisions and other stores.

They were well armed, for in those days no one ever thought of attempting a journey, even though a short one, without being properly prepared for both defence and attack.

On the third day they crossed the Chestnut

Ridge, and encamped that night between it and
the Laurel Hill, in what is now called Ligonier
Valley.

As they were about continuing their journey next
morning, they were unexpectedly attacked by a
small party of Ottawas, whom the French had dispatched to scour the country in search of Peter
and the Doctor. The savages, however, had given
their fire at too great a distance to do any serious
mischief. Two of their shots feebly pierced
through a package of Paddy's furs, and another
slightly wounded one of the horses.

Each of our travelers immediately took to a tree
and kept up such a well directed fire upon their enemies, when any of them dared to appear in sight,
that the latter thought proper about mid-day to
withdraw, after having lost five or six of their number, who were killed on the spot.

Our party then cautiously proceeded onward,
keeping a sharp lookout in all directions which
obliged them to travel so slowly that they only
reached the top of the Laurel Hill that night.
Here they encamped on a spot where they could
not be easily surprised.

The savages had tasted so bitterly of their intrep-
idity the day before that they were not further mo-

lested during the remainder of their journey, which they performed without meeting with any serious disaster in about four weeks.

The account which Addison gave to the Ohio Company of the fate of their expedition, which he ascribed to the jealousy and management of the French, made a great stir in the political world and produced much excitement throughout all the colonies.

But there was none of them that took up the matter with greater spirit than Virginia. That state did then, as indeed it does yet, possess a high-minded and courageous population, that could not tamely submit to any insult or encroachment upon their rights; and the territory thus usurped by a hostile force being then considered as within the bounds of her charter, she felt herself called upon to demand satisfaction for what had been done, and to take measures for resisting such aggressions for the future.

Although during the whole of the spring and summer succeeding the occurrences we have related, the public received fresh and repeated provocations from Indian incursions upon the back settlements, especially in the Virginian territories, yet the colonial governments thought proper to delay making any public effort to restrain or punish these depredations until they should receive instructions on the subject from the government of Great Britain.

With respect to the hostile Indians, small parties of militia and volunteers were immediately employed, but in an altogether insufficient manner, to bring about effective results; and for several months, the terror and sufferings of the Virginia back-woods settlers continued daily to increase.

At length Mr. Dinwiddie, the governor of Virginia, received intelligence that the French government manifested a reluctance to give any satisfaction to the British crown on the subject at issue, and he was authorized to use his discretion in bringing the aggressors to an account for what they had done. A national war at this time was not to be desired. He therefore thought it expedient, before he should resort to actual force, to send an envoy to the commander at Fort Le-Boeuf, to whose instrumentality the late outrages had been particularly charged.

The object of the visit of the envoy was to demand from him, in the name of his Britannic Majesty, an explanation of his hostile conduct towards

British subjects, and that some satisfactory security be given that it should not be repeated.

It was at this crisis very difficult to find any one properly qualified for such an embassy. To one willing to undertake it, the journey of several hundred miles through a trackless forest, inhabited only by savages, the most of whom had of late become inveterately hostile to the English, was not a pleasing anticipation.

No English white man, it was thought, could penetrate into these wilds and return alive, unless by a miracle, for of late even the traders, who had been invited, had been often plundered and sometimes massacred, for no other reason than that of being English subjects.

There were in Virginia numbers of patrotic and gallant spirits, whom danger alone could not have deterred from the undertaking, but various other motives operated upon their minds. They protested against the folly of sending such an embassy into the midst of a barbarous race of men, who neither knew nor cared for the sacred character of an ambassador.

"No," said they, "if we go at all into the haunts of these savages, let us go prepared to drive them and their French allies out together with the bay-

onet and rifle.   We should negotiate with such enemies only with the mouths of cannon."

In short, Governor Dinwiddie, after he had decided on the propriety of the measure, found so
much difficulty in finding any one qualified for the
hazardous service, who would be willing to undertake it, that he began to have thoughts of abandon-
ing the project, especially as the winter season was
approaching.

As he was one day in his private apartment, meditating with considerable anxiety upon this subject,
he was informed that a very respectable looking
young man requested admittance to his presence.
The governor desired him to be shown into a front
chamber, where he in a few minutes awaited upon
him.

Dinwiddie saluted the stranger respectfully, for
notwithstanding his youth, being apparently not
above twenty years of age, there was in his manner
and bearing an air of dignity and intelligence, with
which the governor was forcibly impressed, and
which at once dispelled any feeling of annoyance
that might have arisen at the call of this stranger.

As this young man will play a considerable part
in the remainder of this story, it is presumed that a

description of his appearance on this occasion will not be unacceptable to the reader.

His stature was exactly six feet, and his form a happy medium between the usual slenderness of youth and the more rotundity of middle life. His chest was full and expansive showing plenty of room for a liberal and capacious heart.

His limbs were in just proportion to the rest of his frame, and so free and unincumbered in all their motions, as to give a peculiar gracefulness to his gait and gesture.

His shoulders were broad and finely shaped, indicating great strength. With respect to his countenance, if ever there was one that expressed true nobleness and magnanimity of the soul, it was his. Of the oval form with a remarkably high forehead, it was open, kind and candid.

His sparkling blue eyes displayed the fire of passion, combined with the coolness of wisdom. His nose was of a commanding form, neither exactly Grecian nor Roman, but partaking of both. His mouth and chin were of the pronounced type, and indicated firmness combined with tenderness and generosity.

This young man was a native of Virginia, and descended from one of the most respectable families in that province; but in the opinion of Governor Dinwiddie upon this occasion, such a young man would have made any family respectable.

Reader, you have no doubt guessed the name of this youth who stood before the Governor of Virginia, and, by his bearing, won from that proud dignitary a feeling of high regard and respect. His name which is now synonymous with everything with which our loved country's history is associated, was

GEORGE WASHINGTON.

After the usual salutation was over, Mr. Washington presented an introductory letter from a valued friend of the governor, who perused it with apparently great interest.

When the governor had finished reading the letter, he looked up with a pleased surprise upon his face. "Why, Mr. Washington," he observed, "this is a very complimentary letter indeed, and speaks of you as one well qualified and willing to undertake the hazardous task of carrying a message from me to the French commandant at Le-Boeuf.

"When would it suit you to go on this mission?"

"At a day's notice, whenever your excellency orders—"

"Suppose—let me see," said Dinwiddie, "this is Tuesday, the 23d day of October. In a week from this date could you be ready?"

"To-morrow—to-day—this hour—and at all hours, I am ready for service to my country. You are her monarch's representative; order me when you choose. But if I might suggest anything in this matter, it would be promptness and expedition —your excellency is aware that the season requires it."

"Young man!" replied the governor, "my friend has not been mistaken in his estimate of your character. Your ardor in this case is wisdom. Your country has been fortunate in giving you birth, for I perceive if Providence spares you, that you will be both her blessing and her boast."

"Had I known of you two months sooner, this mission might now have been successfully terminated; but name your day and everything shall be provided."

"It is your excellency's right to name it," said the youth in a modest manner.

"Well then," spoke the governor, "let it be a week from to-day; your commission and instructions shall be immediately prepared.   But, tell me, have you thought of the dangers and difficulties?"

"I have thought of them seriously, sir," replied Washington.

"And they don't cause you to hesitate?" said Dinwiddie.

The reply of the young man should be the living sentiment of every honest youth in the land, as he responded: "Nothing, I trust, will ever make me hesitate to do my duty."

"I am satisfied," remarked the governor.   "It has been, perhaps, fortunate that the perils of the undertaking have deterred others from engaging in it, whose services I should have gladly accepted. My young friend, I shall not detain you longer, but shall be glad if you will spend the evening with me."

"With your excellency's permission, I would rather return to Mount Vernon, to arrange some matters so that nothing on my part may retard the expedition," remarked Washington.

The governor urged upon him to tarry, saying that only one day would make but little or no difference.

To this the young man made reply, "Your excellency will excuse me; but I cannot remain to-night.

unless it be that some public business requires my presence."

"There is no public business to require your stay, I acknowledge," replied the governor, "but I wish to enjoy your conversation and cultivate your friendship—one single evening will be of no consequence."

"I should indeed feel happy and honored in your excellency's society, Governor Dinwiddie," replied the young hero, "but I am now to prepare for a public service which requires expedition; and I have ever made it a rule that, when duty is to be performed, no time should be lost upon pleasure."

"My friend," said Dinwiddie, "be ever thus proof against temptation. I esteem you the more that you have resisted my wishes on this point. Be as expeditious as you please, and may a kind heaven prosper your zeal. I shall try to imitate you in getting everything ready without delay."

Washington now withdrew, and immediately hastened home to make the best use he could of his time in arranging his private affairs and in providing for the performance of his public duty.

When he was out of sight, Dinwiddie could **not**

help exclaiming: "Admirable young man! You will yet be of more service to your country than a thousand mines of gold." Tell me, had he not prophetic vision?

CHAPTER XIV.

WASHINGTON ON HIS WAY TO LE-BOEUF

WHILE Charles Addison was present with the Frasier family, Marie sought to conceal her feelings for the young Englishman. But he was not many hours absent, when his image took such full and forcible possession of her mind, that whether she dreamed by night or meditated by day, it was ever present with her.

Though she dared hardly hope that she would ever see him again, yet without him the world would be cheerless and her life a blank.

She succeeded fairly well in concealing her feelings from the observation of all her friends, except Nora, who was also secretly pining for an absent lover; for Dr. Killbreath had found means, during his short stay at the Frasier's, to not only convince her that she possessed his heart, but also to obtain possession of hers. Although the feeling with which she remembered the doctor was not so deep or acute as that with which Marie remembered Ad-

dison, yet it was sufficient to enable her to sympathize with her sister.

Nearly four months had passed since the departure of Addison and his friends, and Marie had not
heard a word from her lover—for Paddy had not yet
returned from Philadelphia—and she was becoming quite uneasy regarding his safety.

"Surely," thought she, "if they had reached Philadelphia alive, Paddy would have returned before
now, and I should have heard of Charles."

At last to the great joy of all the Frasier family,
Paddy arrived, accompanied by Dr. Killbreath,
whose desire to again see Nora had rendered him
easily persuaded to join her brother in trading with
the Indians.

They therefore brought with them in partnership
a large and valuable assortment of goods, not only
suitable for the Indians, but also for the French,
with whom Paddy was desirous of opening a trade.

On their return near the Laurel Ridge they met
with several Indians who would no doubt have attacked and robbed them, and perhaps massacred
them, had not some of them known Paddy, who
speaking their language freely, managed to engage
them by the present of a few blankets and some
other trinkets, to conduct them home.

Nora was rejoiced to see her dear doctor back again, and he was no less pleased to find himself once more under her father's roof.

Marie was much pleased to learn of her lover's safety.   He had sent her a present of some books of late publication; but the gift which afforded her by far the greatest pleasure was a packet of letters written by her Charles.

In these letters he assured her of his undying love, and expressed a strong desire to return to her presence, that he might enjoy her society.   Duties, however, of a very pressing nature compelled him to remain a few months longer in Philadelphia, but at the first opportunity he would seek her side.

My readers are perhaps all conversant with the tone of a love letter, so we will not continue further than to say that they were read and re-read by Marie, and their contents treasured in her heart.

The summer days passed by without much of event to the Frasier family.

It was a beautiful evening in November, 1753, Indian Summer being then in all its glory and beauty, that two young ladies were walking along the bank of the Monongahela.   Charles Addison and Dr. Killbreath were the topic of their conversation, so the reader can easily guess who they were. They continued their walk for some distance, when, becoming weary, they sat down beneath a tree which grew upon a shelving portion of the bank, and Marie drawing forth one of the books which her lover had sent her she commenced reading in a pleasant tone while Nora listened with great earnestness.

Although Nora was an attentive listener, she allowed her gaze to wander over the landscape. Suddenly she started, for her vision had rested on a white man leaning against a tree not a great distance away. She immediately started to her feet in surprise, crying out:

"Oh, Marie! See, there is a white stranger!"

Marie arose, considerably startled, and the stranger approached with gracefulness, and with admiration strongly expressed in his countenance.

"Ladies!" said he, "I must ask your pardon for my delay in not making my presence known. But how could I interrupt such profitable and refined enjoyment as that in which I found you engaged. And in such a place, too. I have traveled the wilderness nearly two hundred miles without seeing a white woman; and here to find you, and so employed! Ladies, forgive me, but my delight is equal to my astonishment."

"Sir!" replied Marie, "we meet in this wilderness with so few gentlemen like you, that, if we have manifested unusual symptoms of surprise, we trust you will excuse us, for our condition has always been a secluded one. But our father lives near at hand; he always makes the sojourner in the forest welcome. If you would wish, we will show you the way."

"Is your father's name Frasier?" asked the stranger.

"It is, sir," was the reply.

"I was informed that his residence is in this neighborhood, and was just in search of it when I perceived you," he answered.

An idea now entered Marie's mind which caused her to change color and seem embarrassed. "He may be from Philadelphia; he may have news for me, but I dare not ask him." And she unconsciously heaved a sigh, which was noticed by the stranger, who by some subtle influence seemed to be drawn toward her.

A short walk brought them to the lane leading to the house, where they met Gilbert. "That, sir, is my father," said Marie, as Gilbert approached. He saluted the stranger with a friendly welcome, who cordially shook his hand, saying:

"I have heard of you, Mr. Frasier, and was directed to take your house on my way to Fort Le-Boeuf, to which place I am proceeding on public business, by order of the Governor of Virginia."

Marie, hearing this from the stranger, concluded that he had not come from Philadelphia, and the fluttering of her bosom gradually subsided.

The intelligence communicated by the stranger, that he was on official business, only increased the high respect which his appearance had made upon Gilbert.

"Ay, ay! Indian business, na doot," said he. "I wonner the Governor did na lang ere this send to inquire after things; for there hae been unco troublesome doings lately. I.hope no' that ye'll get it a' settled. But come in, come in, I wish I could accommodate ye better, for leevin amang thir woods, ye ken it's no like in a Christian country."

"Your kindness will far more than compensate for any deficiency of accommodation. George Washington, for such, Mr. Frasier, is my name, will never be fastidious in this respect. If he can but procure shelter for himself and his men he will be well satisfied."

"An' whar are yer men?" inquired Gilbert; "I'll

send for them, an' try, wi' a' my heart an' gude will, to mak' ye a' welcome."

"I left my men about a mile up the river, where they halted to refresh themselves, while, with my rifle in hand, I strolled on down the river."

"Your rifle?" said Gilbert, seeing none in Washington's possession. "An' whar is it?"

"It is at the foot of a walnut tree, not far from the place where I met your daughters; for on perceiving them I feared to alarm them by appearing armed in their presence, so I dropped it there."

"I'll send my sin Denny to bring your men doon the river," said Gilbert. "He'll likely find the rifle on his way."

"I think I had better go back myself for the rifle," replied Washington, "and then I can call my men together, and this will save your son unnecessary trouble."

He accordingly retraced his steps to the walnut tree, where he sounded a horn, as a signal for his company to come on, which was immediately answered from no great distance.

Denny, by direction of his father, had followed after Washington, and, reaching him at this crisis, he was informed that he need proceed no farther as his companions would soon be with them.

"If ye'll no' object, I'll push on if ye please, sir, an' meet them," said Denny; "the sight of a white man in thir woods, since the Indians have frightened away the traders, is a pleasure we canna get every day."

So saying, he hastened onward, while Washington returned to the house, desirous to again behold the most beautiful and interesting female he had ever met.

*   *   *   *   *

The young Virginian had left Williamsburg the last of October. His traveling companions were an Indian interpreter named Van Braam, who also spoke French, and a hunter by the name of Christopher Gist who acted as guide; there were also several others, two of whom were Indian traders.

At the mouth of Wills Creek, now Cumberland, Maryland, they bade adieu to civilization and climbed the Allegheny Mountains which, although early in the season, were already covered with snow. They experienced considerable difficulty in pursuing their way, and several weeks had already passed before they arrived at the forks of the Ohio. Here, as the reader has learned, they rested for awhile, enjoying the hospitality of the only white settler in all that region.

*   *   *   *   *

Marie, now being acquainted with the mission of their guest, received him on his return to the house, with an easy, graceful and dignified manner, which won from Washington a silent acknowledgment, which only his eyes revealed.

He felt that he had met with one who was a perfect model of female excellence, and in a place where he least expected it; and looking into her frank, honest eyes, he realized an uncontrollable feeling of confusion, for Washington's heart was made of that material that would not allow him to gaze unmoved upon so rare a combination of those charms, which form that bewitching power many beautiful women possess.

In a short time he was seated with Marie and Nora in the little cosy parlor, with some light refreshment before them, until a more substantial meal could be prepared.

The conversation ran largely upon the disturbed condition of affairs, and as it continued Washington could not help but admire and enjoy the choice language with which Marie clothed all her re-

marks, and he felt that a lifetime spent with such
a companion could not but be one of great enjoyment.

At this juncture they were interrupted by the
arrival of Denny with the remainder of the party
whom Gilbert, with great animation, introduced
into the apartment.

"I am glad," said he, when he had them all
seated, "to see sae mony Christians in my hoose,
an' a' speakin' sae as I can understand.   It's loike
getting back to the world again."

"And I," said Mr. Van Braam, the interpreter,
"I am heartily glad, after wandering so many days
without seeing a house at all, to once more get the
roof of one over my head."

"Mr. Frasier," said Gist, the guide, "I have often
heard the traders talk of your living down here,
and many a time have I wondered at your hardihood, and cannot guess how you have escaped so
long, unless it has been by the protecting aid of the
Mingo prophet, or conjurer, whom they talk so
much about."

"It is indeed remarkable," observed Washington, "that amid all their depredations and barbarities of late, the Indians should have permitted a
family so very much in their power, and belonging

to the nation they so much hate, to remain so long
unmolested. You must surely, Mr. Frasier, have
some rare means of conciliating them."

"I canna say," replied Gilbert, "that I hae ever
used muckle means to please them, but I aye tak'
care no' to offend them. I hae never yet cheated
or affronted any o' them, as the traders hae often
done."

"This plundering and massacreing," said Washington, "have indeed, unhappily taken place; but I
fear they have sometimes been provoked by the
misconduct of our own people. The safety of our
host here, in the midst of the Indians, is a proof of
it."

"He has had the old conjurer, Tonnawingo, at
his back, I guess," said Gist. "Unless the old imp
had helped him, he couldn't have so long escaped
the red devils and their tomahawks. They say he
is a blamed curious old fish, that Indian prophet.
I don't doubt but he has a cloven foot, like his old
ancestor."

"You may examine and see, thou son of levity,"
said a solemn and awful voice, which made the
blood almost stand still in the heart of the startled
and terrified Gist. At the same moment the majestic looking figure of Tonnawingo stood before

them, with one foot advanced as if to invite inspection.

"Look here," continued the prophet, "is there any mark of an evil spirit about me? Examine me and see. Hear me—I am an Indian, and can forbear to be angry when the Great Spirit forbids anger, and for the sake of one here, who is your leader.

"My brother," said he, turning to Washington, "I will say to thee thou mayest go on thy way without fear. Brother, thou hast heard my words."

To this Washington answered:

"Father, I am glad I have met you. I have heard of your virtues, and of your influence over the Indians. You know the object of my mission at present, to this region, is to effect a reconciliation with those of your people who are hostile to us, and to try to put an end to the intrigues of the French in exciting them against us. Father, you have heard me, and you may believe that we do not wish to be at war with your people."

"Brother," replied Tonnawingo, "you are wise and know the true interests of your country; it is refreshing to hear the words of peace from a white man. Behold our Brother Frasier, he is a white man and has lived here long; and because he is peaceable we have not disturbed him. The chiefs of thirteen nations have, at different times, smoked the pipe of peace with him, and he has thirteen strings of wampum in his possession, and they are symbols of protection and peace. Believe me, my white brother, Indians can be kind friends, as well as deadly enemies.

"Hear me further, brother: All our tribes have not declared against your nation. Some of them wish you better than they do the French. The Shannoahs, the Delawares, and the Mingoes are your friends, while the Ottawas, the Chippeways, the Wyandots and other tribes have lent their aid to your white enemies.

"Brother, you have heard me; receive this wampum in testimony of Tonnawingo's friendship. The chief of my tribe, I doubt not, will also give you one; as you are peaceable may you also be prosperous."

So saying, he turned round and abruptly left the apartment.

The impression left by this extraordinary Indian was a mixture of astonishment and reverence. Washington had heard of him before and enjoyed his meeting with him. He was extremely anxious to learn what the Frasier family knew further of him.

The best qualified person to give him the desired information he found to be Marie, and he received this intelligence from the family with a secret pleasure, for it would afford him an excellent plea to draw her into a conversation. But she had left the room immediately upon the entrance of his companions, therefore he could not at once gratify his desire. He resolved, however, to seize the first opportunity that would offer during the evening.

They were discussing the qualities of the departed prophet when Mrs. Frasier's good fare was placed smoking on the table and the party at once applying themselves vigorously to the enjoyment of its disposal, the conversation was discontinued.

During the repast, Paddy Frasier and Dr. Killbreath arrived from a hunting excursion. Paddy, after the meal was over, informed Washington that the Governor at Le-Boeuf was dead, and that an officer named St. Pierre commanded in his place; that in a few days a council of the chiefs of some tribes, mostly friendly to the English, was to be held at a place called Loggstown, about thirty miles down the river. "At the present time," said he, "the only danger your company can have to encounter will arise from the Wyandots and the Connewagoes, part of whom are yet encamped between this and Le-Boeuf, and their chiefs are to attend the council at Loggstown."

"On account of the nature of my mission," observed Washington, "I have a right to demand safe conduct for myself and my followers of the French, which I suppose the Indians will respect. True, the obtaining of that safe conduct may require loss of time and be attended with difficulty; however, it would not be safe for any of my men to venture alone to the fort for that purpose. It will, I think, be better for us to keep close together and trust to Providence."

"There is a small fortification," returned Paddy, "lately erected at Venango, not much above sixty miles from this place, commanded by a Monsieur Joncaire.

"I think I could be there by to-morrow night, for I am well acquainted with the road; and in three days from now, I think, barring accidents, I could meet you at Loggstown with a safe conduct. In the meantime, we can start Dr. Killbreath in a canoe to King Shingiss, about twelve miles down the river with the information that you are here. He will afford you all the protection he can, for he is more strongly attached to the English than any chief in the country."

Washington, seeing the wisdom of Paddy's proposal, at once accepted it.

Paddy, who required no other preparation than to throw on his belt, and a small wallet of provisions, and to see that his rifle was in order, was off in a few minutes. Dr. Killbreath also set out the same evening for King Shingiss' residence.

It was only after these arrangements had been made that Washington was enabled to enjoy an opportunity of conversing with Marie upon the subject of Tonnawingo.

The apartment being finally vacated by all but Marie, Nora and himself, he addressed them, though it must be confessed not without a feeling of some slight agitation at his heart, which, however, he soon overcame.

"Ladies," said he, "my surprise and astonishment is great, in finding so interesting an Indian as the prophet whom you call Tonnawingo. He is surely a credit to his tribe, and appears to be a man with more than ordinary intelligence."

"I am much pleased," replied Marie, "to see that the prophet has produced a favorable impression upon you, Mr. Washington."

"Indeed he has," said the Virginian, "and I have learned from others of the family, that he has been attentive towards you in giving you such instruction as you would not otherwise be able to obtain in this wilderness; but it is strange that his attention in this line is not directed towards members of his own tribe and people."

"I am sorry to say," returned Marie, "that the Indians, although they have often benefitted by his counsel, are too strongly attached to their ancient habits to be willing to receive his instruction. I believe our family is the only one in all this region to whom he has offered to communicate his knowledge, which has been kindly received."

"The mystery is explained!" exclaimed Washington, almost involuntarily. "No wonder, favored maiden, that your mind is so superior when, added to your own natural talents, you have had such an extraordinary instructor. Ah! pardon me, Miss Frasier, I have perhaps said too much; but 'tis very pleasing to meet with such minds as I have met with here!"

"Sir," said Marie, "I know not what may be the privileges of your sex in society; but, if I can credit the authors I have read, your sex has always been accustomed to work upon the vanity of ours, by praising us beyond bounds; and as we who are here in the forest have no means of determining the sincerity of your praise, perhaps it would be the safest method to dispense with terms of adulation and use only such language as will be free from doubt of its truthfulness."

"Oh, Miss Frasier!" quickly replied Washington, with considerable emotion. "Pray, believe me, if I have offended your delicacy, it was done involuntarily, and let me say in my own justification, that I never spoke insincerely in my life, to flatter either man or woman; and concerning you in particular, I have not expressed half—ah! I dare not express half, of my high opinion of your merits."

"Stop, sir," said she; "I will not impeach your sincerity. I believe you to be above uttering opinions you know to be unfounded, but in this instance you are perhaps rather premature in your conclusions—perhaps a little longer acquaintance might change your mind."

"I cannot agree with you in saying I have been premature in my conclusions. Perhaps I may have been incautious in expressing them, but certainly not in forming them, for I cannot resist the evidence of my senses," said Washington.

"Well, then," observed the blushing maiden,

"let the matter rest so; we esteem each other too highly, I hope, to contend about nice distinctions."

Marie felt that their conversation might possibly lead into entanglements which in her present state of mind she would prefer to avoid. Her companion, cautiously avoiding the tempting but forbidden topic of her praise, continued his conversation in another vein. But I have given you enough of this dialogue and will only say, that during the remainder of their conversation our heroine detailed to Washington all she had learned of the prophet's early life, and her opportunities of acquiring knowledge. You, however, know all about this already. I will not tire you with repeating an already-told tale.

I will only add that during this conversation, the whole heart and the affections of Washington were unconditionally surrendered to this "Rose of the Wilderness," and that, although the gratification he enjoyed was great, it was dearly enough purchased by the irretrievable loss of his heart's tranquillity.

CHAPTER XV.

COMPLETES HIS JOURNEY AND RETURNS

THERE will no doubt be many of my fair readers who will think it a great pity that the illustrious character, who had thus become a captive to Marie's charms, should be fated to throw away the affections of his manly heart upon one who could not return them. There may perhaps be some who may criticize her taste in not giving preference to her new lover.

In defense of her, we will say that she clearly saw all of Washington's merits; and although she could not forsee all of his future greatness, she esteemed and respected him as much as if she did, and had he even then been the conqueror of Cornwallis, and the object upon which the eyes of all America looked with pride, although ardently devoted as his whole soul was to her, he could not have made her change in her attachment, or waver in her constancy to Charles Addison.

But Washington was not aware of this. He did not know that another possessed those affections,

for which he felt he could sacrifice every consideration but one to obtain.

For to this young man there was something
more dear, more sacred, than the life within him,
dearer than fame, even more dear than the beautiful Marie, whose loveliness had enchanted his feelings into a sense of bliss he had never known before
—that something was his Duty.

This was his polar star that guided all his actions;
this was the moving spirit within him, to which he
was resolved that every feeling and every wish of
his being should bend.

Being now upon important public business which
required dispatch, he thought it would be wrong
to make such a delay at her father's house as would
justify him in making a declaration of his feelings,
or attempting to engage her affections by attentions
which might require the time he could not then
spare.   After his public duty had been performed,
then he would be master of his own time, and of his
own movements; then he could return to the abode
of this lovely rose and woo her affections, tell her
how he loved her, and ask her to become his own.

Thoughts of this nature filled his mind and kept
him long sleepless after retiring to rest; yet he was
awake with the coming of the dawn, and soon had

his companions at work, grooming the horses and preparing to move onward.

Their good host, Gilbert, however, would not let them depart without breakfast, so a delay was made until the meal was prepared.

At length they set forward, and Washington, for the first time in his life, felt what it was to separate from the object of a tender love. He sighed, as he bid her adieu, and, although she perceived it and suspected its cause, she in a very calm but kind and respectful manner, wished him a safe return.

"Thank you, Miss Frasier," was all he said; but he mentally added, "May a kind Providence soon restore me to her lovely presence."

The travel of a few hours brought them to the Shannapin's town. Here with the eye of a soldier he beheld the point of land where the Allegheny and the Monongahela meet, and was the first person to be impressed with the admirable site it would make for a fort.

Having spent some time in reckoning the height of the banks and the breadth of the rivers at this place, he accompanied King Shingiss, who had met him there with a dozen of his warriors, to his residence upon the banks of Chartier's creek, a few miles down the river, and near the place where Charles Addison had been defeated.

Here he found that Doctor Killbreath, with his party and the baggage, had safely arrived. It was near evening when he reached this place, but as he was desirous of viewing the ground where Addison's disaster had taken place, Shingiss kindly conducted him to the spot, Killbreath, who had acquired a considerable knowledge of the Indian language, acting as interpreter.

Here he saw the remains of the hasty fortification that had been thrown up, and observed some of its logs, showing the stains of the blood of its defenders. Shingiss pointed out to him the spot where Addison slew the young Indian chief, Carrawissa, and gave him an account of the desperate encounter between them. He spoke in such glowing terms of Addison's bravery, that the young man rose high in the opinion of Washington, and from what he heard and saw impressed him with an exalted idea of his character both as a soldier and a man.

The Indian mode of fighting, described to him on this occasion, by keeping up an irregular fire from behind trees, or from an ambuscade, struck him forcibly as the only way suited for this woody country. He felt that Addison had, in a military point of view, committed an error in attempting to defend such a frail fortification, when the density of the forest afforded him such protection for his men.

The next morning, in company with King Shingiss and a few of his warriors, Washington and his entire party proceeded to Loggstown. Here a number of chiefs had already assembled, among whom he distributed the presents he had brought from Virginia for that purpose. These presents were received graciously, and Washington was assured that he had nothing to fear for his party, as all the chiefs present wished to be on friendly terms with the English. A large wigwam was constructed for him and his men, around which some of Shingiss' warriors kept guard, for fear of any surprise during the night.

The next morning several other chiefs and sachems arrived; among these were those of the Wyandots and Connewagoes, who were hostile to the English. These hostile chiefs, after being told that Washington had come for the purpose of making peace, accepted of his presents and agreed to listen to his proposals without molesting him.

A council feast was now prepared, of which

Washington and his party were invited to partake; after which all the chiefs smoked the calumet with him, except those of the hostile tribes, who refused, saying they could not do so until they learned the terms of peace he should offer, or until their allies, the French, had accepted and ratified the treaty.

At length the council was organized, and a chief sachem of the Mingoes addressed Washington. We will not be able to give the readers the address as delivered, only to say that the speech of the Mingo chief was friendly, and at its close he handed Washington a belt of wampum in token of his friendship.

Washington received the belt, and made rep'y to the chief, saying, "I am ordered by your white brother, the Governor of Virginia, to proceed with all possible haste to visit the French commandant, to deliver to him a letter of great importance to a'l, and that he was there to call upon the sachems of the nations, to inform them of his errand, and to ask advice and assistance to enable him to proceed by the best and nearest road to the French. He also informed them that he was to apply to them for provisions, and for some of their young men to conduct him on his way, to be a safe-guard against the Indians who were favorable to the French.

At the close of Washington's address, one of the chiefs of the Wyandots addressed the council in such inflammatory language that his followers, as well as those of the Connewagoe chieftains, became aroused and their attitude became very unfriendly. They conceived a plan to surround Washington and his little party and make the attempt to beat off the Delawares, who firmly kept their ground as their protectors.

A great clamor and confusion arose and blows would no doubt soon have been exchanged which might have proved disastrous to Washington and his friends, when the approach of Tonnawingo was announced.

He entered the council ring hastily, fire seemed to flash from his eyes, his white hair streamed in the wind, his awful wand extended forward, as though he were rushing to arrest a great calamity that was about to befall them. A marked silence had taken place from the moment his name was announced, and even the boldest of the council, perceiving that displeasure rested upon his countenance, sat speechless before him.

"Brothers, brothers!" he exclaimed passionately, "what were ye about to do? Thank the Great Spirit that he has sent me to stay the work of your impious hands. Oh, Maneto!" he cried directing his eyes and lifting his holy wand toward heaven, "forgive these people of the crime they were about to commit, and assure us of thy forgiveness by some sign or token from the French, that we may know that this man and his people are under thy care, and that to harm them will be to displease thee."

At this moment, to the great astonishment of every one present, Paddy Frasier entered the council ring with a written paper addressed to the chiefs and warriors of all nations friendly to the French, requesting them to respect and hold sacred the person and effects of George Washington and those of his company, while employed in proceeding to or from Fort Le-Boeuf. This document was signed by Le Gardeur de St. Pierre, commanding officer at the fort.

We will here explain that Paddy had accidentally met this officer at Venango, and obtained from him the above passport without difficulty.

The opposing chiefs and sachems now expressed their sorrow for their rashness, and withdrew all further opposition to Washington and his party.

The council then broke up and our friends remained for the night at Loggstown, enjoying the hospitality of the Mingo chieftain and the protection of his tribe.

We feel that we cannot give a more clear and concise description of the remainder of this journey to the French fort and the return of Washington to the home of the Frasiers', than by an extract from "The history of our country," by Ellis.

Leaving Loggstown with a number of Indian chiefs in the character of companions more than protectors, for it was believed that for the present no protection was needed, and encountering all manner of hardships and perils the party early in December reached Fort Venango, now Franklin, which was a French outpost in charge of M. Joncaire.

He received the white men with courtesy, but tried to persuade, although without success, the Indians to desert them.

Ascending French Creek, the party reached Fort Le-Boeuf, where they found the French commandant. He was a polite old soldier, who treated his visitors with much courtesy, entertaining them for four days, at the end of which he handed his sealed reply to Washington.

Expressing his thanks to M. de St. Pierre for his hospitality, Washington and his companions set out on their return journey to Williamsburg.

It was now the depths of winter and the return was thus a great deal harder than had been their coming. The weather became intensely cold, and the snow was in many places several feet deep.

When the party reached Venango the pack-horses were so exhausted that they gave out. Washington and Paddy Frasier dismounted and turned over their animals to assist in carrying the baggage, and Washington deeming it unnecessary to proceed at the slow pace the pack-horses were obliged to travel and no doubt impatient to again behold Marie, and forward his dispatches, he delegated to the guide the charge of bringing them to Frasier's house where he intended to remain until they arrived.

Strapping a few articles on their backs, Washington and Paddy Frasier bade their friends good bye and pressed forward on foot through the sleet and snow.

In crossing the streams, the ice which bore them for some distance from the shore sometimes gave way farther out and let them sink to the arm-pits in the chilly current beneath. Many times on rising in the morning their wet clothing was frozen to their bodies.

Not one man in a thousand could have undergone what young Washington and his companion, Paddy Frasier, passed through, but they bravely pushed on until they stood on the bank of the Allegheny River, whose swollen current was filled with masses of rushing ice.

There was only one way of crossing the stream, and that was by means of a raft. They spent the day in putting one together, and, as the wintry day was coming to a close, they shoved out from the shore. Washington was plying a pole with all his strength when the action of the ice flung him into the water a dozen feet deep.

On his back was his pack, with his rifle strapped to it and his clothing was thick and cumbrous, so that despite his great strength and skill, he might have been drowned had he not seized one of the logs of the raft that was knocked apart by the current.

Both men were flung upon a small island, where they lay all night without a fire or a particle of food, and almost frozen. Washington suffered no serious injury but his companion suffered by having his fingers and toes badly frozen.

PERILOUS CROSSING OF THE ALLEGHANY RIVER

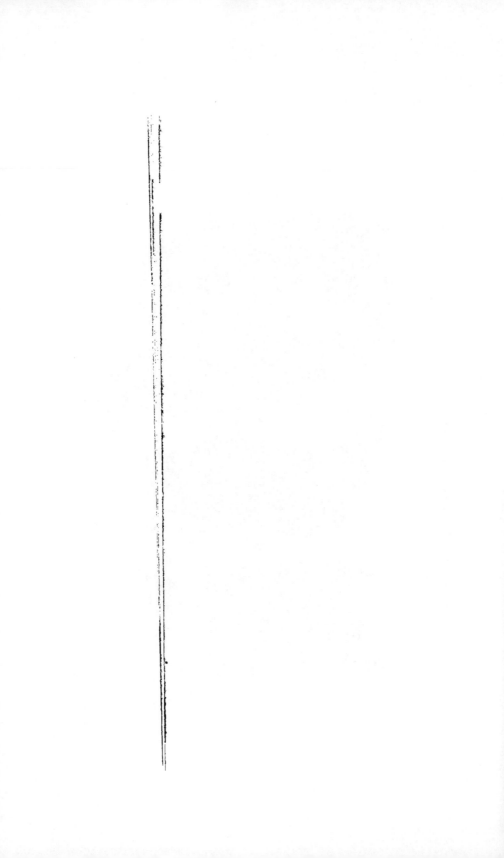

This island near Lawrenceville, Pa., is still known as Washington's Island. In the morning the surface of the river was frozen solid and the two men walked from the island to the mainland. Encountering an Indian, they pressed him into their service as a guide. He was a treacherous rogue, who was very friendly at first, so much so, that the white men became suspicious of him.

One afternoon he deliberately raised his rifle and fired at Washington, who was barely fifty feet distant, but missed him. Paddy Frasier at once leaped upon the savage and bore him to the ground, and would have killed him had not Washington interfered. He was allowed to go and, fearful that he might lead a party in pursuit, the two traveled all night. Nothing was, however, seen or heard of the fellow.

With the coming of day they were enabled to travel faster, and as Paddy knew the best and nearest road, they reached his father's house sooner than he had predicted.

Refreshments and a change of raiment for each were soon produced, and Washington having ascertained that the papers in his pack, which had been fastened to his shoulders, had suffered no damage, he felt, after the dangers and difficulties he had passed through, truly thankful, and his enjoyment was increased by the thought that he was safe under the same roof and in the presence of one so dear to him.

He felt great satisfaction to hear her express her gratitude to heaven and her joy for his escape from the dangers that had surrounded him. It made his heart beat with joy to know that she was concerned regarding his welfare.

"Ah!" said he to himself, "surely this interest in me must be more than mere friendship could inspire, when she has so little hesitation in expressing it. She is altogether the child of nature and truth, and I must believe that she feels all, perhaps more, than she expresses."

Thus it is that love can blind minds of the most acute and accurate discernment. Often times the very freedom from embarrassment, with which the object of our love expresses an interest in our concerns, is fondly mistaken for a mark of passion, when it denotes nothing more than friendship and respect.

Washington was not fully sure that the sweet Marie would be ready or willing to acknowledge a feeling of affection for him, neither did he feel like breaking the resolution he had formed of not, at this time, making a formal declaration of his own feelings toward her, and thus learning the true condition of her own. The desire to make his public duty now the chief, if not the sole object of his attention, to a certain extent restrained him.

Washington's resolution not to reveal his heart's feelings to this sweet rose of the wilderness met with a trial of its strength and firmness next day for, the day being a pleasant one, shortly after breakfast the beloved of his soul invited him to accompany her on a visit to the Indian queen, Alliquippa. How his heart beat at the thought of it. Yes, reader, this was a great pleasure for him to contemplate, and yet it was a temptation. He could not refuse her, but he was determined not to allow a declaration of his passion to disturb her, come what may.

As they walked along, Marie told him that the Indian Queen they were going to visit was one of her dearest friends. She also told him that Alliquippa was attached to the cause of his nation, and, when she learned of his visit to the chiefs at Loggstown, she had felt mortified that he had not paid his respects to her

"She has conversed with me several times about

you," continued the maiden, "and desired me as soon as you returned to bring you to her residence.

"I promised I would, and I am now fulfilling my promise and, as I believe you do not speak Indian, I will, if you have no objections, be your interpreter."

"Miss Frasier," responded Washington, "my delight will—but pardon me, I must restrain the expression of my feelings—object to you being my interpreter?   I do not—I cannot, for being unable to speak Indian, I shall, of course, be glad of your assistance.   I have learned from your brother that she is favorable to our cause, and I should think myself deficient in my duty did I not call upon her, and assure her that we appreciate her favorable feelings toward us, for I fear ere long we shall require all the friends we can make in this locality."

"I hope," said Marie, "that matters will not be pushed to an open rupture, for war is a shocking calamity."

"I fear the outcome," returned her companion, "for it appears to be the intention of the French to drive us into war.   Oh, Marie! ere the sword is drawn I wish you were safe out of this wilderness."

"And why do you wish so?" said the fair girl, affecting a tone of surprise.   "Here live my parents, and to leave them you surely would not consider as pardonable or even practicable."

"I only express the simple wish of my heart," returned Washington, "and that, too, without having any excusable grounds to explain it." At this juncture Marie exclaimed, "Yonder is the Queen's residence; she will no doubt be waiting our arrival." So they walked onward in silence, neither Washington nor his companion referring to the sub jeet they had abruptly dropped, although the fair maiden felt convinced that her companion was more interested in her welfare than a casual acquaintance would warrant her to expect.

Her Shannoah majesty received Washington very graciously, although she gave him a slight reprimand for not visiting her as he had passed so near her residence.

Washington assured her that when he passed that way before, he was not aware that her wigwam was so near; "besides," said he, "I did not then, as now, have an interpreter to enable me to converse with you. But, as a proof of my regard, I hope you will accept of some presents I shall send you as soon as my baggage arrives at Mr. Frasier's. In the meantime, receive these few rings as a token of my personal regard, and this string of wampum

as a cement to the amity between you and my nation."

The queen, on her part, presented him with a
wampum, thanking him for the rings and the presents he had promised, and assured him that she had
always felt a high regard for his countrymen; and
that on his account, that regard in time to come
would be still higher.

Washington took his leave, and returned to Frasier's with Marie, much pleased with the result of
his visit.

CHAPTER XVI.

LOVE-MAKING IN THE WILDERNESS

AS they were returning from their visit to the Indian Queen, when about half way on their return journey, they perceived a company of about thirty or forty men, and as many horses laden with baggage, making their way slowly down the bank of the river.

Washington at once conjectured them to be a second party which he had heard the Ohio Company contemplated sending, to make another attempt to take possession of their territory. He and his companion quickened their pace, that they might meet with them at the place where the different ways crossed.

When Marie had advanced near enough to be able to distinguish the different members of the party she suddenly stopped, and from the crimson that swept over her face there was evidently some considerable mental emotion. She, however, by a strong effort recovered herself quickly, and although Washington had noticed her confusion he did not consider it anything extraordinary, but presumed it was no doubt due to a maidenly timidity in approaching so large a company of strangers.

"Fear nothing, Miss Frasier," said he; "these I doubt not are our friends, and will offer us no injury."

She assured him that she felt no alarm and that she had—here she suddenly paused, for the person who appeared to be the leader of the party, at this moment perceiving them, suddenly turned his horse, and was riding swiftly through the brush toward them.

As he neared them she remarked in a low voice to Washington: "This gentleman coming is Mr. Addison, who commanded the Ohio expedition last year. I am glad he has arrived before you leave us, that you may become acquainted with each other."

"I am glad of it, too, for I have heard much in his praise," replied Washington.

By this time Addison had approached and alighted from his horse, and it was with a great effort that Marie assumed an appearance of composed cordiality of manner, as she approached him and bid him welcome.   She then added:

"This gentleman, Mr. Addison, is my friend, Mr.

Washington, from Virginia." Addison coldly saluted Washington, and dryly observed that he should "always be glad to meet with any friend of Miss Frasier's."

Washington, however, responded with great sincerity and warmth of feeling.

"Mr. Addison, I am really pleased to meet you, for both public and private report have enabled me to determine the worth of your character, and I trust, as we may both be interested in this section of country, that we may be able to lend protection to our friends from the assaults of the enemy."

"Mr. Washington," replied Addison, with more warmth of tone, "the testimony of the public voice in your favor, since you so gallantly embarked in the arduous mission to Le-Boeuf, is too flattering for me to repeat it, but I feel that in reality it is hardly what you deserve. I shall indeed feel proud of your friendship and trust that it may be long continued.

"And now, Miss Frasier, may I ask how it has fared with yourself and your father's family since I saw you?"

"None of us have met with any harm, although we have many times been in great alarm and anxiety, on account of the Indian outrages that were committed on the border settlers."

After some further conversation, Addison informed them that he was at the head of another ex-ｌedition, that although he had failed in the first attempt, the Ohio Company had still confidence in him; and had sent him forth to establish, if possible, a trading post.

At this juncture Washington asked him if he had any particular point in view as to where he would locate his fort.

Addison replied that he had not, and it was then that Washington pointed out to him the advantages offered at the forks of the river over the heights at Chartiers Creek, where Addison had made his first attempt.

About this time they came up to the company that Addison had left, who were then resting at the juncture of the road. Introductions were given, and Peter McFall, who was with the party, recognizing the young lady, flung his cap high in the air, rushed forward and grasping her hand in a true Irish fashion, exclaimed:

"By the powers, mistress, but I am glad to see you living again, for I thought the savages had killed every sowl of a Christian in the wilderness."

Marie assured him that the Frasier family were all safe and would be glad to see him back again, and when she informed him that Dr. Killbreath was with them, Peter was ready to start off in a run to see his dear doctor.

The way being short, the entire company soon arrived at the house of Gilbert Frasier, and the host and his wife had once more the pleasure, and they did not fail to inform their guests, of beholding some of the blood of Maughrygowan under their roof.

Towards evening of the following day, Vanbraam arrived with Washington's baggage and the rest of his followers. The presents promised to the Shannoah Queen were given over to the care of Paddy Frasier, who immediately proceeded to her residence and delivered them to her majesty; and the next morning Washington prepared to leave Marie and this spot in the wilderness, which was now to him the dearest spot in all the wide world. Before he set off, however, Charles Addison had left with his party to take possession of the forks at Shannapins, Washington's reasoning having convinced him of its being the better place to erect the fort he contemplated.

These two young heroes bade farewell to each

other, impressed with the strongest feelings of mutual respect, but little dreaming that they were each other's rival in a matter upon which each felt at that time, that the happiness of his whole life depended. True, that Addison at the time of meeting Washington and Marie together in the woods, had permitted a slight suspicion to alarm his mind, which his manner had almost betrayed, but after a moment's reflection, confidence in her fidelity was fully restored and the ease, candor, and cordiality of Washington's manner of addressing him confirmed it.

Just before Washington set off he seized a favorable opportunity for a short, private interview with Marie.

"Miss Frasier," said he, "I must now bid you farewell for a time. Permit me, before I depart, to present you with a small volume of poems, which has for many months past been my constant companion. I have marked with a pencil those passages of my favorite poem, which I shall often call to mind when at a distance from you; and may I request that, for my sake, you will frequently read them? They will depict to you the feelings which, until I see you again, will strongly agitate my mind.

Farewell, and may heaven protect you from all danger."

So saying, he pressed her hand and departed.

The book which Washington left with our heroine was a handsomely bound copy of Spencer's Poems, and the passages he had marked for her attention she found to be the most beautiful and expressive of all tender poetic sentiment.

We would be pleased to here record the lines for the benefit of the reader, but strange to say Washington's own journal, from which much of this is taken, does not give them for our perusal; hence we must be content in the exercise of our imagination as to what they were. However, had not Marie been before convinced from the conduct of her illustrious visitor that he loved her, the lines of the poem he had marked for her would have left no room for doubt on the subject.

The condition of affairs caused the lovely maiden to grieve, for she respected, esteemed, and almost revered those talents and virtues which she recognized in him.

But that high degree of respect and esteem which poets call love, she could not bestow upon him, for the reader well knows that another engrossed all her heart's passion and tenderness.

·"How rejoiced I should be," she would say to herself, "if this excellent, this admirable young man could place his affections on some one who is free to return him her own. I know from my own feelings how much the happiness of his life depends upon this; for if ever a man deserved love and happiness, it is he."

One might think from expressions like these that Marie's attachment to Addison was not deeply founded. Far from it; she felt it both a duty and a delight to be true to him, and while she cherished a warm friendship for the now absent Washington, her heart was wholly with her Charles, who having encamped his men at Shannapin's town, and marked out the ground for the fort, returned the next day to visit his sweetheart.

Those of you who have passed through the experience of "love's young dream," know that during the period of courtship, where hearts respond in unison to each other, no matter what season of the year, the days are delightful and the sky of a roseate hue, and so it was with Charles Addison and Marie Frasier. But we will not weary those who peruse these pages with a recital of the sweet things said, or the delight of their solitary rambles.

Addison, on his part, was anxious for Marie to

name the day when the marriage vows would be consummated, declaring he had brought with his company a person legally qualified to perform the ceremony.

But the maiden bade him be patient, seeing that as yet he had not broached the matter to his father whom he had left behind in Philadelphia, and that it might be possible that the paternal blessing would be withheld.

Her lover assured her that his father would certainly receive her as a daughter, but notwithstanding all his persuasion, Marie could not feel secure in her mind that she would hold as high a place in the esteem of the father as she did in the heart of his son, and until she could be assured of this, although she loved Charles Addison dearly, she preferred to be his sweetheart rather than his wife.

Her lover was disconsolate, he even grew despondent, and would take long walks by himself, that he might uninterruptedly ponder over his unfortunate situation.

A day or two after his conversation with Marie upon the matter we have referred to, he set out from the camp at Shannapin's on a favorite walk, for meditation. It was one of those days of sunshine which sometimes come in midwinter, to gladden the heart, after long days of intense cold.

His way lay along the bank of the river whose broad glassy surface reflected the bright sunshine like a mirror. He had rambled for some distance, and becoming weary had seated himself upon a jutting rock to rest and call to his mind the charming graces of the one whose image filled his entire being.

He had scarcely seated himself when he heard the sounds of approaching footsteps, and soon the form of Tonnawingo, the prophet, whom he had not seen since his return, stood before him. ,

"Hail to thee, my son!" said the prophet. "I am glad to see thee yet safe. But thou comest in an evil hour to visit this land, for thy safety will be endangered."

"Father," replied Addison, "since my arrival, I have longed much to see you. The dangers you speak of I have anticipated, but if they delay until we have raised our defences we will not fear them."

"Then haste to prepare your ramparts, my son," said the prophet, earnestly. "From behind them you may at least treat for safety, if you cannot fight for victory. I come to warn you, that you may be wary, for your foe is stronger than you."

So saying, Tonnawingo ascended the banks, leaving Charles fixed to the spot by the suddenness of his departure. But recalling the warning he had received, he hastily returned to the camp and encouraged his men to greater expedition in forwarding the work on the fortification.

CHAPTER XVII.

A STRUGGLE NOT RECORDED IN HISTORY

THE warning Tonnawingo had given Addison in regard to the enemy was not lost upon him. He engaged the services of Paddy Frasier as a scout to hover round the French station at Le-Boeuf in order to watch their actions, and give him the earliest information of what they were about to do.

He also kept four or five of his men constantly employed in ranging the country round about so as to prevent a sudden attack. The balance of his forces were busily engaged in digging trenches, and preparing long pointed stakes to set in the ground to form their stockade.

From the friendly Indians he at first received considerable aid, but in a few days their ardor began to diminish, and, fearing that some unfriendly feeling existed toward him, he thought it would be proper to pay a visit to King Shingiss and talk with him on the subject.

His Delaware Majesty received him kindly and stated that he still preferred his nation to the French, but as he was now imitating them, by building strong-holds in the country, many of his people were beginning to fear the consequence, and that this strong-hold might some day be used against them instead of the French.

Addison assured him that his force would never be employed against his friends. He further made promises to the Chief that, if his nation would compel the French to leave the country, those tribes that had been friendly would be amply compensated and protected from their enemies.

The result of this interview was that Shingiss promised to talk with his people and urge upon them to still be friendly to the English.

Matters were in this condition when Paddy Frasier arrived in haste one evening with the news that a large body of French, possibly between four and five hundred, were proceeding down the river.

This word was indeed alarming, as their defenses were far from completion, and the few Indians were not to be depended upon. Addison, however, determined to do his best to resist his enemies as long as he could, although he had little hope of being successful.

He despatched a messenger to Shingiss, requesting the aid of the Delaware warriors. Shingiss responded personally with about thirty men, this
number being all he could muster on the emergency.

Addison soon concentrated all his force within
the partially completed stockade, and every man
was in full expectation of a severe conflict. They
kept all night on the alert, only one-half resting at
one time.

They were not disturbed during the night, but
morning had scarcely dawned when they perceived
in the woods, scarcely five hundred yards away, the
glittering of the arms and uniforms of the French
soldiers.

In a short time a man approached with a white
flag. He said he was sent to demand from Mr.
Addison an absolute surrender of himself and all
the men and stores under his command, in return
for which his own life, and the lives of all his followers, should be protected from the Indians, although they would have to submit to be sent to
Canada, perhaps to France, as prisoners of war.

Addison at once rejected these terms. His refusal was scarcely communicated to the French
commander when the trumpets sounded, and the

attack commenced by a heavy fire of musketry upon their defences which were so incomplete as to afford them very imperfect shelter. They fought, however, with great bravery, returning the fire of their enemies with such promptness and steadiness that the French dared not advance to storm the works, as was their intention at first.

The French knew that the English had no cannon, hence did not choose to spend time in transporting any of their own over such a difficult country as lay between Le-Boeuf and the forks of the Ohio, lest the English might become too well fortified before they would reach them.

- They were, therefore, obliged to wholly depend upon the fire of their muskets which was kept up incessantly, with a constant return.

The French saved themselves as much as possible by seeking shelter behind the trees of the forest, which afforded them as secure a protection as the unfinished stockade did the English.

Their number, however, being so large, prevented them all from securing shelter, thus a great number were exposed and these suffered severely during the attack.

St. Pierre, about one o'clock in the afternoon, resolved to change the mode of combat. He accordingly drew off his men from the reach of the English fire, and divided them into two parties, ordering Captain Joncaire to proceed with one portion, out of view of the enemy, towards the Monongahela, and under cover of its high bank to repair to the junction of the rivers where the stockade was most incomplete.

He then himself conducted a similar party under the protection of the overhanging banks of the Allegheny, toward the same point.

The intention was to unite and make an assault upon the unprotected side of the English.   However, as either party considerably outnumbered the force to be attacked, the orders were that no time should be lost in moving forward, for no matter which party should reach the ground first, the other party could not be far off with its assistance.

St. Pierre's own command reached the point first, but on scaling the bank, which was at that place very steep, nearly thirty of his men were killed by a well directed fire from the English, and the rest shrank back under cover of the bank, to wait the coming of the other party.

In a brief space of time Joncaire's division arrived and at once scaled the bank, not, however, without some loss, which they repaid by a heavy volley upon Addison's men, who were practically without any shelter. At this juncture, St. Pierre's men also appeared upon the contested ground; and Addison seeing that further resistance would only bring destruction to his followers, submitted to the necessity of the case and surrendered himself and his party as prisoners of war.

Addison had lost nearly half his men. Five or six others were wounded, and he himself had received a slight wound in the thigh by a musket ball. Of his Indian auxiliaries, ten or twelve were killed, and among this number was King Shingiss, whose death Addison greatly regretted.

The French had between forty and fifty slain, and nearly as many wounded; but their victory was decisive, and the object of their expedition completely attained. The French commander now resolved to keep possession of the ground he had taken. He therefore immediately set his men to work, assisted by a great number of Indians, to finish the fort which the English had begun, for he deemed it an excellent position from which he could over-awe the Indians, and prevent any further attempt of the Ohio company to locate there.

During the ensuing spring this post assumed a

very formidable aspect, under the name of Fort DuQuesne, which for years set at defiance the whole power of the British in America.

St. Pierre at once perceived the advantage of making friends with all the neighboring tribes and drawing them away from their alliance with the English. He therefore set at liberty all the Delawares, whom he had made prisoners in the late battle, and King Shingiss being now dead, he had no difficulty in forming an alliance with his successor.

Not having accommodations for the English prisoners at Fort DuQuesne, he in a few days after the battle sent the greater number of them under a strong escort to Le-Boeuf. Addison, however, was detained until his wound should be so far healed as to permit him to travel without inconvenience.

He was treated kindly by the French commander, who permitted him to retain all his private baggage, and allowed him every accommodation for his personal comfort that the place could afford. He bore his misfortunes heroically, for he had done all that was possible for him to do. His employers had not furnished him with a sufficient force to accomplish their designs, hence their failure. But then he did not blame the company; they had given

him all the force they could muster for the enterprise, and his own anxiety to return to this section
had induced him to accept its command.

The French commander knew nothing about
Addison's intimacy with the Frasier family, nor
even of their partiality for the English. And as
for Paddy's agency in behalf of our hero's cause, it
was conducted by that wily woodsman in such a
way that no one in the interest of the French suspected him. He was, therefore, permitted to trade
at the fort without hindrance.

As to Tonnawingo, although the French commandant placed no confidence in his prophetic pretensions, yet he respected him as a man of extraordinary talents and information, and, on account
of the influence he knew him to possess over the
various tribes, he was allowed to come and go at
will. The prophet thus being under no restraint
at DuQuesne or the various other forts was enabled
to keep thoroughly posted.

In a few weeks, Addison being quite recovered
from his wound, St. Pierre thought proper to send
him under a guard of six soldiers to his fellow prisoners at Le-Boeuf. This was disagreeable news
to the young man, for he cherished the hope that
as he was so near to the Frasier's he might possibly

some day gain permission, on his parole, to visit
the family and again see his Marie.

He had, however, to submit to the will of his
conqueror, and march away from DuQuesne with
a very heavy heart, in company with a guard of
soldiers.

It was in the month of February and the weather
was cold and dry, with a depth of about two feet of
snow; but the party was hardy and active and well
equipped for the journey.   They proceeded on
their way for nearly two days, without meeting
with any accident; but on the evening of the second day, when they reached Bear Creek, a branch
of the Allegheny, and about forty miles from Du-
Quesne, their progress was unexpectedly checked
by a volley of musketry fired by men in ambush,
which killed four of the guard upon the spot.

The assailants immediately leaped from their
concealment, with loud cheers; and to Addison's
great surprise and delight, he beheld in his rescuers, his friends, Paddy and Denny Frasier, Peter
McFall and Dr. Killbreath.   Denny, Paddy and
the Doctor, threw away their rifles, and each seizing a loaded musket from the fallen soldiers gave
instant chase to the two survivors, who had taken
flight the moment their companions fell, without

waiting to see whether they were attacked by Indians or white men.

Peter McFall ran directly to loosen the cords that bound his master's wrists. Addison, the instant he was set at liberty, dashed after his friends hoping to prevent any further sacrifice of life, but he had not ran far until two or three shots were heard, and again loud cheers rang out upon the air. He soon arrived at the spot, and found to his chagrin that the objects of his solicitude had received their death wounds.

He thanked his friends heartily for the services they had rendered him, but felt grieved that it necessitated such a loss of life. Paddy replied that he would take no risk in allowing a man to escape, as their report might not be for his future welfare, closing with the remark that by shooting them he breathed easier and was likely to breathe longer.

Addison was in a quandary to know how McFall comprised one of the party of rescuers, but that worthy soon informed him that this time he did not escape by the underground route as on a previous occasion, but that a rope swung across the top of one of the pickets in the stockade, and a dark rainy night had enabled him to both scale and descend from the wall that surrounded the fort.

Although night was closing about them, they only halted long enough to partake of some refreshment, when they took up their return march to the home of Gilbert Frasier. We will not follow their return, only to say they met with no interruption on their way, and in due time Charles Addison found himself once more in the presence of his beloved. What tender sensations filled his breast as he sat by her side and gazed upon her charms. He could think of no luxury on earth equal to it, especially when he compared his present surroundings with those of only a few days before.

But Marie did not feel so perfectly at ease. Rejoiced as she was at his escape from his enemies, she greatly feared his falling into their hands, for she believed they would no doubt soon hear or suspect something of his rescue and use every means to discover the place of his concealment.

She did her utmost to impress this fact upon her lover's mind, but he seemed disposed to consider her fears groundless, for he could not bear the thought of again leaving her.

"You are aware," said the maiden, "that as soon as the French suspect your escape they will search for you here. They will naturally suppose that, if you be at all in this region, your countrymen will know something of you.   I wish you to assume a secure disguise, remove to some distance from us, and visit us but seldom, at least until the search for you will have abated.   Tonnawingo, I know, can furnish you with a retreat, for he knows all the secret places in the forest.

"Our family will supply you with everything they can to render your hiding place comfortable."

"Oh, Marie! this is almost banishment," he replied.   "I cannot bear to be driven from your presence."

"But it is necessary under the present circumstances," said she, "to submit to this inconvenience, unless you wish to be captured again; and the sooner you submit, Charles, the sooner I will feel at ease in regard to your safety."

He remonstrated further, but finally yielded to her entreaties, saying, "I shall do as you wish, for your sake I will attend Tonnawingo wherever he chooses to lead me."

"Now I am satisfied," said the lovely Marie. "Under the prophet's care you will be safe.   He will be here to-night and direct you."

That evening Tonnawingo made his appearance at the Frasier home.   Addressing Charles he said:

"My son, you are once more out of the power of
your enemies, and it now only requires prudence
to keep you so.   My son, this maiden has told me
what you have purposed to do, and I rejoice that
you have allowed her to influence you.   If you are
ready, follow me—but first bid the maiden farewell,
for you will not see her for many weeks."

For a moment our hero relented his promise and
began to make a protest, but the prophet bade him
be at rest as all was being done with a view alone to
his welfare.

Addison realizing the necessity of the movement sorrowfully bade the maiden farewell, pressing her hand to his lips, then quickly followed
Tonnawingo out of the apartment.

It was a beautiful moonlight night, myriads of
stars sparkled in the clear sky, and the pure white
snow glittered on the frozen ground.   The queen
of the night coursed along in all her splendor,
beaming down upon rivers and rivulets all frozen
as hard as iron, with a surface like polished steel

Reader, you can easily recall nights like this, unless you be of a southern clime, when our hero
started forth with the old Indian prophet to seek
a place of security.   Tonnawingo led the way, and
Addison followed in silent meditation.

They kept nearly northward along the river
bank of Turtle Creek. The stream soon became
enclosed by high precipitous bluffs, and they
crossed on the ice to its left bank, along which they
proceeded about half a mile, when they suddenly
took a path that led in an easterly direction up a
high hill. On gaining its summit they kept along
the ridge, still in an easterly direction for half a
mile, then they turned to the left and descended
into a deep valley, at the bottom of which they
crossed a small run, and turned into a deep ravine
which they ascended, until about half way up,
when they came to a large rock, which seemed to
obstruct their further progress.

Here the prophet spoke to Addison for the first
time since they had left Frasier's.

"Now, my son," said he, "you will see the retreat I have, when I desire concealment. There
are only two individuals, besides myself, who know
it, and in these I can repose implicit confidence.
You will be the third; consequently you will understand that the confidence I have in you is not
small. The security you will here enjoy from
either French or Indians will be all that you can
desire. Within you will find the lodging I am
about to offer you, and its entrance, except to

those who know of it, can only be found by a miracle.

So saying, Tonnawingo caught hold of the branch of a small pine tree, that seemed to be growing in the angle of the rock, and pulling it downward he separated the upper side of the root some distance from the earth, revealing a dark opening beneath.

The tree remaining in this posture, the old Indian bade his companion follow him, and they found upon entering the opening a short flight of steps leading downward.

These steps seemed to be the work of human hands and they led to a small platform or landing place having a smooth earthen bottom.

"Remain here a few minutes until I strike a light," said Tonnawingo, as he proceeded into a dark passage, to what distance, Addison was unable to tell, but he knew from the sound of receding footsteps that it must be of some length.

The prophet, however, was absent only a short time and soon the flickering of a light announced his coming. "My son," said he, when he approached with a flaming taper. "draw the rope which winds through that pulley."

Our hero did so, and the root of the tree instantly

returned to its place, closing up the opening and the rays of the moon were no longer visible.

The prophet now led the way through a long, narrow, and rather damp passage, which at length brought them into a large dry and airy chamber. In an angle of this apartment, to the left of its entrance, the embers of a wood fire not quite extinguished were seen, the faint wreaths of smoke passing out through a funnel shaped opening, which Addison afterward discovered led into another ravine on the opposite side of the ridge from that on which they had entered.

The furniture was simple and scanty, comprising only a few articles of prime necessity for the comfort of one or two individuals at most. There were a bed and bedding, a plain table, two or three rough chairs, a large chest, and two or three shelves that answered for a cupboard.

"Be seated, my son," said Tonnawingo; "you are now in my abode. I must make it comfortable for you."

So saying, he withdrew into the passage and soon returned with several billets of wood in his arms which he cast upon the fire, and to the delight of Addison, who had began to feel rather uncomfortably chilly, the flames soon began **to** crackle and enliven the chamber with its genial warmth.

"My son, you perhaps need refreshment," said the prophet, "and I shall supply you, for within this cavern there is at present enough for all our wants."

"Father," said Addison, "I need no food, but I acknowledge I need repose, for my mind is filled with a sense of sadness."

The prophet looked at the young man with a feeling of disappointment. "Are you sad, my son, because you are safe? If so, you are under no restraint here, and may rush again into danger, if it will give you pleasure.

"My son, you have promised to be ruled by me, and it is the wish of her whom you love that you should be under my care. Will you vex her by your imprudence and by being dissatisfied with what is being done for your good?

"Know you not, that your enemies are numerous and powerful in the country, and if you should fall again into their hands they likely would not treat you with as much indulgence as they did before. My son, be wise, be content to remain here a few weeks and all will be well. You will want for neither food nor drink. You will have a bed to lie upon, and books to read, as liberally as this wilderness can afford. For your own sake, and for the sake of one beloved, I request you to reconcile yourself to only a temporary privation of her society and of the outside world.

"My son, I offer you food, but if you prefer retiring to rest, it is well; I will direct you."

Addison preferred retiring, and begged the prophet to excuse his apparent dissatisfaction with his present abode.

Tonnawingo made no reply, but picking up a light conducted his guest through the passage by which they had entered, and turning abruptly to the right, entered a small room, much cleaner and more comfortable than the one they had left.

Here Addison beheld a bed prepared for his reception with a small table and chair, both exhibiting very rude workmanship, but suitable enough for the place and the purpose intended.

The prophet having pronounced a short benediction upon his guest, left the light with him and retired. It was at this juncture that our hero perceived a letter lying upon the table, which, upon closer examination he found to be addressed to himself and in the handwriting of his own Marie. He opened it with some emotion and—well, we will not give the substance of the epistle, but merely state that it was an appeal from the beautiful girl, for him to bear with composure his seclusion from her society, assuring him that if he would bear his present lot without repining it would contribute much to her peace of mind.

Addison read the letter through carefully, dwelling at some length on the expressions of endearment which it contained, for the lovely, warm-hearted maiden had written without reserve of feeling.

When the letter was finished Addison was in a different frame of mind from that on entering the room; he now longed for the opportunity to assure the beloved of his heart that he was content to isolate himself from the entire world if he had but the knowledge that it was pleasing to her.

But this he could not enjoy till the morning, without interrupting the prophet in his devotions or it might be his slumbers.

He had therefore nothing to do but betake himself to his bed, and possibly in happy dreams enjoy the society of, to him, the one woman in existence.

CHAPTER XVIII.

A FRONTIER WEDDING

ONNAWINGO was surprised in the morning to see his guest in such good spirits, although he divined the cause of it, for he had himself been the bearer of . Marie's letter to her lover, and had placed it where he would be most likely to find it.

"You have been refreshed from your night's repose," said the prophet.

"Yes, father," replied Addison; "I am much better than I was last night. But, father, could you oblige me with materials for writing?"

"I can, my son, with much pleasure," replied the prophet. "I am glad you desire to write, for by reading and writing I trust you will be able to spend your time here without feeling it irksome."

Addison assured him that he would, and having possessed himself with pen, ink and paper, he retired with a light heart to his bed-chamber to write his epistle. We will not insert his address to his loved one, for it was lengthy, and filled with such expressions as were only intended for the perusal of Marie Frasier, and not for the entertainment of the reader of these pages.

Having finished his letter he put it into the hands of the prophet who promised that it should be conveyed to Marie that very day.

Tonnawingo now broached the subject of the safety of Addison's servant, Peter McFall, for realizing the rashness of the young man he feared that he might subject himself to the risk of being recaptured.

"Father," replied Addison, "the certainty of his safety would give me great pleasure, and I shall be thankful for whatever in your wisdom you may think proper to do for him."

Tonnawingo replied that he would consult with Paddy Frasier as to the best disposal of McFall. Then preparing himself for the outer atmosphere he left the cave, taking care to continue the tracks of the footsteps in the snow leading up to the pine tree aforementioned, by proceeding onward, thus making a circuitous route to the Frasier's.

Having delivered to Marie the letter he carried, he took Paddy Frasier aside and explained to him his views with respect to Peter McFall.

Paddy replied, "I have been myself alarmed on

this subject, lest the fellow's long tongue should some time or other betray to the French the whole affair of Mr. Addison's rescue. So far as the capture of McFall is concerned," Paddy remarked, "that would be of little consequence as the world would likely jog on pretty well without him. Although, father, I agree with you that, for the general good, we must get him out of the way as soon as possible."

It was therefore planned between the prophet and Paddy that McFall should be sent with a package of furs to the plantation of Gist, one of the characters who has appeared in this story in preceding pages. McFall was to carry a sealed letter to Gist in which the fur trader was advised that for all practical purposes the return of Peter be delayed some months.

McFall was accordingly summoned and made acquainted with what they desired him to perform.

Peter, upon hearing their request looked perplexed, then suddenly breaking forth, "Arrah now, by the powers how can Peter McFall do this without first consulting his master, Charles Addison, and, prophet, may I make free to ask you just where you have stuffed my poor master out of the way? For sure, shouldn't Peter attend him where-ever he goes even if it be into a catamount's den in this howling wilderness?"

"I know your regard for your master," replied the prophet, "but as to his present residence, my son, I am not at liberty to reveal it."

"But, dear Prophet, cannot I see my master, to get from his sweet self the directions for this trip ye are wishing for me to take?"

"My son, on the present errand, Paddy here will accompany you part of the way, and give you such explicit directions that you cannot fail to find the plantation of Christopher Gist. It is only about a hundred miles up the river, and your master wishes you to remain there for a couple of months, when he shall in all probability call for you."

"Holy St. Patrick!" exclaimed Peter. "See him in a couple of months? Why, sure now, he may be in heaven before that time, and Peter in purgatory, and I may never see him at all again."

"That may all be, Peter," broke in Paddy Frasier; "you must be content to abide by the wishes of your master and wait for him at Gist's, or perhaps if you should be removed to Purgatory you may bid them adieu there and come to see your master, like you have twice done to the French at Le-Boeuf. But in either place take care that you say nothing about us rescuing him from the French. It will do Gist no good to know of it, and as to the inhabitants of Purgatory, they already know all about it there from the blathering of the half-dozen Frenchmen we sent there quite suddenly a short time ago."

Peter promised to attend to this caution, and everything being prepared that evening for their journey, they set out with the dawn of the following day for Gist's habitation, Paddy by the entreaties of Peter, accompanying him the entire way. Reaching Gist's he barely tarried over night, leaving his companion to fall in love with one of Gist's daughters, which Peter actually did, allowing the charms of the fair Esther Gist to entirely obliterate from his recollection those of Mollie McNickel to whom he had sworn constancy before leaving the shores of Old Erin.

Paddy returned to his father's house with his mind at ease as to the present security of both Charles Addison and his man, Peter, from the power of the French. He had, indeed, in a short time afterward reason to congratulate himself on Peter's removal; for the French, beginning to entertain some suspicion as to the fate of Addison's escort, had employed a number of Indians to range the whole country in search of them, or some information as to their fate.

Some of the remains of the French soldiers were at length found, very much mangled and torn by wild beasts, but still in a condition to admit of their being identified. Paddy Frasier, by sly management, succeeded in throwing suspicion upon some of the Delaware Indians who were supposed to still harbor a secret partiality for the English interest. It was even believed that Charles Addison was secreted among them. Their chiefs were in consequence summoned to Fort DuQuesne to undergo an investigation, and to answer to charges founded on these surmises. But the French commandant failed to learn anything that would implicate the tribe.

The search for both Addison and McFall, whose escape from Le-Boeuf was known at DuQuesne, was carried on for some time in the neighborhood of both forts, but all to no avail. Finally it was abandoned as fruitless and Marie Frasier began to feel quite at ease in respect to her lover's security.

He had often written to her, and in every letter had earnestly entreated her to visit him.

At length, as soon as she felt that the search made for him by his enemies had ceased, she yielded to his request, and accompanied the prophet to his cavern. The meeting of the lovers was a joyous one, but what passed between them we are unable to record, this much, however, we conjecture, that Charles insisted upon a return with the fair maiden; but in this he was doomed to disappointment, for the young lady did not yet feel that he might be entirely safe within her father's house. However, with the promise that she would come again he reluctantly bade her farewell, and accompanied by the prophet she returned home.

Shortly after this visit of Marie to her lover, the first marriage that ever took place between the adherents to the British crown in this section was celebrated. It was no less than the joining of the hands (for the hearts were long before united) of Dr. Alexander Killbreath, late of the city of Philadelphia, and Leonora Frasier, eldest daughter of Gilbert and Nellie Frasier, of Frasier's Field, at the forks of the Turtle Creek and the Monongahela.

We will not prolong our story by going into a full detail of this marriage, as we have much yet to say of the other principal characters in our narrative. But we cannot allow an event of so much significance, and so rare in this region, to entirely pass without a comment. The seeming great trouble was to secure the services of a Protestant minister, and as the one that accompanied the ill-fated expedition led by Charles Addison had been taken prisoner, and carried with his unfortunate companions to Canada, the necessary contingent to unite these two in wedlock was sadly wanting.

The doctor had obtained the consent of both Gilbert and his wife, Nellie. The only impediment in the way was the absence of a clergyman of the Protestant faith. The only available personage was the chaplain at the fort; but as this man was a Roman Catholic priest, Gilbert, with his Scotch views, could not be reconciled to his performing the ceremony. However, at last these scruples gave way on the part of the parent, before the weight of the Doctor's rhetoric, and a day was set for the wedding, and the chaplain at the fort notified that his presence was in much need at the Frasier residence.

Monsieur d' Abbeville had been too long a military priest to feel any great scruple of conscience in uniting two young lovers like these in the wilderness—even though they should be heretics.

He therefore consented to spend a merry night at Frasier's and make the doctor happy.

The preparation for celebrating a day so important in the annals of Gilbert's family occupied the attention of his whole household for nearly a week. Gilbert having given his consent to have the thing done, resolved to put forth every effort to have it done in a manner becoming the Frasier's, and therefore spared no pains on the occasion.

Paddy also exerted himself, and as at this time he was on intimate footing with the officers of the garrison, he procured from their stores a supply of luxuries which could not then have been procured elsewhere. In order to further ingratiate himself into their good graces he invited several of the officers and their ladies to witness the ceremony. For, ever since the affair at Bear Creek, he had been extremely assiduous in cultivating their good will.

Marie had for her part, the regulating of the bride's dress, the decorating of the rooms and the arrangement of the table. As for Mrs. Frasier, every good housewife who has had the preparation of a marriage feast knows she had a hundred and one things to do, and if we are correctly informed, she neglected none of them.

The eventful day at length came, and just about the hour of noon, the "holy man," accompanied by five officers and three ladies, arrived at the Frasier residence.

Nora, who was in a small room being decorated by Marie for the occasion, perceiving this strange party so gaily dressed passing the window, felt a misgiving in her heart of being able to face such a company, and for the instant regretted that she was to be one of the principals in the ceremony.

But being assured by her sister that these strangers would be delighted to witness the affair, and that, so far as appearances went, Nora need not be ashamed to show herself in any place and before any company.   With this assurance the maiden took fresh courage, although she still felt a dread of passing through the ordeal, and heartily wished it were over.   No doubt some of the fair readers of these pages has had a like experience, and of course can realize the feelings of this frontier girl, who declared she knew there would be a great deal of blundering, for she never had any experience in the matter of weddings.

At this moment the mother entered to inquire if

Nora was ready to be introduced to the company. It only required a few more touches of the deft hands of Marie, and blushing "like the dawning of morn," this fair wood-nymph attended by her still fairer sister, was ushered into the presence of the gay French ladies and gentlemen, who were burning with curiosity to see her.

Expecting to behold only raw, clownish and coarse girls, little superior in appearance or cultivation to the squaws that performed their menial service, the reader may judge how great was their astonishment when these connoiseurs saw entering their presence, in simple, neat attire, two beautiful females, so attractive, and yet so modest that their presence would have graced an assemblage of royalty.

Bows were made in profusion and compliments without number were passed by the officers, with all the volubility and politeness characteristic of the French school. The French ladies received these two buds of the forest with politeness and good humor, although they could not help being conscious of the fact that they were surpassed in personal charms and graces by these two maidens of the wilderness.

Nora understood a little French, and Maric could speak it almost as freely as English.

We will not be able to give the conversation carried on as it would prolong this story beyond our limit of time and space. Suffice it to say that the conversation flowed freely, and was only interrupted by the suggestion of Monsieur d' Abbeville that the marriage ceremony had better be performed before dinner, and then they would have nothing to do afterwards but enjoy themselves.

The priest took his station, when just at this juncture the sound of horses' feet were heard at the door. Paddy Frasier at once left the room to learn the cause of interruption to the ceremony, and in a few moments returned with two companions whom he introduced to the company as Mr. Washington and Mr. Vanbraam.

Two of the French officers, Joncaire and De Vamploise, had seen Washington before, and immediately recognized him.

"What! This you, Mr. Washington?" exclaimed Joncaire pleasantly, as he shook him by the hand. "You remember Venango yet, I hope?"

"Very well," replied Washington, "and I remember you, too, and a remark you then made of a desire to secure the site at Shannapin's. You have kept good your word, I hear, but no matter—it is the fate of war."

"You remember correctly, Mr. Washington. But I hope you have not come among us this time with any proposal to drive us from this pleasant country?"

"You may rest at ease on that subject at present," replied Washington politely, "I come on no official business; I am merely a private visitor."

"Then let us fling public concerns to the winds for this day at least," said Joncaire. "We are come to a wedding, and have nothing to do here to-day but be merry. I hope you will have no objection to join us?"

Washington, who had been hastily informed by Paddy, previous to their entering the room, of what was going on, pleasantly made reply, "I will have no objection in the world Monsieur Joncaire."

He then hastily proceeded to pay his respects to each individual in the room. When he came to Marie he for a moment changed color, and evinced a slight agitation, but so slight that no one observed it but Marie herself. It called forth from the fair maiden, however, a responsive blush, which did not escape the quick eye of Washington, and caused his heart to throb with a feeling of delight, for a hope had at once arisen in his heart that he was more to her than a mere acquaintance.

Everything being in readiness before the advent of Washington and his companion, all that was left to do was for the priest to put on his sanctified vestments, and the doctor and his betrothed to kneel together before him.

The whole company also knelt; when, having gone through what Gilbert considered the profane and idolatrous ceremony of the mass, the priest proceeded to the more interesting and essential ceremony of receiving the mutual vows of the bridal pair, and then, with as much haste as the forms of his church would permit, he pronounced them to be man and wife, and desired the husband to imprint the seal of the sacred union upon his wife's lips. The doctor eagerly obeyed, the priest imitated him and then the congratulations of all present were in order.

This was followed by a plentiful and luxurious repast, which was the work of the industrious hands of Mrs. Frasier, Marie and Denny assisting her in placing it before her assembled guests.

The French showed themselves as good at feasting as jesting and devoured Mrs. Frasier's fare with a keen relish. Paddy had succeeded in procuring some old Burgundy from the garrison, and when the exhilarating influence of the wine was felt, the gayety and jollity of the company, particularly the French part of it, rose correspondingly.

This overflowing of spirits soon brought an inclination for dancing, and as Paddy possessed a violin, and both he and Vanbraam being tolerably good performers, there was no lack of music, and away went the merry Frenchmen to the regions of airiness and joy.

Soon a regular cotillion was gotten up for which Mr. Washington had the good fortune to secure Marie as a partner.

The noble appearance and accomplished manners of Washington rendered him a great favorite with the French ladies, while the beauty and grace which adorned Marie excited the unbounded admiration of the officers. Washington was happy, for Marie, anxious to give him no cause for uneasiness, paid him every attention, and spared no pains to make everything pleasant and agreeable.

Indeed, so marked were the attentions these two paid to each other during the evening that the French, both men and women, observed it and became satisfied that Washington's present visit was altogether a visit of love.

The sports and enjoyments of the night were kept up until the moon arose, which was about one o'clock in the morning, when the French departed as gaily as they had come, and a couple of hours found them snugly stowed away in their quarters at Fort DuQuesne, while those at the Frasier residence were a good way into dreamland.

CHAPTER XIX.

AN ILLUSTRIOUS LOVER

ASHINGTON was up with the dawn, the morning following the day that witnessed the marriage ceremony, for his heart was far from being at ease.

"Alas!" said he, as he walked out along the banks of Turtle Creek, "if this most lovely of all maidens refuses my love how wretched I shall be. My heart will bleed at the desolation of its hope. And it will be still more miserable at the thought of the trouble and danger which will surround her, if war shocking and fierce with these barbarous savages penetrates this section, which I fear it will.

"But I will prevail on her, and heaven grant that she may consent to become my own, that I may carry her to a place of security."

In such contemplation, this ardent and illustrious lover spent upwards of an hour as he walked to and fro. He at length returned to the house, resolved to embrace the first opportunity that should offer, to make known to the mistress of his heart's affection his fears, his wishes, his warmth of admiration, and his sincerity of love.

When he reached the house he found that Marie had risen. He met her, smiling sweetly in all the blooming charms of maiden youthfulness. She was busily preparing the breakfast, and as she went through the various movements of household economy required by the occasion, he perceived in every turn and gesture of this lovely "Rose of the Wilderness" gracefulness and ease, which showed that she could render any task interesting, and that she was peculiarly fitted to preside with dignity and grace over all kinds of domestic concerns.

As the young Virginian followed her various movements with admiring eyes, he murmured to himself, "Oh, that she were once the mistress of my household, how doubly sweet and delightful would the shades of Mount Vernon then be to me. It may be so; and the time may not be far distant. To-day, I am resolved to ascertain the state of her feelings, and I pray a kind Providence may grant that they may be favorable."

But an unforseen circumstance prevented him from learning his fate that day. For the morning meal was scarcely over, when news came that Queen Alliquippa was quite ill and requested the presence of Marie, as the Queen feared she had not many hours to live.

Our heroine immediately set out in obedience to this summons, accompanied by the messenger who had brought the sad news. When Marie reached the wigwam she found Alliquippa just recovering from a strong convulsion which had left her much exhausted.

Marie wept over her, for she felt that she was about to lose forever one of her dearest and most valued friends.

The Queen was sensible of the presence of her favorite, and pressed her hand in token of the satisfaction she enjoyed of her being by her side. The violent tremors of her muscles that had agitated her frame, had apparently deprived her of her vocal powers, but after a few moments of rest, they seemingly recovered for a time and enabled her to say, "Marie, my daughter, thou art kind. It pleases me to see that thou lovest me. But do not grieve for me. I am going to meet my husband Shannalow in the happy hunting grounds, and I shall be happy."

The lovely, tender-hearted girl at her bedside could hardly speak for weeping. She sank upon her knees beside the couch upon which the Queen lay and in broken tones, sobbed: "My ever affectionate and kind mother, art thou going to leave me? Oh, canst thou not bless me before thou goest?"

In a faint murmur the Queen prayed, "Oh, Maneto, bless my child." She was unable to proceed further, for at this instant another convulsion seized her, during which the soul fled its frail tenement of clay, and Marie gazed upon the inanimate form of her dear friend.

She stooped and imprinted a kiss upon the cold lips, then withdrew with a heart full of sorrow.

When the news of Alliquippa's death reached Frasier's, Washington and Paddy set out for the purpose of lending whatever aid they could, and to accompany Marie home. As Paddy chose to remain for some time at the wigwam, for the purpose of showing the Indians his respect for their deceased Queen, Washington was delegated to act as his sister's escort on the way home, a task that was full of pleasure to him, and which he performed with all the gallantry that became his high, noble self.

True, he would have greatly desired to speak to her on the subject nearest his heart, but under the existing circumstances he feared she might consider him both selfish and out of place.

Their conversation during the walk home was, therefore, confined largely to the history and character of the deceased.

The next day Washington attended the funeral of Alliquippa. All the great men and warriors of her tribe were present.

The bier upon which she was carried to the grave, consisted of two long poles, joined together by wicker work, covered with decorated skins of the catamount.

Tonnawingo, as prophet of the tribe, walked before the procession, with his sacred wand extended.

Following the bier came the sages and the elder chiefs, then the most celebrated warriors, after which came the younger braves and the females. Washington and those of the Frasier family who attended brought up in the rear of the procession.

The burial ground was a little way up the side of a hill fronting the east and not far from Turtle Creek. Here a grave was dug in such a manner that when the body would be placed therein it would be in a half perpendicular position and facing the rising sun.

When the procession reached this last resting

place of the dead Queen they placed the bier alongside of the grave, when Tonnawingo, after waving his wand in the air three times, addressed the assembly.

"Brothers and sisters, before you commence your funeral dance, before you convey your beloved Queen into her last resting place and sing over her the songs of your sadness, listen to my words.

"Ye grieve for Alliquippa; ye think she has been unfortunate in being thus separated from you whom she loved to reside among. But hear me: She has been fortunate in the transition, because she was virtuous and good-hearted, and did her duty, and for these things her spirit is now receiving a glorious recompense from the Almighty Maneto. When you think of her who lies here, let it be to imitate her virtues, and then you will have no cause to fear the approach of death, and when it comes you will go to obtain the reward the Great Spirit has in store for you, in the happy hunting grounds to which your fathers and our dead Queen have gone.

"Now, brothers and sisters, you may perform your burial ceremonies. I go to worship the Great Father."

So saying, he waved his wand three times towards heaven, blessed the assembly, and departed.

Susquelooma, the chief who would succeed Alliquippa, now took upon himself the management of the proceedings, and the death dance immediately begun.

After this was over, the body was lowered into the grave, after which the antlers of a deer, the wing of a dove, a pair of moccasins, a string of beads, together with some twigs of spice wood and branches of the spruce pine were thrown in.

Susqueloona and several other chiefs now chanted the death-song, while a number of warriors proceeded to fill in the dark mould.

After the filling up of the grave, a heap of stones was piled upon it, in order to mark it, so that any of her tribe passing by might know where to pay the customary honor to the remains of one who had been long beloved and respected among them. The procession then returned to their wigwams, and Washington in company with Paddy, Denny and Dr. Killbreath, returned to the Frasier's.

Marie had not attended the funeral, but had remained at home; therefore it was not until the afternoon of the following day that Washington had an opportunity to make to her an open avowal of his feelings.

He asked her to walk out with him along the bank of the river, and it being one of those premature spring days which sometimes in Pennsylvania enliven the generally severe month of March and make a ramble very inviting and agreeable, she therefore readily consented, and they set out together.

Washington intentionally directed their steps toward the walnut tree beneath whose branches he had first lingered to gaze upon those charms that had made such an impression upon his heart.

"Here, Marie," said he, "is the place where I first beheld you; and from that moment to this the image that was impressed upon my mind has never for one instant left it, and never, never will leave it."

"Mr. Washington," said she, "I do not doubt your assertion, for I know you are above flattery, and because I believe you and know you are sincere, I will say candidly, that I am sorry you have allowed such lasting impression of unworthy me to find a place in your heart and mind."

"Oh, Marie!" he interrupted her, "do not use such chilly expressions.   How can you, if you esteem me and wish for my welfare, regret that which has afforded me the sweetest sensations of my life? Pray, do not say you are sorry for this."

"Alas, Mr. Washington," she replied, "if I respected you less I might feel less sorrow on this subject. But you deserve to be happy, and to make you so the woman of your choice should be capable of loving you with an ardor equal to your own. In short, sir, it is my earnest wish that you should bestow upon a more suitable object those affections of which I am but too conscious I am not worthy."

"Not worthy!" he exclaimed; "not worthy of my affections? Ah, then, what woman on earth can be worthy of them? To draw the picture which my imagination has formed of your person and your virtues would excite a doubt in your mind of my sincerity, but may I assure you I have never been insincere with any one."

"I do not question your sincerity," replied the fair maid, "but permit me to say that you do not know me sufficiently to judge of me accurately. If you did, you would see the necessity of forming a better choice."

"No, no," exclaimed her companion, "I swear that, unless thou dost peremptorily and finally refuse to be mine, I shall never form another choice. Oh, Marie! wilt thou not yield to my persuasion and agree to become mine?   This wilderness is unfit—"

"Mr. Washington," said she, "excuse me; but I must undeceive you—or rather remind you that I have already said I cannot return you that love and affection your noble self deserves."

"Give me but time, my fair companion," cried her lover, "time and my long and earnest concern for your welfare would first excite gratitude, and my patient waiting would evoke pity, and gratitude and pity would soon produce love.   You would not be long so cold, so indifferent, towards one so devoted to you.   It is not in your nature."

"Ah, sir!" said she, "you know not, you cannot know my feelings on this subject.   That I feel pity, for you just now, heaven is my witness; but that I never can feel love, heaven well knows."

"Marie, you talk mysteriously," said he.   "I really cannot understand you.   You say you pity me and in the same breath you say you cannot love me.   But, enchanting maiden, although you say it, I will hope against it; and trust that time will soften your heart, and make it favorably disposed to my suit."

"Never, never! I cannot," she exclaimed, evidently much agitated.

"Pray do not use such cruel words," said he, interrupting her; "I will not ask you at present to be mine. I will have hope—I will have patience. But, oh, let me ask of you to fly from this wilderness, for there will soon be no safety for you here. The legions of a powerful nation will soon carry their thunders into this forest to drive their enemies out of it, and the conflict will be dreadful. Ah, Miss Frasier, I indeed tremble for your safety unless you can be prevailed upon to leave this place before the bloody era commences."

"Mr. Washington," she replied, "you know that my father is on terms of intimacy with both the French and the Indians. Our feelings and sympathies are with the English, it is true, and the French may possibly suspect this, yet so long as we join neither party I think neither party will injure us. But you may lay your fears before my father and perhaps may induce him to consent to a removal."

"I will try the experiment," said he. "I may be able to prevail with your father, and by this means have the satisfaction of securing your safety, which really has been the main object of my present visit."

Marie expressed her thanks for his solicitude in her behalf. They then returned to the house, and Washington soon found opportunity to have a conversation with Gilbert Frasier.

Gilbert had long enjoyed so much safety amidst the tribes of warring Indians, and felt himself at the present time so secure in the friendship of both the French and the English, that he could not think of leaving what had been so long his home in the wilderness.

Paddy, who was present, confirmed his father in his desires to remain, by saying that he doubted very much if they could take their departure from the place now, without the knowledge of the French, who might in all probability interfere with their going.

"The day we should attempt to leave," said he, "you may depend upon it, that a troop of horsemen and a tribe of Indians would surround us, and force us to take up our abode, perhaps not in our own dwelling again, but in Fort DuQuesne, so that all we could gain by the attempt would be to make enemies of those who are now our friends. Besides, I think we can be of more service to the British cause by remaining here, and watching the movements of their enemies."

Washington, finding that he could not prevail on the family to accede to his wishes, and feeling that his duty to his country required his immediate return to Virginia, concluded not to delay his departure any longer.

Therefore the next morning he bade a tender adieu to Marie, and, accompanied by Vanbraam, left the Frasier residence with a heavy and anxious heart, and pursued his way to Mount Vernon, where he arrived in about two weeks, without meeting with any accident.

CHAPTER XX.

BEGINNING OF A GREAT STRUGGLE

THE news of Charles Addison's second defeat, and the establishment of the French fort at the head of the Ohio, had reached the cities along the Atlantic coast and caused a fever of excitement all over the country east of the Allegheny Mountains.

Hostilities were not yet formally declared between Great Britain and France; but the British Secretary of State had written to Governor Dinwiddie, that the attack of the French upon the Ohio Company's people, and their fortifying themselves at DuQuesne, was equivalent to the commencement of hostilities on their part; and therefore his majesty's colonies should feel at full liberty to attack and drive off the aggressors by any means in their power.

Upon Washington's return to Mount Vernon he had the satisfaction to find that a regiment of four hundred regulars had been raised by the authority of the Virginia Legislature, for the express purpose of proceeding against the enemy as soon as the season would permit. He felt himself honored in receiving the commission of Lieutenant-colonel. Mr. Fry, a military gentleman, supposed to have a knowledge of Indian affairs, having been appointed Colonel.

Washington had received word from Paddy Frasier that the French stronghold at DuQuesne was not yet complete, but was every day getting stronger, and as soon as the season opened the garrison expected to receive from Canada a strong reinforcement of arms and men.

In consequence of this knowledge he earnestly solicited of Dinwiddie permission to march against Fort DuQuesne, which after due consideration on the part of the Governor was granted.

Washington was extremely anxious for the capture of this fort, for several reasons. One of which was that by its coming into possession of the English the seat of war would be removed from the neighborhood, where one lived who was the object of anxious solicitude on his part.

True policy also called for prompt action, for a small force might be able to do then what a much larger force might fail to accomplish later on.

Colonel Washington was authorized to proceed

about the middle of April, with two hundred regulars and some militia, to attack Fort DuQuesne. If he found his force insufficient, he was to throw up entrenchments and await the arrival of Colonel Fry, with the remainder of the army, who would hasten after him as soon as it should be ready for marching.

The young hero lost no time, and in something less than two weeks he and his little force were encamped at a place called the Great Meadows, a few miles west of the Laurel Hill.   Here, finding an eligible position he determined to erect a fort, for the purpose of protecting his horses and provisions; and also as refuge for a retreat for his men in case of disaster.   This stronghold, from the haste and circumstance under which it was erected, he called "Fort Necessity."

While his soldiers were employed at this work, being anxious to learn the real condition and strength of the French garrison, he set out on foot accompanied by Vanbraam, both dressed as Indians.   When he reached Turtle Creek, he found Paddy Frasier had just come that very day from DuQuesne, and therefore was able to give him all the information he desired.

The news he received was not very encouraging.

The stockade of the fort on the side toward the two rivers was still incomplete, but a day or two before a re-inforcement of nearly five hundred men had left Fort Le-Boeuf and were descending the Allegheny river, and a large supply of cannon and other military stores was reported to be on its way from Canada.

Regarding Washington's approach, Paddy rather believed that the French were yet unaware of it. Washington tarried for the night at the Frasier residence, and during the evening had the pleasure of enjoying in private a short conversation with the woman he adored; but he found her as much averse to his protestations of love as formerly, although he pleaded his case more energetically and eloquently than ever before.

In the morning as Washington was taking a short walk along the river he perceived the prophet Tonnawingo approaching.

"Hail, my son," said he, extending his hand, "thou art again with us, and thou art welcome, for thy presence is an inspiration."

Washington took the hand of the old Indian in his own, giving it a hearty shake, remarking that he was pleased to greet the prophet, and hoped that he might in some way be able to serve him.

"Your coming is opportune, my son," said Tonnawingo, "else I would have been obliged to seek thee in thy camp.

"There is a person concealed in these woods from the enmity of the French.   He is of a generous, daring turn of mind, and like thyself a soldier.

"He has heard of thy coming with an armed force, and longs to join thee against the enemies of his country.   Wilt thou receive him?"

"With great pleasure, and a hearty welcome," replied Washington.   "May I ask his name?"

"Charles Addison," answered the prophet.

"I am glad of it," said Washington.   "He is a young man of indeed a gallant spirit, and will be a valuable acquisition to me.   I have often of late wondered where he was concealed; for I learned of his rescue from the French, and could not think he had made his way to Philadelphia, or it would have been publicly known.   But where shall I see him?"

"At this place to-night at ten o'clock, if that hour answers," said Tonnawingo.

"I shall make it answer," replied Washington.

"Then farewell, my son," said the prophet, and he disappeared, going in the direction of Turtle Creek, while Washington returned to the house, to enjoy the pleasure of conversing with Marie, although he knew he must avoid the subject of greatest concern to his heart.

He was doomed to disappointment, for she was not present when he returned, and he had too much delicacy of feeling to inquire of her whereabouts.

He was, therefore, forced to pass a rather dull day in the company of Gilbert Frasier and Mr. Vanbraam.

To explain the absence of Marie, we will say that previous to Tonnawingo's meeting with Washington he had visited the Frasier home, and at that time informed Marie of the desire of her lover to join the forces of Washington.

Therefore it was to the place where her heart was treasured that she had gone, at the request of her lover to bid him a farewell, while another was longing for her presence.

A little before sunset she returned much to the gratification of Washington, who had begun to entertain fears that he would not be permitted to see her again before his departure.

He had conversed with her but a brief space of time, when they were interrupted by the entrance of Paddy, who had just returned from a visit to the garrison at DuQuesne.

Washington, although very loth to do so, asked the fair maid to excuse him for the present and, taking Paddy's arm they walked a short distance from the house in silence.

As soon as they were out of hearing of the inmates Paddy broke the silence.

·"Some Indians have informed the Commandant at the fort, this very day," said he, "that you are approaching with several hundred Virginians to make an attack. The whole garrison has in consequence been all afternoon in great commotion; and I waited as long as I possibly could to learn what they proposed to do. I found that after holding several councils of war, with plenty of speeches and drinking wine in abundance, they resolved to send a detachment of about a hundred men to watch your movements and impede your progress if possible. These fellows started at a quick pace about an hour ago, under command of Major Jumonville."

"I must then return immediately to my camp, to prepare for their reception," said Washington.

"Yes," replied Paddy, "but you must take great care not to fall into their hands on the way."

"The sooner we are off now the better," said

Washington. "If Mr. Addison was here, I think we might proceed at once."

"Mr. Addison!" exclaimed Paddy, with some show of surprise; "does he go with you?"

"I am told that such is his desire," said Washington.

"You will find him a brave fellow,' replied Paddy, "worth a dozen Frenchmen, so long as he has nothing to do but fight."

"I do not doubt his courage, in the least," remarked Washington, in reply to Paddy. "But tell me, is it not near ten o'clock?"

"I'll see," replied Paddy, drawing a watch from his pocket. "I just set this by the dial at the garrison to-day." The moonlight being quite clear, Paddy made out the time to be close to the hour of ten.

"We must be off," said Washington. "Let us call Vanbraam and bid adieu to our friends."

"Yes, and I deem it proper that I should aecompany you as a guide," returned Paddy. "You may need my services in steering clear of the French, who are now traveling in the same direction."

Washington thanked the brave young man for his kindly offer, saying he would be only too glad to accept his services.

He then hurried into the house, bade a hasty farewell to Marie and the rest of the family, and set out for the walnut tree, followed by Vanbraam and Paddy.

Tonnawingo and Addison had arrived there a few minutes before them. The two young men received each other with a warm and hearty greeting; and the prophet pronouncing his benediction upon them they set forward, Paddy leading the way, through unfrequented paths, and sometimes no path at all, until they arrived at the objective point of their journey.

During their return they neither heard nor saw anything of the French detachment, nor had any intelligence of the coming of the enemy reached the fort.

During the night Washington took effectual measures to prevent a surprise, and the next morning Paddy Frasier, together with several scouts, were sent to range the country in search of the enemy.

A few days before, Washington had the misfortune to lose by sickness one of his officers, a captain, by the name of Stewart. He had now an opportunity of showing his regard for Charles Addison by bestowing upon him the vacant place, and Charles was commissioned a captain.

He was now a soldier, and an officer in the service of his country, and under a leader who honored him with his friendship, and who impressed him with the most profound admiration and respect.

It was about nine o'clock at night when Paddy Frasier entered Washington's quarters, with the news that he had discovered the enemy encamped in a narrow defile to the east of them, and only about two hours' march from the fort.

Paddy described the ground on which Jumonville had encamped his men, in such a manner that Washington at once perceived the practicability of seizing, during the night, upon the heights that surrounded them, and surprising them into a surrender in the morning, perhaps, without bloodshed.

He accordingly, without delay, placed himself at the head of his men, and proceeded to the place designated by Paddy.

Here he found the enemy occupying a flat piece of ground, not more than fifty yards wide and protected on each side by high hills, which made it one of the best places for concealment that could be found, but one of the worst for an escape.

After cautiously reconnoitering the ground, Washington detached nearly one-half of his troops and sent them under charge of a trusty officer, by a circuitous route, to take possession of the western height, while he himself with the remainder proceeded to occupy the range on the east.

His humanity prevented him from attacking the French during the night; for he reasonably expected that in the morning, when they would find themselves surrounded, and completely hemmed in by a superior force, with no means left for an escape, they would surrender without causing unnecessary sacrifice of life.

The French were indeed much astonished when morning dawned, and revealed to their view the surrounding heights glittering with the weapons of the soldiers, and the British colors floating at intervals around them.

Their commander was a brave but rather rash officer. Full of chagrin and irritation, at his being caught in a trap, he rejected Washington's summons to surrender. With the forlorn hope of throwing the Virginians into some confusion, which might facilitate his escape, he ordered an attack to be made upon a company that had been placed to guard the lower entrance to the defile. This body was under the command of Captain Addison, beside whom Paddy Frasier had taken his station.

"See that scoundrel Jumonville!" cried Paddy, as soon as he observed the movements of the French. "He will sacrifice his men to his madness and give us trouble as well. But I'll just pop a bit of lead into his cap, to teach him some sense."

The next instant Paddy's rifle was leveled and the French officer fell with a bullet in his brain. This fatality befalling the commanding officer, the attack was suspended, when, after some little parleying, the French surrendered themselves unconditionally prisoners of war, and were soon lodged in Fort Necessity.

The day following the capture of the French detachment the remainder of the Virginia regiment, that was to follow under Colonel Fry, joined their companions; but the colonel had sickened and died on the march, before reaching them. The entire command now devolved upon Washington, very much to the satisfaction of all his officers and men.

The number of his troops was also augmented a few days afterward by the arrival of two companies, one from the colony of New York, and the other from South Carolina; for by this time all the colonies had become interested in the struggle, and resolved to support Virginia in her efforts against the common enemy.

Having now a force of nearly six hundred men, fairly well equipped for war, except cannon, though Washington knew that DuQuesne was also destitute of this ordnance, he resolved to push on and attack the post.

A scarcity of provisions was beginning to be felt, and this was the only thing that seemed to call for a postponement of his plans. But he trusted that a supply would soon follow him, for he had written an urgent letter to Governor Dinwiddie on the subject.

Leaving one company of his men in charge of Fort Necessity, to protect it from any surprise, he commenced his march with the remainder of his troops.

The army had reached a point, at the close of the second day's march, a few miles west of the Laurel Hill, when they were met by Paddy Frasier with intelligence of such a nature as to stop their progress.

His report was that the French had received

their long expected supplies from Canada, and were now, with a force of nearly a thousand whites and as many Indians, on the march to meet the British and could not be more than a half day's journey distant. Under the circumstances, Washington deemed this alarming intelligence. Their bread was about exhausted and their supply of meat had become very scanty. If the French should by any means get between him and his expected supply of provisions, or other stores that might be sent him from Virginia, they would be intercepted, and his little army deprived of necessary subsistence.

He was very reluctant, however, to commence a retrograde movement, but he felt that the force of the enemy being so overwhelming, his best move would be to fall back upon Fort Necessity and there make a defense until help would reach him.

He called a council of war, and addressed his officers, laying before them their situation. The council, after a very brief deliberation, resolved unanimously that a retreat was necessary to afford them any chance of avoiding capture. It was, therefore, immediately begun, and Fort Necessity saw them again enter its ramparts, about four days after their departure.

There was only one individual in the entire army who felt the disappointment occasioned by this turn of affairs as acutely as Washington himself, and he did so because his feelings arose from the same cause.   This man was Captain Addison.

With high hopes in his breast, he had expected in a few days to again be beside his Marie, not as one who feared to show his head above ground, but as an avowed soldier of his country, able to protect the object of his affection.

Washington's feelings ran much along the same line, only he had an additional burden of public solicitude and grief for the miseries to which he saw that thousands of his countrymen would be doomed, in consequence of his failure in this enterprise.

Expecting soon to sustain an attack, he kept his men busily engaged in fortifying and improving the strength of the stockade which had been hastily erected and was still far from being complete. His troops were all zealous in obeying his every direction, the officers themselves setting an example for their men in performing manual labor.

Captain Addison had worked very perseveringly at the trench, when one day towards evening, feeling that he would like to enjoy an hour of rest, he strolled away a short distance from the fort, and had seated himself upon a mossy rock to enjoy a few moments of quiet meditation, when to his sudden surprise two men rushed from out the bushes close by and seized him before he had time to arise.

Being a young man, both strong and active, he very quickly managed to get one of his adversaries beneath him; at the same time the other drew a dagger and was about plunging it into his body, when all of a sudden he was forcibly seized around the waist by a man who lifted him dagger and all high in the air, exclaiming: "May the divil take ye, but two on one is foul play, my honey. And, by St. Patrick, it's my own master ye would murder," cried the now infuriated Peter McFall, for such it proved to be, as he dashed the Frenchman to the ground, and quickly seizing the dagger that had dropped from the man's hand, he buried it in the bosom of his fallen foe.

"Huzza for old Ireland!" cried Peter. "Now, master, for the other rascal."

"Not so fast, my brave Peter," cried Addison; "he calls for quarter."

"By the powers of Killarney! then I'll quarter

20

him in a jiffy," replied Peter, attempting to strike at the Frenchman.

"Hold, my rash fellow!" said Addison, protecting the man's body with his own. "It would be murder to kill a disarmed and defenseless man."

"Murder to kill a Frenchman!" exclaimed Peter. "By my soul, that's a new doctrine. But what will ye do with him?"

"I would have you take him in charge," said Addison, "and conduct him to the fort yonder, where we will dispose of him as may be found suitable."

Peter leaped upon the captive as a tiger would upon his prey, and seizing him by the collar drove him before him in great triumph, occasionally giving him a shake, which caused the Frenchman to roar lustily, much to the delight of his tormentor.

Upon their entrance to the fort, the prisoner was at once examined, and acknowledged that he and his slain companion had been sent forward by Monsieur DeVilliers, who was at the head of an army of French and Indians, numbering nearly two thousand men, to reconnoitre the position and learn the strength of the force under Washington's command.

To account for the unexpected and timely approach of Peter McFall to his master's rescue, I must inform the reader that Mr. Gist, to whose house it will be remembered Peter had been conveyed by Paddy Frasier, having learned of Charles Addison joining the ranks of Washington's army, had communicated this intelligence to Peter, who immediately resolved to join his master. He accordingly bade a tender adieu to the fair Esther Gist, whose charms had made him forget those of Molly McNickle, and starting for Fort Necessity, which was not more than fifteen miles distant, he arrived as we have seen, just at the critical moment to save his master's life. Greatly to his own satisfaction as well as that of his master he resumed his old station as the faithful and favorite servant of Charles Addison.

CHAPTER XXI.

BATTLE OF FORT NECESSITY

THE day had scarcely dawned when information was carried to Washington that the enemy was approaching, and that the woods seemed to be alive with French and Indians. The garrison was immediately called to arms, and every man stationed where he could render the most effective resistance.

As the foe seemed to be advancing in the direction where the trench was deepest, although there were other places, where it would offer no resistance, being but a few feet deep, Captain Addison was directed to place his command there, which order was immediately carried out, each man carrying in addition to his rifle a loaded musket.

They had scarcely taken their places when the savage war whoop was heard and the enemy was seen advancing in battle array until they were within about six hundred yards of the ditch, when they halted and poured a rain of bullets from a thousand muskets upon the stockade.

Some of the badly placed piles were overthrown, and five or six Virginians killed by this discharge. Those in the ditch coolly reserved their fire, until encouraged by their silence the assailants advanced rapidly to about one hundred yards of the place where Captain Addison had stationed his men, when he gave a preconcerted signal to his marksmen, and at that instant a hundred reports were heard as one discharge, and as many Frenchmen bit the dust.

DeVilliers, supposing the rifles of the Virginians to be now empty, urged his men forward to storm the fort, when they were again saluted by a volley from both the ditches and stockade, which sent nearly one hundred and fifty more to earth never to rise again.

The French commander now deemed it prudent to avoid that fatal ditch and attack the fort in another quarter. He accordingly drew off his men out of reach of the fire of the Virginians, which allowed Addison's marksmen an opportunity to reload.

The enemy now keeping at a respectful distance from the fort, marched towards its southeast quarter, where they hoped to find it more easy to assail. Although they were able to see that the ramparts here were less formidable than elsewhere, yet being ignorant of the depth of the ditch that fronted it, they were very slow in approaching, lest they would meet with a similar volley to the one on the other side.

At last after several hours spent in manoeuvring and trying to draw the fire from the fort, which had maintained a mysterious silence all the while, De-Villiers, becoming at last aroused, gave the command, and his whole force rushed forward, seemingly resolved to take the place regardless of the cost.

The Virginian marksmen lay in wait for them and discharged their rifles as before, but the enemy not being so compact, their fire was not so fatal, although it made the French recoil for a moment. However, they gathered fresh courage and pushed forward regardless of danger.

Although the fire from the ditch fell with telling effect they came on up to the very edge, and, led by DeVilliers in person, upwards of five hundred entered the ditch, and would perhaps have overcome the few stationed there, had not Washington at this critical juncture led a bayonet charge, which forced the French to withdraw, leaving behind some sixty of their number dead on the spot.

Not content with forcing the enemy out of the ditch, Captain Addison sprang out upon the bank, and calling on his men to follow him, which they did to a man, he led a charge with clubbed rifles upon the enemy. The brave fellow was too impetuous, for the enemy were at least three to one against him, and turning upon him he and his little band would have been almost, if not entirely annihilated, had not Washington who, perceiving his danger, rushed to his aid with a band of Virginians, and drove the enemy to the cover of the woods, not however, before Captain Addison and Monsieur Joncairé had crossed swords in single combat with the result that the Frenchman was stricken to the earth, receiving a dreadful fracture of the skull, of which he died a few days afterwards.

Both Washington and Addison with their men withdrew to the protection of the fort, and a cessation of the attack now took place, affording Washington time to learn the condition of affairs.

Between sixty and seventy of his men were killed, and upwards of a hundred so badly wounded as to be unfit for service. The enemy was repulsed, it is true, but there was every probability that the attack would be renewed the next day. If the enemy would direct their attack against the

weaker portion of the stockade, surrender or an-
nihilation, semed inevitable. The only hope would
lie in the attack being made upon the same points
as heretofore. This would enable Washington's
men to better repel the attack, and perhaps compel
them to abandon the enterprise.

It was, therefore, his great object to prevent
them from discovering the weak parts of his defense, and he accordingly ordered that during the
night the weaker places should be particularly
guarded from the approach of spies.

While he was making arrangements for preventing a surprise, a trumpeter approached from the
woods where the French were stationed, and de-
manded a parley, and permission for an officer to
enter the fort in order to negotiate for a surrender.

Washington refused to grant the last request.
He declared he would permit none of the enemy to
enter the fort without detaining them as prisoners
of war, and that if the French commander was serious in his desire to negotiate, he must give a passport for a British officer to proceed to his camp for
this purpose, and his guarantee of a safe return.

Washington's caution in the matter arose from
his unwillingness to expose the imperfect condition of the fort to the enemy, besides he feared it

might be a trick of DeVilliers to discover any available quarter for a new attack.

The French commander granted the parole required, and Captain Addison was appointed to wait upon him, and ascertain the terms he had to propose. These terms, being very little short of unconditional surrender, were absolutely refused by Washington, and Addison was instructed to inform DeVilliers that his terms would have to be much more reasonable to receive a consideration.

The French officer then in a second message stated that he would permit the garrison to leave, upon both officers and privates giving their parole not to serve in the country again during the present contest against the French. They were to take with them only enough provisions for their return to their several homes, but to depart without taking any of their arms or munitions of war.

Washington was indignant at this proposal, and with some warmth of feeling, said: "Tell Monsieur DeVilliers that he very much mistakes both our situation and our disposition, if he calculates on our accepting such terms.

"The only terms I shall accept are these: That we shall be allowed the honors of war, be permitted to retain our arms, baggage and stores of every

kind, and to march without molestation back to
our homes.   Tell DeVilliers that rather than ca-
pitulate on any other conditions, I shall bury myself and every man who will stand by me, in the
ruins of this fort.   And further say, that if this is
not acceptable, we will terminate our negotiations
and resume the contest."

When Captain Addison reported this reply to
the French commander, he arched his brows and
shrugged his shoulders, then after a few minutes'
silence he remarked: "That young Washington is
an obstinate fellow, but I see he is a brave man, and
I believe I can make nothing more out of him
without considerable slaughter; therefore I will let
him have his terms, so that I may get him entirely
out of this country."

The terms of the capitulation were accordingly
drawn up in French, and then translated in English, when it was signed by the officers on both
sides.

The next morning, after the burial of their dead,
the British removed all their stores from the fort,
and with their colors flying, and drums beating,
they marched out in martial array, and paraded at
some distance from the French encampment.

As their horses were chiefly all killed or crippled

during the engagement, they found themselves unable to carry off all their stores. Therefore, in order to prevent them from falling into the hands of the French, they destroyed all but what they were able to carry away upon their shoulders. They then continued their march homeward, and in about three days arrived within the inhabited parts of Virginia.

Washington and his men were highly complimented for their spirited and gallant conduct on the march and in the battle. When the legislature met, they expressed their satisfaction for what had been done, by presenting a sum of money to be distributed among the soldiers, and tendered a vote of thanks to Colonel Washington and the officers under his command, for the credit which their conduct had reflected upon their country.

To this vote of thanks we give Washington's reply, taken from "Marshall's Life of Washington."

We, the officers of the Virginia regiment, are highly sensible of the particular mark of distinction with which you have honored us in returning your thanks for our behavior in the late action; and we cannot help expressing our grateful acknowledgment for your 'high sense' of what we shall always esteem a duty to our country and our worthy King.

Favored with your regard, we shall zealously endeavor to deserve your applause, and by our future actions strive to

convince the worshipful house of burgess how much we esteem their approbation, and, as it ought to be, regard it as
the voice of our country.
   Signed for the entire corps
                    GEORGE WASHINGTON.

We would naturally suppose that the applause
bestowed upon this young hero, on this occasion,
would strengthen his desire for a military life, yet
we find that shortly after this, owing to some cause
unknown to the writer, Washington for the present relinquished any military aspirations he may
have cherished and retired to private life.

DeVilliers, satisfied with having driven Washington out of the wilderness, and deeming the occupation of Fort Necessity unnecessary, relinquished it the day after its capture, and retraced
his steps back to Fort DuQuesne.

Great Britain had now publicly declared war
against France, and large bodies of European
troops were expected soon to arrive in the colonies, yet there was so much perplexing delay that
nothing was attempted that season, and during the
whole of the autumn and winter of 1754 the French
remained unmolested in the possession of all the
territory embracing the head-waters of the Ohio
river.

The family of Frasier continued as usual to follow their employment undisturbed by the French, with whom Paddy managed to keep on the most friendly footing. The assistance he had rendered Washington never became known to them, and both he and Doctor Killbreath continued to trade with them and the Indians as freely, and with as little fear, as if they had never taken any part with their enemies.

With respect to Marie Frasier, she had learned of the conflict at Fort Necessity, and felt proud of the honorable part her lover had performed under the noble Washington, but since the return of Paddy and the doctor, she was without news regarding his danger or safety.

At length fortune had compassion upon her, and relieved her anxiety by throwing in her way a Philadelphia newspaper, which Paddy had managed to procure from a trader who had been on a visit to the east with some furs.

This paper contained the following paragraph, which gave Marie great joy in perusing.

It is with pleasure that we announce the arrival in our city of that gallant young man, Charles Addison, who commanded the party sent out in the beginning of last winter to take possession of the lands belonging to the Ohio Company, in our western wilderness, and upon whom the French garrison of Le-Boeuf committed the daring outrage which has often been mentioned in our paper in terms of indignation, and which we rejoice that our mother country has at length determined to resent, in a manner becoming her rank and dignity among the nations.

Mr. Addison's friends had been for several months uncertain of his fate, and their joy on being again blessed with the society of one so much valued and beloved, after he had, as many supposed, fallen a victim to savage revenge and cruelty, will not be easily imagined.

This gentleman's adventures in the western wilderness, during the past winter, we are informed, have been of the most singular and romantic character. Until the coming of the gallant Washington to the quarter, when an opportunity permitted him to join his countrymen, he owed his safety only to concealment in the lonely dells and darksome caverns that abound in that wild and savage country.

Great, indeed, must have been his sufferings, and miraculous his escape.

We trust that Mr. Addison, or some of his friends, will one day favor the public with a narrative of his adventures, during his stay in the west. We are persuaded that there are many who would feel extremely interested in the perusal of such a work.

This information was of great value to the lovely maiden so far removed from the avenues of civilization, and it will be difficult for those who read these lines at the present day to fully realize how much information of this kind was prized by those who in that day did not have the facilities afforded in this advanced age for the interchange of news.

CHAPTER XXII.

MARCH AND DEFEAT OF BRADDOCK

THE joy of Charles Addison's father and mother on meeting again with their only son, whom they looked upon as one restored from the grave, was indeed great, and parties and receptions were given by the overjoyed parents, at all of which Captain Addison was the flattered and petted hero of the occasion.

The compliments and smiles of admiration bestowed upon him by the fair sex were well calculated to not only turn the head of the ordinary young man, but to shake the constancy of an affcetion not firmly grounded in true love.

But the lover of Marie Frasier meritoriously held fast to his heart's integrity. I say meritoriously, for not a few were the aspirants for a place in the esteem of this young man who seemed to be riding upon the tidal wave of popularity.

Wealth and beauty bowed before him, but, if he felt his heart warming under the seductive influence of his surroundings, one single reflection upon the charms of a "Rose"that was blooming in the Wilderness for him alone, was enough to restore to him those feelings of true affection which he delighted to cherish.

All through the fall and winter young Addison lived a life of enchantment, which to one of his genial temperament was very enjoyable; but at times he felt an irresistible desire to be away from the gay crowd that surrounded him and to bask in the sunshine of the fair maid that had won his heart.

When the spring time came he felt an almost uncontrollable desire to see her.   To inform his father of his wishes, with a view to obtain his permission to return to the western wilds, he knew would be fruitless.   His only hope lay in the contemplated march of a British army against Fort DuQuesne, the landing of which was looked for every day.

He had not long to wait, for in a short time the joyful intelligence reached him that a respectable army of English soldiers, under General Edward Braddock had reached the shores of Virginia with the avowed intention of proceeding against the French.

Here was his opportunity, and he at once solicited the consent of his father to join this army as a volunteer, which was reluctantly granted by the elder Addison, who was not partial to warlike measures although he was heartily in favor of forcing the French from what he believed to be English territory.

Charles was elated with the prospect of soon again beholding the beloved of his heart, and assisting to expel the enemy from the neighborhood in which she resided. He accordingly hastened to Alexandria, where Braddock had agreed to meet a convention of the different governors of the colouies, in order to settle upon a plan for the campaign.

Here Addison met with his former commander, Colonel Washington, whom Braddock, anxious for his services, had appointed as one of his aids-de-camp. Washington's influence and friendship soon procured for him the appointment of captain of a company of Virginia Rangers, that were to be attached to the army.

After many vexatious delays, on account of the difficulty in obtaining sufficient supplies of provisions, wagons and other articles necessary for the expedition, the army was set in motion, and proceeded to a fort at Will's Creek, afterward called Fort Cumberland, which was at that time the most western post held by the English in America.

From this place there was no road on which wagons could pass, and it begun to be feared that too much time would be lost in cutting a way through the rough and wooded country, thus giving their enemies longer time to fortify.

The army, however, courageously struggled with all obstacles, until it had advanced as far as the Great Meadows, where the difficulties of the way were found to increase so much that Gen. Braddock, who at first rejected the advice of Washington, to carry only such baggage as could be taken forward on horses and to leave his long train of wagons behind, was now compelled to adopt it so far as to take with him only the lighter wagons and tumbrils. They were constantly obliged to construct a passage, evidences of which the writer has observed while traveling over their line of march, although the remains of what is known in Western Pennsylvania as "Braddock's Road," are fast disappearing from view.

The force of Braddock, including regulars and provincial troops, was about two thousand men. Their general was a quick-tempered, conceited man, very overbearing and harsh in his manner, though resolute and brave. He looked upon provincial troops with contempt, but he could not resist the sensible advice of Washington in this particular. So selecting twelve hundred of his best troops, with what baggage and military stores that could be more easily carried, he placed himself at their head and began his march for Fort DuQuesne, one hundred and thirty miles away.

The remainder of his army was left at the Great Meadows, under charge of Colonel Dunbar, with instructions to follow with the more heavy baggage, by slow and easy marches.

Ellis, in his work entitled "History of our Country," states that the marching pageant of the portion led by Braddock was strung out a distance of four miles, although we do not wonder at this, knowing the unbroken nature of the land along the line of march.

Their progress was so slow that the French were allowed all the time they wanted to prepare for their coming. History tells us that it was on the last day of May that the army left Fort Cumberland and it was not until the eighth day of July that they came in sight of the ford below the mouth of Turtle Creek where they were to cross the Monongahela.

Here they stopped a short time to rest and refresh themselves, before they attempted the crossing of the ford. Fort DuQuesne, their objective point of march, lay some twelve miles away, but they expected to be in possession of it before the close of the next day.

Washington, knowing full well the danger of advancing in the way Braddock was doing, urged upon him to dispose of his army in open order. The British commander turned upon him and angrily retorted: "What! do you, a provincial colonel, presume to teach a British General how to advance against a foe?" Washington bit his lips and held his peace, but his heart was heavy for he felt the shadow of impending danger around them.

From where the army lay, the Frasier residence was visible, and the smoke was seen lazily curling from its chimney. The sight of it caused at least the hearts of two in that vast concourse to beat faster as they recalled the face and form of a fair one who was perhaps standing before the fire at that very moment in preparation of the noon-day meal.

Up to this time the army of Braddock had met with no opposition from an armed force, and the greater part of them did not dream of meeting with any resistance until the day they reached Du-Quesne.

Washington was an exception; he knew that the Indians in the employ of the French would not be content to wait until the attack was made upon the fort, but would seek to ambush the approaching army, and how true this was the reader of history well knows, and what a sacrifice of human life.

Before proceeding to detail the events of the battle we will take the liberty of describing in brief the famous field of conflict in the early annals of our country's history.

The stream of the Monongahela at this place runs nearly from east to west. That of Turtle Creek issuing out of a narrow and deep glen enters it from the north. This glen widens as the stream approaches the river, gradually reaching back for almost half a mile.

Where Turtle Creek flows into the Monongahela, a flat tract of land extends back from each side of the river, with here and there several declining tables of fertile land, the lower one reaching along the river where the ford was situated. Less than a mile below the mouth of Turtle Creek this stretch of flat land ends, and the banks become more high and precipitous, especially on the north side of the river, and for some distance on the south

side until they reach Pittsburg, the site of Fort Du-
Quesne at that time.

A short distance below the junction of Turtle
Creek with the Monongahela, is a rise in the land
above the adjacent flat, and embraced by two ravines running parallel to each other, about three
hundred yards apart.

It was in these gullies the Indians laid their fatal
ambush on that ill-fated ninth day of July, 1755.

Standing on this ground, a most pleasant landscape, not very extensive however, but certainly
very romantic, opens to the view. To the north
the ridge rises above you; to the west, the view
down the river is limited by the high banks already
mentioned. Directly south the broad expanse of
the Monongahela lies glittering before you, while
on the other shore, where Braddock's army halted
before he attempted to ford the river, the land rises
gradually, leaving no extensive margin, as it does
on the north side. To the east the view is clear for
quite a distance up the river. The spot in all this
expanse of territory in which was centered the
greatest interest at that time to many of the characters in our story, is the little peninsula of land
lying between the waters of Turtle Creek and those
of the Monongahela. It was of triangular shape

and consisted of several hundred acres of rich bottom land, and on this spot stood the home of the only white settler in all that region, namely, our friend Gilbert Frasier.

A visitor to this spot to-day would find a great transformation.

One continuous stretch of manufactories extends for miles both east and west. At night the sky is livid with the reflection of the sheets of flame issuing from the tall chimneys. Everywhere can be seen and heard the evidence of a great work going on, in which thousands find employment, while the hill sides and every other available space are thickly studded with the homes of the industrious.

The beholder can hardly conceive that here, a little less than a century and half ago, the wild beast was startled in his lair within the tangled morass of a dark forest, by the war-whoop of a no less wild and fierce savage and the deafening report of the discharge of musketry, as the powers of one great nation strove against the other for supremacy.

*   *   *   *   *

The situation of the French garrison at Fort DuQuesne during the opening and early part of the summer of 1755 was rather perplexing.

Monsieur DeVilliers, who had succeeded St. Pierre as its governor, had at this time only about four hundred French soldiers under his command; most of those who had fought at Great Meadows had been sent to other forts.

He had repeatedly written to the Canadian government for reinforcements, but as yet they had not reached him. Matters were in this state at the garrison, about the beginning of July when some Indian scouts informed him of the approach of Braddock. He at once sent out three trusty scouts to watch the motions of the British.

In a few days they reported to him that the army of Braddock had reached the south bank of the river. In order to acquaint himself with the ground over which the British were expected to march, he had before the arrival of the enemy, paid a visit to that locality and while there visited the Frasier residence, when he unluckily came face to face with Marie Frasier and beheld with surprise and admiration the beauty of this lovely maiden.

A violent passion for the fair maid seized upon him, and he resolved that as soon as the coming crisis would be past he would seek her out and pay his court to her. DeVilliers was a widower of about forty years of age, of a temper bold, sanguine and irritable. He was a man who permitted no scruples of religion or morality to stand in the way of his gratification.

On viewing the ford, he perceived at once that he had not a force sufficient to contest its passage by the army that he understood was coming against him. He resolved to adopt a plan whereby the Indians could render him efficient service.

This was to form an ambuscade, into which the British might be ensnared. He accordingly selected the ground we have before described, for that purpose, and there proposed to place his Indian allies.

He returned to the fort, and having assembled four hundred savages, who were all excellent marksmen, he informed them of his design, and at once received their ready assent to its execution. To each of these Indians he gave two loaded rifles and eighteen charges of powder and ball.

This band of savages then assembled outside the fort, and loudly chanted a war song. Then with their rifles over their shoulders and their tomahawks and scalping knives slung by their sides, they proceeded on the evening of the 8th of July from the fort to the place of ambush, in order to prepare it during the night, as the British were expected to cross the ford the next day. DeVilliers, at the head of three hundred of his best French soldiers, accompanied them.

They arrived at their destination long before daybreak. The French commander gave the Indians the necessary instructions how to act, and having placed two hundred of them in each of the two ravines before noticed, he concealed himself and his French soldiers at some distance and waited for the approach of the enemy.

About noon, General Braddock gave orders to cross over the river. His advance, composed of some light companies, and a company of grenadiers, to the number of three hundred men, were not more than half way over, when they were unexpectedly fired upon by a small party of French, who showed themselves among the trees near the river bank.

After firing, this party immediately retired back from the river, and Braddock, never dreaming of an ambuscade, ordered his men to hasten after them.

On perceiving this state of affairs, Colonel Washington rode up to the commander-in-chief, and begged him not to follow the French, as evidently such a small number of troops acting as they did, by just showing themselves and then retiring, were only intended as a decoy to lead them into some ambush.

"My orders are to pursue those fellows," replied Braddock curtly; "and Colonel Washington, I hope I have not been so long a soldier without knowing how to lead an army over a ford not more than knee deep, in the face of no stronger opposition than that of a few Frenchmen, without asking advice from any man. I shall ask your opinion only when I think I need it."

Washington made no reply. He only sighed as he perceived Colonel Gage, who commanded the advance, leading it onward.

"Alas!" said he, riding forward to Captain Addison, who was leading on his company of Virginia rangers; "this is indeed madness; I am afraid we shall pay dearly for it. We must do our duty, however."

"I shall obey your directions alone, Colonel," replied Addison, "for I know they will not be inconsistent with my duty." This feeling was endorsed by all the Virginia captains.

At that instant, the entire command had gained the beach, and Braddock gave the orders for all the companies to follow the track taken by the advance detachment.

Washington gave the signal for the provincials also to advance; for he was determined not to forsake the regulars although he greatly disapproved of making an advance in this way after a few fleeting Frenchmen.

Only a few scattering shots had as yet been fired by the French, as they retreated. Their object was only to lure the British after them, between the gullies where the Indians lay hidden, and silently watching for their prey. In this they succeeded to their utmost desires, for the van-guard of the British ascended the strip of land lying between these two gullies with rapidity.

Suddenly a terrific war-whoop was heard, and two hundred rifles from the ground upon their left poured their fire upon them, and the next instant two hundred more from their right sent forth their death dealing missiles. Two-thirds of the advance guard lay prostrate upon the earth, and the remainder were wildly firing into the trees and bushes in the vain hope of reaching some unseen foe.

The firing from the ravines appeared to cease, and Braddock conceiving the danger to be over, and anxious to avenge the slaughter already made, and as well rescue the remaining portion of the advance, ordered a large division of the main body to ascend the height, and there form into two parties, and with fixed bayonets charge into each ravine and destroy or drive out the invisible foe.

This corps gallantly ascended to the scene of death, when the firing was again opened with as much fury as before. At the same time the French from the heights above began an attack upon the advance guard who fell hastily back upon their companions, throwing them into confusion, so much so that they failed to make the charge ordered, and dreading another volley, every man able to march, hastened back from the fatal spot to the low ground.

This created a panic, and the whole body of regulars would soon have crossed the river in full flight had not their officers by great exertion restrained them.

General Braddock, mad with vexation and mortification at the loss already of so many brave men, rushed in among his troops and earnestly entreated them to stand their ground, and it was only through his indomitable will and exertion that order was again restored.

At this crisis, Washington again offered his advice, that the army should not attempt to dislodge their assailants, but draw off out of the reach of their fire, and continue their march to Fort DuQuesne, without paying these concealed enemies any more attention.

But Braddock was deaf to all advice. He resolved to take another course. He detached about two hundred and fifty men, and sent them around by the left of the ambush ground, in order to come upon the hidden enemy in another direction, and thus have them hemmed in between two fires.

This movement, however, was soon discovered by DeVilliers, who seized upon a favorable position by which he knew this detachment must pass; he met it there and cut off every man, without the loss of a single soldier on his side.

Braddock now resolved to make a stronger and more irresistible charge with his entire force upon the enemy. He therefore called upon his troops to come on a third time, and leading the way himself, he was followed by his devoted soldiers, and the death dealing ravines had victims once more within their reach.

Had this body boldly pushed on with fixed bayonets the moment they ascended the ground, they would no doubt have dislodged the savages from their concealment. But instead of doing this, Braddock imprudently took time to form them into two columns, with as much deliberation and formality as if he were parading them at a review in Hyde Park.

This delay restored the courage of the Indians, who, perceiving so large a body advancing with so much eagerness, had become intimidated, as the French were at this time engaged by the party sent out to attack the ravine in another quarter and not having them to rely upon, they were fast losing courage, although everything so far had gone to their entire satisfaction.

This blunder on the part of the British General gave them time to restore their confidence and energy, and once more they opened fire upon the crowded troops with dreadful fatality. Here one-third of Braddock's officers were killed, and he himself had three horses successively shot under him, and soon his entire division began to lose that compact order which he had taken so much trouble to form.

In a short time they fell into absolute confusion and fled, some of them back to the lower ground, and some forward to the ground lately occupied by the French. Braddock, wild with rage and furious with hot displeasure at the conduct of his men, was borne back with those who retreated to the lower ground. Near a spring, which to this day bears the name of "Braddock's Spring," and at the lower point of the western ravine, he again attempted to rally his troops, when a fourth horse was shot under him, and while he was mounting another, he received a ball in his breast.

The Indians had seen him fall, and about a hundred of them rushed forward out of the ravine to seize him, and here occurred a desperate encounter over the body of the prostrate commander. Washington, resolving to save the fallen Braddock at any risk, rushed to his side calling on Addison to charge with his Virginians, which order he promptly obeyed, but a volley from the other ravine soon prostrated nearly one-half of his men.

Washington himself shot one of the Indians who was attempting to drag the body of the prostrate officer away, and plunged his sword into the body of another, when his own horse was killed under him, and he came to the ground as a dozen of shots were fired at his head at close range.

In this fire his hat was perforated and part of its plumes and other decoration carried away. Addison, seeing his danger, rushed furiously forward with the remnant of his company to his rescue, and with one stroke of his great broadsword cleft in twain the skull of a savage, who was leveling a murderous aim at Washington only a few feet away. The Indian's rifle, however, went off, but the direction of the aim had been changed by Addison's blow, and the ball only tore off the epaulette from Washington's left shoulder.

In a few moments an orderly rushed up with another horse, and Washington remounted, when perceiving that a number of Indians had again laid hold of the wounded Braddock, he plunged in among them with tremendous fury, and leveled three or four of them to the earth, with the irresistible sweep of his broadsword.

Another volley from the Indians was poured in upon him, for they perceived that until he was destroyed they could not capture the General. His horse was again shot, and his coat perforated in a number of places.

Addison's few surviving troops would not have been able to hold out against the rush made by the Indians had not another company of Virginians under command of Captain Poulson, rushed to their rescue, when the savages were driven back into their retreat, not however, until they had un-horsed Captain Addison, and carried him off, to-gether with five or six of his men as prisoners.

All this time the battle was raging, but with no apparent success to the British arms, for the regu-lars stood huddled together like frightened sheep, the soldiers firing their pieces wherever a puff of smoke became visible, which in some instances proved as destructive to friend as to foe.

While the regulars were acting in this disorgan-ized manner, the Virginians had deployed and, taking shelter behind trees, were able to some ex-tent to punish the hidden foe.

Washington pressed close up to where his com-mander lay, and bending over him, heard him mur-mur, as though speaking to himself: "Who would have thought it?"

The stricken officer, at this moment recognizing the presence of Washington, looked up and feebly asked: "What shall we do now?"

"We must retreat at once," replied Washington. Braddock was unwilling to do this, and partly re-gaining his strength, he continued to issue his orders.

At length he grew too weak to give further com-mands, and Washington calling some soldiers, had

the wounded General tenderly placed in a light
tumbril which was called into service, and hurried
out of the reach of the enemy's fire.

`That portion of the regulars who had ascended
the glade instead of retiring to the lower grounds
had, during the contest around Braddock, been
busily engaged with such of the enemy as occupied
the eastern ravine, thus making it more easy for
the Virginians who fought around Braddock to
grapple with those who sought to carry him off.

But Braddock was scarcely borne off the field
when the situation of these men became extremely
critical. The French were seen returning in triumph, after the slaughter of the unfortunate detachment that had been sent to attack them in the
rear.

The active and vigilant eye of Washington soon
perceived their danger, and he resolved to rescue
them or perish with them. At least two hundred
of the regulars had already recrossed the river, and
could not be rallied, but there were about three
hundred, including his Virginians, still holding
their ground.

"Come on, my brave fellows," said he, "we must
rescue our companions yonder from impending
destruction.

"If we only can engage the Indians in the ravines our soldiers may escape. Hark! the French above yonder have fired upon our men already. At it, my boys, and every man do his best by firing or by bayonet. Widen your ranks—the less compactly you rush on, the better. Forward!"

The soldiers gave a loud shout, for they now felt a confidence they had not experienced before. In a minute the eastern ravine was attacked.

"Keep these Indians in play, my brave fellows, for a few minutes," cried Washington, "and with the blessing of a kind Providence I shall soon return to you." So saying, he clapped spurs to his horse, and ascended between the ravines at a full gallop towards those he wished to rescue. Three gallant fellows on horseback, named Pomroy, Burton and Craig, voluntarily followed him. As he passed the length of the ravines, a volley was fired at him from that on the west, but he was at too great a distance from it to be injured.

The attention of the savages on the east was occupied in resisting the attack of the troops; they, therefore, gave him but little attention. Several of them, however, fired at him and his followers, two of whom, Pomroy and Burton, were killed. But the fleetness of Washington's horse, or rather

·the protecting hand of a kind Providence, saved
him to his country.

The troops to whom he advanced received him
with a cheer. "Follow me rapidly," said he, to
them. "Keep on, no matter what comes, and
shoot every savage you can see."

The entire party rushed down the decline, dis-
charging their muskets into the eastern ravine as
they passed it. They received in reply some scattering shots from the savages, which killed but one
or two of their number.

"To the bank of the river now, my brave men!"
cried Washington to the whole of the troops.

They obeyed him, and in a few minutes he re-
formed them into ranks, and ordered them to reload their pieces, as he perceived the Indians manifested a disposition to pursue them. Seeing the
British prepared to receive them on open ground,
neither the savages nor the French thought proper
to advance, and the entire remnant of Braddock's
army passed to the other side, where they were
joined by those who had previously fled from the
engagement.

On reviewing the remainder of that fine body of
men, which only a few hours before had crossed the
river with flying pennons, firm in the belief that on

the eve of the same day they would expel the enemy and rest in Fort DuQuesne, it was found that little more than five hundred of the rank and file remained, and of the officers twenty-six were killed and thirty-seven wounded out of a total of eighty-two.

The artillery, all the military stores and baggage of every kind, even the private cabinet of General Braddock which contained his instructions, were left in the possession of the enemy.

The enemy lost three officers and thirty men killed and about the same number wounded. The bravery of the Virginia troops was attested by the fact that out of three companies only thirty men escaped death or wounds.

The survivors of that proud army were allowed the chance to retreat unmolested, because the savages stayed behind to revel in the spoils that had fallen into their hands. When they straggled with war-whoops back to Fort DuQuesne, they presented a singular sight, laden with scalps, wearing laced coats and brilliant uniforms, swords belted on to them in various ways, and carrying extra fire-arms, and an endless variety of plunder.

The retreat of the survivors of Braddock's army was kept up through the night, the General being

n.ade as comfortable as possible on the way.   But
it was evident to all that his proud heart was
broken by the reverse he had met; this with his
wound, which proved a serious one, terminated his
life before the dawn of the coming day.   His last
words were: "We shall know better how to deal
with them next time."

The remains of the brave general were wrapped
in his military cloak, and at midnight of the following day he was accorded a soldier's burial, Washington reading by the light of the flickering torches
the solemn burial services of the church of England.   History tells us that the retreating wagons
drove over his grave in order to obliterate all trace
of it from the eyes of the prowling savages.   It
was effectively lost sight of for many years, but in
the construction of the National pike, running
through that region, his remains were found and
re-interred.   His grave may be seen to this day,
near the fifty-fifth milestone.

After the burial of Braddock, Washington continued the retreat until it reached Dunbar's camp
at Fort Cumberland.

A word more in connection with this chapter.
Washington's escape from wounds or death in this
battle is deemed miraculous.   His tall figure at-

tracted attention everywhere, and an Indian chief not only singled him out for death, but ordered his warriors to do the same.

Years afterward, this chief acknowledged that he had fired at least a dozen times at Washington, and became convinced that he was under the protection of the Great Spirit. Who dares to doubt the convictions of the red man?

LAST RESTING PLACE OF THE ILL-FATED BRADDOCK

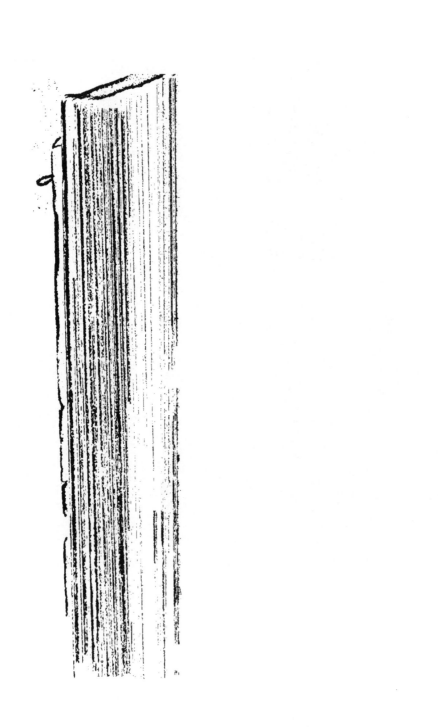

CHAPTER XXIII.

A NEW LOVER APPEARS

ASHINGTON felt keenly the defeat his countrymen had sustained, and his heart bled within him at the fearful sacrifice of so many brave men. His hopes of seeing the French driven from the territory were blasted, and he feared that in some way or other this defeat might be attended with the worst of consequences to one in that region very dear to him.

During the whole of the battle her image had never been absent from his mind, and sadly did he grieve that the defeat brought such a situation of affairs that, although her residence was in view of the very ground upon which they fought, he was obliged to depart with the remnant of the vanquished army without enjoying a single moment's interview with her.

While mustering the defeated troops, after conducting them to the south bank of the river, he cast an anxious look across the stream in the direction of the Frasier residence and beheld her with the rest of the Frasier family gazing earnestly, and he thought with sadness, at the unfortunate army. He politely lifted his chapeau and bowed, as he sat on his horse, and his heart beat with quickened pulsations, as he saw her wave her kerchief in response. Gilbert and his sons took off their fur caps and returned the salute.   Oh, how he longed to visit them, but duty compelled him to proceed with the shattered army and their wounded General back to Great Meadows without delay.

The line of march had hardly passed out of sight of the battlefield when he heard a voice calling his name.   Washington reined in his steed with great surprise, as the prophet Tonnawingo arose out of a thicket that was close by him.

"Most noble sir!" cried the prophet; "I will not detain you, for I know you desire all haste possible. Alas! this has been a day of calamity.   I thank the Great Spirit for your escape.   But my son, Charles Addison, has not been so fortunate.   Farewell, my son, I will not detain you."

"Father," said Washington, "if thou lovest me, I pray thee watch over the safety of Marie Frasier. She is too beautiful and tender a flower to be safe amidst scenes like these. Let me know wherever I may be if aught befalls her."

"I shall watch over her," said the prophet, "and shall let you know if she be unfortunate. I concealed myself here that I might salute and bless you as you passed. Farewell, and may the Great Spirit still protect you as he has done this day."

"Farewell, father," replied Washington, as the prophet disappeared among the bushes.

*   *   *   *   *

The feelings of the Frasier family during the turbulent scenes which had been enacted that day within their sight, can better be imagined than described. Gilbert's whole soul was with his countrymen, and his heart warmed when he beheld their red uniforms.

"Ah, Nelly," said he, "they are something like Christian soldiers. They put me in min' o' Ireland and Maughrygowan. Oh, may the dear Lord help them against the savages."

"Amen," said Nellie, and she lifted her eyes toward heaven.

As to Paddy Frasier and Doctor Killbreath, the vigilance of the French prevented them, during the whole of the preceding spring, from venturing any show of their partiality for the British cause.

They were not aware of the ambuscade, for it
had been laid in the night, and DeVilliers had been
so cautious as to communicate the scheme to none
but those who were to be employed in its execution. They, therefore, were greatly disappointed,
grieved and shocked at the result of the battle of
which they had been spectators.

But who can speak the agony of Marie Frasier's
mind during the incessant peals of rifles and musketry, which for three long hours rung in her ears,
and which seemed to her imagination to carry destruction to everything within reach.

She knew that her lover was among the combatants; for had not her anxious and affectionate eye
singled him out, as seated upon his prancing steed
he led his company of rangers across the river, and
her eye had followed him until the firing commenced, when her alarm and agitation became so
great that, unable to behold more, she was obliged
to retire to her chamber.

When she was informed that the troops were re-
crossing the river, with the hope of again seeing
her Charles, she hastened to the porch before the
house, from which the rest of the family were viewing the scene. Here she perceived Washington,
and returned the salute as before mentioned, but

she had not perceived the form of the one so dear to her, and her mind was filled with suspense as to his fate.

She had retired to her room with her heart filled with anxious solicitude, when Mrs. Killbreath informed her that the French commander was in the house and had expressed a wish to see her.

"Tell him, my dear Nora," said she, "that I am really indisposed. The terrible scenes of this day have rendered me incapable of seeing anybody. Oh, Nora, Nora! God only knows how my heart is at this moment torn with agony and suspense."

Nora made her apology to DeVilliers. It was of too reasonable a nature not to be believed, and he was of too gallant a spirit not to admit it. He remarked that he was not surprised at her being terrified, and he was very sorry that the affair had taken place so near them, but he hoped that both Miss Frasier and the entire family, in whose welfare he declared himself to have a great interest, would have recovered from their terrors by the time he would next have the pleasure of visiting them.

He then partook of some refreshments offered by Mrs. Frasier, and returned to the scene of the contest where the victors were employed, some in scalping the slain, and others in collecting the spoils.

He soon called them together, and as the day was well advanced, the greater part of the Indians accompanied him to Fort DuQuesne, which they reached in triumph towards the evening.

Not Marie alone, but the whole of the Frasier family, felt anxious to learn the fate of Charles Addison, whom they had seen advancing to the fight, but not returning from it. Therefore, as soon as the victors had withdrawn from the field, Paddy, Denny and Doctor Killbreath hastened to the scene to ascertain the number of the slain, and whether their friend Addison was among them.

The sight that met their gaze was well calculated to arouse their emotions, for around them lay in silent death the flower of a once proud army. Hundreds of human beings, who had in the morning of that day rejoiced in all the vigor of health and strength, now lay cold and insensible to feeling as the earth on which they were stretched, for the savages not with a feeling of humanity, but from a different motive we think, had either plunged bayonets or driven tomahawks into the bodies of all such, who on account of their wounds could not be carried away as captives.

Upon every one of these unfortunate men the scalping knife had performed its barbarous office, and the head stripped of its natural covering, in order to furnish the savage conquerors with trophies of their victory.

The conquerors, although they had carried off a great proportion of the spoils, had still left a considerable quantity behind; enough, indeed, to have made the fortunes of the Frasier family, but at this time the feelings of Paddy himself, who was not in general very scrupulous in such matters, were so much affected and shocked to behold such an awful havoc of human life, that all mercenary desires were stifled in his breast and he could not think of carrying away a single article.

After making a close examination of the slain, much to their relief, they failed to find the body of Charles Addison, and returned home to impart the joyful intelligence.

This was a great relief to the agitated mind of the sorrowing maiden, still she was ignorant of his fate. She was holding converse with Nora in her room regarding the probable whereabouts of her lover, when the voice of Tonnawingo was heard in the outer room.

"Oh, Nora!" said she, "if there is any one on
earth that can administer comfort to me it is that
holy man. Would to heaven that all Indians had
hearts like his. Tell him, my sister, that I wish to
see him.'

The prophet was soon with her. "Oh, father,"
said she, "what a relief I feel in your presence. I
thank a kind Providence that you at least have met
with no misfortune."

"My daughter," said the prophet, "I have indeed felt for your situation to-day. The youth
whom you love was in the midst of the fight; but
be comforted, for he did not fall, neither is he a
prisoner at Fort DuQuesne. But I shall take
steps at once to learn where his captors have taken
him, and I doubt not the Great Spirit will protect
him.

"My daughter, let us be thankful. Washington,
that noble and glorious youth, has this day been
miraculously preserved, while hundreds fell around
him. He is safe and the Great Father has shown
his kindness to the children of men."

"I know it, father," she replied; "I have beheld
this excellent young man out of reach of his enemies, and I felt consolation at the sight."

"My daughter, I rejoice that you so respect this hero, although you know not half his virtues, or half his worth to the world; for, my daughter, while he lives the cause of freedom may possibly suffer, but need never despair."

"I know, father," she replied, "that great public good is likely to result from Colonel Washington's career, if a kind Providence prolongs it. I am aware of his worth, and greatly do I rejoice in his safety, and ardently hope for his prosperity. But there are at present, griefs that have come close to my heart. Charles Addison is in great danger, and while it is so I cannot be comforted."

"My daughter, I know your heart, and I sympathize with you," said the prophet; "Charles Addison I esteem and love, for he is worthy of both. But despair not of his deliverance from danger. The Great Spirit preserved him before, when in as much peril as now, and he is as mighty to save as ever.

"My daughter, be of good cheer; I go to discover where they have taken him for whom you grieve. Farewell!"

Marie's mind was much composed after this interview, and during the evening she joined the rest

The Rose of the Wilderness

of the family in their conversation on the disasters of the day.

*　　*　　*　　*　　*

The charms of Marie Frasier had made too deep an impression upon the mind of the governor of Fort DuQuesne to permit him long delay the repetition of his visit to Frasier's. His thoughts of her had kept him awake most of the night. "How has it been possible," said he to himself, "that I have been so long ignorant of such a lovely rose blooming near me and not know of its beauty or fragrance. But I am a fortunate man to have discovered her at last. I will make her my wife, for it would be a villainous thing to think of any other relation, nor do I suppose she would fall a willing victim, for she appears as modest as she is beautiful.

"By heavens, I will offer her my hand. She surely can not refuse to become mistress of Fort DuQuesne; and I shall be happy in the enjoyment of such a treasure. I will not be content till I know her mind, and have made her my own."

At an early hour in the morning, he set off for Frasier's. Marie had walked out upon the bank of Turtle Creek, with the expectation of deriving some benefit from the fresh morning air and the quietness and beauty of the scene, for a heavy sorrow lay upon her heart.   DeVilliers perceived her before he came to the house, and tying his horse to a tree, he approached her before she was aware of his presence.

He bowed politely, and with a pleasant smile addressed her: "Miss Frasier, I am really happy to meet you here all alone, in this charming spot.   I hope you have recovered from your fright of yesterday.   I could not be at ease, until I had come to see you."

"You are very kind, sir," said she; "but I presume more important business brought you at so early an hour, than merely to inquire after the state of a stranger's mind."

"Upon my honor, Miss Frasier, no other business in the world than just to see, and converse with you, has brought me from the fort this morning.   Believe me, my charming girl, I think no business half so sweet, or so delightful as to be in conversation with you; had I only known you sooner, we should by this time have better understood each other."

"It might have been so," she replied, looking at him in surprise; "for I protest, sir, that I cannot understand you now."

"Ah! my dear Miss Frasier, you may say so, but

I cannot believe you, for your pretty tell-tale eyes say that you well understand the nature of my visit. But I will make it plainer to you. Ever since I first beheld you, I have been so fascinated I could think of nothing else. Even in the heat of the battle yesterday, I could not drive you from my mind, and as soon as the enemy was driven off I hastened to see you. My dear, I feel as if I could live by looking upon you."

"You would derive very little benefit from such diet, I fear," said the maiden, scarcely thinking it worth while to reply seriously to such flippant language; "and I am afraid that ere long you should find it very little to your satisfaction."

"Nay, Miss Frasier," said the French commander, in a fond tone, "by my soul, those pretty cheeks, those ruby lips, those sparkling eyes, I would never grow weary of looking upon, for I confess I never saw anything in the world I loved half so much."

"Monsieur DeVilliers," said she, "my heart is too much laden with sorrow at the present to feel amused at such unmeaning, such frivolous, and pardon me if I say such ridiculous nonsense, that I feel is beneath your dignity and unsuited to my present state of feelings."

"Ah, my pretty maiden," returned he, "your charms have warmed my heart to a sincere, uncontrollable passion. I love you—by my life, I adore you! I have never seen a woman I could love as I do you."

The lovely girl began to perceive that the officer before her was in dead earnest, and as the true situation dawned upon her mind, she felt indignant with herself that she had allowed him to proceed so far, and she addressed him with some show of feeling.

"Sir, this language seems as mad as that which you uttered a short time ago was foolish, and both, I must say, are unworthy of you, and disagreeable to me."

"Pardon me, madam," he replied. "Can it be unworthy of me to love so much excellence? My hand is free, my.fortune respectable, and my heart devoted to you. I offer them all to you, and shall feel myself the happiest of mortals if you accept of them."

"Then hear my reply," said she, "and set it down on the tablets of your memory—that I utterly and decisively reject them."

"You do?" said he, beginning to feel that he did not stand on such eligible ground with her as he supposed. "Then it comes to this issue, my fair tempter, that as I feel I cannot live without you, you must become mine in spite of yourself, though I would wish for your voluntary consent; for, upon my honor, I should be very loth to compel you."

"Sir," said she, "we may as well drop the conversation. My voluntary consent you can never have; you have already my answer, and it is final, unalterable, and need not be repeated."

"Then," said the despairing officer, "proud girl, you would doom me to wretchedness. Permit me at least to kiss your hand before you would drive me from your side," and here he quickly seized and pressed it to his lips.

Her soul was filled with indignation and horror at his rudeness, and as soon as he relaxed his hold upon her hand, she turned abruptly from him and without answering his farewell, she hastened back to the house in great distress of mind. While De-Villiers, having resolved in his heart the measures he would adopt, proceeded to his horse, mounted, and more to lull away any suspicion of his visit, rode on up the glen, and returned to DuQuesne, by a different direction.

Marie hesitated when she reached home whether or not she should relate the incident to her friends.

She did not wish to arouse any feeling of uneasiness in their minds, as the governor, receiving so decided a refusal, might never disturb her again. True, he had thrown out a hint that he might persevere in his designs, but if so, how could her few friends resist the Governor of Fort DuQuesne, if he should follow the import of his insinuations. She resolved to lay the matter before Tonnawingo, the prophet, and be guided by his advice.

As for DeVilliers, there was nothing further from his intentions than to relinquish the pursuit of her. He saw clearly that nothing was to be gained by mere solicitation, and his passion for her was too violent to brook much delay. He therefore resolved to employ active and prompt measures.

Therefore, as soon as he returned to the garrison, he ordered a lieutenant, Rantell, a man whom he knew to be fit for his purpose, to report to him immediately. The officer appeared, and with a low bow, remarked: "Your servant, sir."

"I want you on a special service, Lieutenant," said the Governor, "and I shall expect you to manage the thing exactly as you are directed."

"To a fraction, if possible," said the lieutenant.

"There is a lady in the case, Rantell," said De-Villiers.

"Ah, sir, a pleasant affair; next to shooting an Englishman, and a deuced sight better than burning them, as those devils of Indians purpose doing."

"A captain's commission, Rantell, will be yours my brave fellow," said the Governor, "the moment the lady is brought into the fort."

"Good as done, your honor," replied the Lieutenant; "neat job, by St. Dennis! Where is the dove's nest, Monsieur LeGovernor?"

"At the junction of Turtle Creek with the Monongahela; she is a daughter of the old Irishman living there," replied DeVilliers.

"What! Not Dr. Killbreath's wife, I hope?" exclaimed Rantell.

"You mistake me, Lieutenant Rantell," said De-Villiers, affecting offense at the insinuation. "I trust I am not yet so much of a rascal as to lay claim to another man's wife. No, Lieutenant, it is her sister."

"I most humbly crave your pardon, Governor; I suppose it is the pretty sweet-faced lady, the Doctor's sister-in-law, that I saw last winter when out there hunting. I tell you she is dainty, and had I been the doctor, I know which of the two sisters I should have chosen for a help-mate," replied Rantell.

"Your taste is good," said DeVilliers. "I am glad you know the lady. I love her to distraction; I wish to marry her. I told her so but she is rather shy about the matter. I want to bring her here; as I think I could better persuade her if here, than in the woods under her father's wing yonder. You need not ask her consent to come nor any of the family's. Take twenty smart fellows with you, enter the house boldly, and bring her off without question. But, take care Rantell, offer her no insult, if you would avoid getting a bullet in your brain. Remember she is to be my wife."

"It shall be done to the Queen's taste," replied the lieutenant. "But when shall we set out, Monsieur Le Governor?"

DeVilliers pulled out his watch and consulted it. "It is not twelve yet. You had better set off in a half hour. Give each man a dose of rum when you start, and another when you come in sight of your destination, and I shall expect you back by sundown. Good-day, be polite to the lady, and civil to the family."

"I'll manage it all neatly," said the lieutenant, bowing himself out of the Governor's presence.

CHAPTER XXIV.

ABDUCTION OF "THE ROSE"

IT was between three and four o'clock in the afternoon, when Denny Frasier, who had been out in the woods west of the house, came hurriedly in saying that a troop of French soldiers were in sight. Marie, who was in her apartment, for she had scarcely stirred out of it since her meeting with DeVilliers, did not hear the intelligence communicated by Denny.

The balance of the family who were at home, ran to the door, more from curiosity than alarm; they met Rantell, rather cordially, who after having ordered the body of his men to keep at a distance, unless called forward, had approached the house accompanied by only three soldiers. Paddy and Doctor Killbreath had left early in the morning on a hunting excursion and were not expected home till night. Gilbert and Denny were therefore the only male portion of the family present, and so far as any opposition might come from these two, Lieutenant Rantell had little, if any, concern.

As neither Gilbert nor his wife could speak French, Mrs. Killbreath had to return the officer's salutation and answer his interrogations.

"Good day! my friend Frasier, my best wishes for the welfare of your family," was Rantell's salutation, accompanied by a ceremonious bow.

"We thank you," replied Nora, "but as my father does not understand or speak French, you will excuse his silence."

"With all my heart, Mrs. Killbreath. But pray, dear madam, where are all the rest of your people? I hope our fighting here yesterday has not driven them away?"

"My brother Paddy, and my husband, the doctor, have been out hunting since morning, and I believe we are all present except them and my sister, who is rather indisposed from the alarm she experienced during yesterday's battle."

"Is your sister so sick as to permit no visitor?" questioned the lieutenant. "I have a message I wish to deliver to her."

"A message for Marie!" exclaimed Nora. "Pray, sir, who can it be from?"

"From a most true and earnest friend she has at the garrison," replied the officer.

"Inform me of it please, and I shall communicate

it to her, and immediately let you know her answer," said Nora.

"I am instructed to communicate it to her alone," was the reply. "I shall tell her so," said Nora, as she arose and hastened to Marie's apartment. But to her astonishment, the officer was there almost as soon as herself.

"Excuse me, ladies!" said he, smiling and bowing very politely to Marie; "excuse me for this unmannerly intrusion. But I must plead the necessity I am under of obeying my superior officer. My dear madam," said he, addressing Marie exclusively, "I have to inform you of Governor DeVillier's request, that you will honor him with your company this evening, at Fort DuQuesne. I have been ordered out with a party of soldiers to escort you there."

"Alas!" exclaimed Marie, in violent agitation, "I see I am undone. Oh! Nora, Nora, they are going to take me from you! I might have known it, and I might have concealed myself, but I did not think he would have resorted so quickly to this outrage."

"What is the meaning of this, Lieutenant Rantell?" asked Nora. "What do you want with my sister? She cannot have done anything either to injure or offend the Governor."

"Nor does the Governor, my dear madam, wish or intend to do anything to injure or offend her. It is pure love, Mrs. Killbreath, that is at the bottom of this affair." Then turning to Marie, the officer addressed her: "My fair lady, I am under strict orders to show you all possible politeness, and I have a fine horse to carry you to the fort. Pray, now will you permit me to help you mount him?"

"Oh! sir, have mercy!" pleaded the lovely Marie, for she shuddered at the thought of being in the power of DeVilliers. "I beseech you, for the love of heaven, do not assist in plunging me into ruin? Heaven will bless you if you let me escape."

"I am a soldier, madam," said the lieutenant, "and must obey orders, you know. But we must make haste, and please let us go in good humor together, for confound me, if I enjoy being at variance with a lady."

By this time Gilbert, hearing something of an altercation between the Frenchman and his daughter, advanced into the room.

"What's wrang, Marie, my bairn?" said he. "I hope the officer wants naething uncivil wi' ye?"

"Alas, father, my dear father!" she replied, "I am undone."

"Sir," said the officer, who perceived that Gilbert was displeased, "there is no use fussing about the matter, Monsieur DeVilliers has taken a fancy to your daughter, and has ordered me to carry her to the fort. He will, I assure you, offer her no harm. On the contrary, he wishes to make her his wife, and will treat her tenderly as the pupil of his eye."

"What says he?" asked Gilbert, who did not understand the language addressed to him.

Nora briefly explained its import.

"Wants my dochter into the fort amang the soldiers?" exclaimed he, "an' without her consent, too! Get oot o' my hoose this precious moment, ye rascal to come here on sich an errand! Get oot! or by the power givin me by the Lord Almichty, I'll turn ye oot by the heels and neck."

"My friends, all this is to no purpose. There are twenty brave fellows out yonder who will enforce my commands. So my fair lady," said he, making a bow to Marie, while at the same time he laid hold upon her arm, saying, "you had as well come along without giving us more trouble, or allowing this old gentleman to get into a scrape."

At this juncture Marie fell upon her knees in the attitude of supplication. Gilbert could endure it no longer; his rage overpowered his reason, and running into an adjacent room, he seized upon an axe that he happened to find there, and rushing back swung it over his head and shouted in an angry tone.

"I'll cleave you to the yearth this moment, if ye get not oot, an' no vex my bairn,'' and as he said this he actually wielded a blow which would have been fatal to the lieutenant, had not one of the soldiers who had entered the house with him, caught the axe ere it descended, and attempted to wrest it out of his grasp.

Gilbert, however, although advanced in life, was a strong man, and in a moment he overturned the soldier. But another of the soldiers seized upon the axe, and had just taken it from Gilbert's hold, when Denny Frasier, hearing the scuffle, darted forward upon him, and with a kick upon the stomach overturned him upon his companion. Rantell, himself now closed with Denny, and the third soldier having called forward the remainder of the troop, seized upon Gilbert who, with Denny, was soon overpowered. Rantell ordered a sergeant's guard to enter the house, and Gilbert and his son were securely tied hand and foot with ropes.

"Now, my lady," said he (hastening to Marie, who was just recovering from a swoon, for she thought her father was killed), "let us be going. I am sorry for the scuffle, but it was the hot-headedness of that foolish old man that caused it. Mrs. Killbreath here can loosen these thongs as soon as we are gone, and see to it that they don't attempt to follow us, for if they do—we shall shoot them down.

"Pardon me, Mrs. Killbreath," said he, "if I interfere in a woman's concerns, but I see there is one thing we almost forgot; the lady's stay in the garrison will, perhaps, require some change of raiment."

Mrs. Killbreath took the hint; but first throwing her arms around Marie's neck, she kissed her, while her eyes overflowed with tears.

"Farewell, my dearest, dearest sister!" said she. "Oh, may a kind Providence deliver you from these men."

She then hastened to pack up some clothing for Marie, which done she handed to the lieutenant. While Nora was thus employed Marie had alternately embraced her father and her mother. She was at length separated from them, and proceeded as far as the porch, when her mother running after her again caught her in her arms.

"Oh! my bairn, my lovely bairn! I canna let

you leave me. I will go wi' you. Where'er they pit you, canna be owre bad for me. I will watch owre you, and comfort ye amang the soldiers."

"Pardon me, ladies!" said Rantell, "but we have no time now to discuss matters; and my instructions relate to only one lady. So my good mother you had better walk within doors, and pacify old crack-brain yonder, who will no doubt pronounce many a solid curse upon us before we reach Du-Quesne.

"Now my fair one, you were the prize I was sent to capture, and yon gallant steed impatiently champs his bit, as if he longed for his lovely burden."

Here he separated her from the arms of the clinging mother who, with a wild, despairing cry, fell flat upon the floor of the porch in an unconscious condition while Gilbert and Denny within the house tugged at their thongs with the ferocity of madmen. No one can tell what the consequence would have been had they succeeded in freeing themselves.

Marie, with a bursting heart and burning brain, was soon placed upon the horse provided for her, and the troops with their lovely prize hastened toward Fort DuQuesne.

Gilbert and his wife felt the calamity that had on this day befallen them all the more acutely, as they had, since their settlement in the wilderness, experienced no loss or separation from any of their family. Their children had grown up under their care, healthy and prosperous, and now to be rudely deprived of this loved one, perhaps carried off to a fate worse than death, was a shock they were scarcely able to bear.

Gilbert and his son were soon loosened by Mrs. Killbreath, from their bonds after the departure of the French. But the folly of giving pursuit was too apparent for them to attempt it, and all they could do was to weep bitterly for their lost Marie. As for Mrs. Frasier, it was a considerable time after her fall before she regained consciousness, and when that was effected, it was found that her mind had sustained so severe a shock as to render her delirious. They laid her in her bed for she was in a high fever, and Gilbert had no other thought during the sorrowful evening, but that he had lost both wife and daughter forever.

As he looked upon Nellie in her raving moments, fierce rage would overpower him and he would involuntarily exclaim:

"Curse such fiends! They hae robbed me o' a'

comfort. But God forgive me, I should curse nae yen. I leave them in thy hands, oh Lord! Deal wi' them according to thy own pleasure; but, oh, have compassion upon this afflicted family. Proteet my bairn, an' restore my wife!"

It was late in the evening when the fond mother's mind became tranquil, and they all rejoiced. At this moment the door opened and the prophet Tonnawingo entered.   He was at once informed of the sad state of affairs in the Frasier family. The prophet was thunderstruck on receiving the intelligence. He threw himself upon a bench beside a table and buried his face in his hands while his breast heaved with strong emotion. At length he threw himself upon his knees (the entire family except the mother following him), and stretching out his hands and lifting his burning eyes toward heaven, exclaimed:

"Oh! Great Spirit and Father of the universe! Grant me success, in what thou hast suggested to me this hour. I depend upon thee, and thee alone, to protect that suffering maiden and restore her again to her parents."

He then arose and inquired for Paddy Frasier, and when told that Paddy had not been home since morning, he seemed greatly disappointed, and paced the floor impatiently.

In a short time Paddy and Dr. Killbreath arrived, and Tonnawingo seemed much gratified. The rage of both these hunters of the forest, when they heard of their sister's misfortune, need not be described. They both swore eternal hatred to the French. But the prophet did not give Paddy much time to vent forth the vehemence of his rage, for he at once took him out of doors, where he conversed with him for about ten minutes. When they re-entered the house, Paddy hastily provided himself with a flask of rum, and some provisions, which he deposited in a pouch at his side, and throwing his rifle on his shoulder, set off again at full speed, as though he had enjoyed a long rest.

After supper, the prophet took Dr. Killbreath aside and requested him to proceed early in the morning towards the head waters of Chartier's Creek in order to watch a party of Connewagoes who had carried Charles Addison in that direction, and to lose no time in bringing him back intelligence of their intentions concerning their prisoner.

"My son," said he, "show this wampum to the Sachem Taksuma, who is their leader. He will protect you from any injury, and perhaps give you all the information you require. I would have gone myself, but Marie, the child of my heart, is now in distress and I cannot forsake her.

"Tell the sachem that Tonnawingo, the prophet of Maneto, requests that, if the council should condemn the prisoner to be burned, that he grant him, what no prophet of Maneto has ever been refused when he asked it for a condemned prisoner, namely, that he have seven days after his condemnation to make his peace with Maneto before he be given to the flames."

The Doctor promised to obey the prophet's instructions, and early the next morning set out upon his errand.

CHAPTER XXV.

THE DOVE IN THE EAGLE'S NEST

HE sun was almost hidden from sight, to the occupants of Fort DuQuesne, when the lovely object of its governor's passion was brought an unhappy captive within its walls.

DeVilliers heard the sound of the bugle announcing the arrival of Rantell's party, and with a feeling of some embarrassment he hastened to salute the enchanter of his soul, and to conduct her into his residence. When he held out his hand to assist her in dismounting, she for a moment, shrunk from his touch with an instinctive shudder, but instantly recollecting that there was no possibility of then avoiding it, without perhaps subjecting herself to greater rudeness, she silently accepted his assistance, and suffered herself to be led, an uncomplaining victim, to the lodging that had been prepared for her.

This was a moderately neat room on the second floor of the Governor's house overlooking the Mo-

FORT DUQUESNE

nongahela. The view from its front window took in the parade ground of the stockade. The furniture of the room, although not in great profusion, was of good quality and on the wall were a few shelves filled with books.

"Miss Frasier," said DeVilliers, as he conducted her into the room, "I am really very sorry that you should have compelled me to take this step. But I felt that I could not live without you, and I had no alternative. Endeavor to make yourself comfortable in this abode, such as it is, but I wish, yes I wish it was a palace for your sake."

"Sir," said she, "comfort is now a matter of no concern to me, for to enter a palace under such circumstances, would be the same as a dungeon." Here the energy which had sustained her during her journey forsook her, and she burst into tears.

"Oh, my dear father and mother," said she, "what must you not feel at this moment! Heaven support you under this trial."

"Be calm, my lovely maiden," said DeVilliers in a soothing tone, for he really felt affected at her sorrow. . "The urgency of my love for you alone constrained me to separate you from your friends, but, believe me, it was not to make either you or them unhappy; and, upon my honor as a soldier, I promise that anything short of parting with **you** I shall submit to, in order to make your residence with me agreeable."

"Then I need expect no relief from my misery," she replied, "for nothing short of a separation from you and a restoration to my friends can afford such relief. Oh! restore me to them, and I shall never cease to bless you, I shall never cease to pray for your happiness."

"Maiden! you have already said you will never promise to be mine, and now you say your greatest desire is to be separated from me. I can, if I please, dispense with a promise, and though you desire to leave me, I can still be happy—for I have you with me, and you are at this moment mine, to all intents and for all purposes, as completely and absolutely as if the priest had made you so.

"It is for your own sake, my fair one, and not for mine, that I wish the forms to be gone through with. What say you? Will you consult your own reputation, your own purity, and pronounce the vow which will make me happy without making you wretched."

"Never!" she replied in a tone of firmness and decision; "never sir, if I am to be doomed to wretchedness, no act of my own shall with my knowledge be ever necessary to it."

"Foolish, obstinate girl!" he replied, with some show of irritation, "if I did not love you sincerely I would seize upon your charms without ceremony this very hour. But harsh and inconsiderate as you are, your purity is worth something in my estimation; it is worth at least a few days' postponement of my happiness, for I swear it shall come with your own consent, if I shake your very soul to its centre in order to extort that consent from you. I shall now leave you to reflect upon it, but before I go your lovely hand shall feel the imprint of my lips." So saying, he forcibly kissed her hand and left the apartment.

Marie threw herself upon the bed and burst into tears. The full sense of her wretched situation, and still more wretched prospects, rushed violently upon her mind, and she poured forth the sorrows of her soul to her Maker, asking that if possible some miraculous deliverance would be granted her. Nature at length became wearied with the poignancy of her sorrow, and she sunk into a troubled and disturbed slumber.

She arose in the morning, rejoiced to find herself

restored to a degree of resolution and fortitude which she had been devoid of the previous evening.

She had been offered refreshment the night before, but was too grief stricken to partake of it, but now she was beginning to feel the promptings of hunger.

In due time the same squaw that had brought her the food which she had refused the night before again appeared, with a request from the Governor that she would favor him with her company at breakfast, which was waiting in the dining room.

This invitation she declined on the plea of indisposition. The squaw retired, but in a short time returned to prepare breakfast for her in her own apartment, and in a few minutes was followed by DeVilliers himself, who saluted her with great politeness, remarking that as she was unable to afford him the pleasure of her presence at the breakfast below, he would crave the liberty of enjoying it with her in her own room.

"You are master here, sir," said she, "and no doubt despotic enough, to make all matters bend to your will. My opposition to your taking this liberty would be fruitless, and would not relieve me of your presence, let me feel it as disagreeable as I may."

"Then my presence is still disagreeable to you?" he observed. "Well, let it be so, since yours affords me delight. But, my fair one, I wish you to join me in this breakfast, for by my faith, I did not bring you here to starve you."

"Sir," said she, "on condition that you avoid the subject so painful to my feeling, I shall partake with you, but on no other terms."

He bowed a complacent assent, and she sat down to breakfast with him. But the meal was scarcely over when the sound of a trumpet was heard.

"Curse those Indians," said he, starting to his feet; "they are now going to hold a council concerning our English prisoners, a number of whom they have resolved to burn. I have been trying to persuade them from it, but it won't do. They must be gratified; otherwise they will go off in high dudgeon, and I cannot spare them at present, lest the British under Dunbar should think proper to make a trip this way. I must attend this council now and save as many lives as I can."

Marie shuddered at this intelligence, and at that moment her mind reverted to the condition of Charles Addison, whose fate at that moment, for aught she knew, might be dependent upon the decision of this very council. She caught the Governor's arm as he was about leaving and exclaimed:

"Oh, for the love of heaven! Monsieur DeVilliers, save these unfortunate men. God will surely bless you for the deed."

"Since it is your wish, my sweet one," said he, "I shall do my utmost; but these savages claim so much for their fighting the other day that I fear I shall accomplish but little, especially as they captured the men themselves. So eager are they for burning their prisoners, Miss Frasier, that I am told a party of them left the field of battle with one or two captives whom they feared to bring to the garrison, lest I should interfere to save them. But I perceive the old Mingo prophet, Tonnawingo, among them. This promises well, as he is always averse to burning prisoners, and he has more power over them than I have. However, between us I think we shall be able to save some of these unfortunate Englishmen."

"Oh, I beseech you to save them all, if you can," cried Marie.

"That is impossible," he returned; "I have already conceded that they should have at least twelve at their disposal; they claim this as a reward for their conduct in the late battle, and I could not

refuse them.   The present council is to determine
how many more they shall have, as well as a selec-
tion of the twelve already promised.   If the Mingo
prophet assists me, I think we shall be able to save
the remainder."

"That prophet is a good man," remarked Marie.
"I know he will assist you, and may heaven also
assist you in this benevolent work."

"Amen," said DeVilliers.   "Good morning,
Miss Frasier, I will remember your wishes, and if
possible protect these men."

Shortly after DeVilliers departed, the tender-
hearted girl beheld from her window the wretched
prisoners, nearly forty in number, tied together, in
pairs, and surrounded by several hundred savages,
who were dancing, singing and shouting their triumph over their unfortunate captives.   Her heart
grew heavy, and her eyes dimmed with tears as she
recalled that while her lover was not among this
unhappy lot, he was perhaps elsewhere doomed to
a like fate.

She could no longer gaze upon the scene that
filled her with so much sadness, and retired from
the window.

An hour passed by and she was again visited by
DeVilliers.

"Miss Frasier," said he, "as he entered her apartment, "I am heartily glad to get rid of this unpleasant business, and once more enjoy the delight of your presence. It is like changing the company of fiends for that of an angel."

"Ah, sir, tell me!" she exclaimed, "has anything been done for the poor Englishmen? Have you secured their safety?"

"They are all safe," he replied, "except the twelve I mentioned to you who have been selected by lot. I exerted myself greatly since I knew it would please you."

"And what—what," she asked with emotion, "is to become of these unfortunate twelve?"

"Why, I fear the savages will burn them, according to their custom in such cases," replied DeVilliers.

"Oh, Monsieur DeVilliers," said she, "is there no way left to save them from such a cruel fate? Have you not force enough to protect them? Oh, think that these men may have fathers and mothers, wives and children, whose hearts are filled with anxiety for their welfare. Think, oh, feel, if thou canst feel for the misery of others, what will be their suffering when they learn that those dear to them have met such a terrible fate. Oh, do something to save them, I entreat of thee if thou wouldst expect salvation thyself !"

"Why, my sweet enchantress," said he, "why plead so strongly in behalf of men of whom thou knowest nothing, and who neither know nor care anything about thee; and yet be so indifferent to the prayers and entreaties of one who adores thee? Why accuse the savages of barbarity to their victims, who are their enemies, when thou art thyself as barbarous and hard-hearted towards one who loves you with a passion too violent to go unrequited and live?"

"Sir," said she, "it is to no·purpose for you to talk this way. Tell me, yes tell me, can you do anything to save these unfortunate men?"

"First inform me, my angel," said he, "can you, will you do anything to save me from a worse fate?"

"Alas, sir, to what straits would you drive me, say —say—for heaven's sake can you save these men?"

"If you give me your hand at the altar," said he, after a little meditation, "as the price of their lives, you shall have them, if I should turn out the entire garrison to rescue them from the stake."

"Oh, blessed Father!" she exclaimed, "to what a situation I am reduced! Alas, sir, I cannot, I cannot give my pledge.   I think I would give it to you to save these victims, but I cannot, it is already given irrevocably to another."

"Your hand pledged to another!" exclaimed De-Villiers, rising from his seat in surprise, and pacing the room in great agitation. "Your hand pledged to another, and no doubt your heart too— Miss Frasier, is it not so?"

"Alas, sir, I cannot deny it.   But surely, surely, if it be in your power, you will not let these unhappy prisoners die."

"Die!" he repeated, "yes—that they must. But but, perhaps, no," said he, suddenly changing his manner. It may be still in your power to save them.   You are not married I hope?"

"No, sir," was her reply.

"Then, my lovely fair one, these men may yet be safe.   Let your hand be mine, and their lives shall be yours."

"But, sir, I have told you that my hand is already pledged."

"Merely pledged," cried he; "what signifies that? A mere verbal promise. Miss Frasier, you will surely not place such a trifle in competition with the lives of twelve human beings. Say but the word, my loveliest of women, and they are safe."

"Oh, please sir, it is impossible.   I cannot unsay what I have said.   I cannot forfeit my word of honor!   No, no, rather than that, let me die the death allotted to these men!"

"No, they whom you devote to the flames shall die!" and he hastened out of the room in a paroxysm of rage.

In about twenty minutes the sound of trumpets was heard, and a guard of soldiers appeared conducting twelve prisoners across the parade ground in the direction of our heroine's place of imprisonment.   At the distance of about twenty yards from her window the party halted, and the prisoners at a command given them kneeled with their heads uncovered, and looked up to Marie as if earnestly supplicating her intercession.

DeVilliers hastened to her side.   "Look," said he, "hard-hearted girl, at those poor men now under sentence, to suffer within one hour the most terrible of all deaths, burning at the stake!   Look at them on their knees imploring thee to deliver them from a cruel and fast approaching death.   I have told them that their destiny is in thy hands, that if it pleaseth thee I will defend them and restore them again to their people.   Wilt thou save them, or wilt thou let them perish?"

Marie looked at the men. Their uniforms of red, in times of prosperity the most brilliant and imposing of all warlike colors, were now stained and tattered; their countenances woe-begone and their forms wearied and drooping, their supplicating posture, their hair blown to and fro by the changing winds, all bespoke the extremes of hardship, misery and terror, to the imagination of the distracted Marie.

She burst into tears as she beheld them, for she reflected that these very men had, perhaps, once been in the enjoyment of happy homes and the society of loved ones, which they might never, never enjoy again, for were they not on the very verge of a termination of all the enjoyment of life, and that, too, in the most barbarous and cruel manner known?

She beheld them imploring her, who had it in her power to save them by foregoing her own happiness, and becoming the wife of this man at her side. What was she to do? Could she refuse De-Villiers, and have these poor supplicants carried off to a cruel death? Or could she yield to his desires and make her life forever miserable, and what was worst of all, be unfaithful to the beloved of her heart, Charles Addison?

DeVilliers perceived her wavering, and he urged her to a decision. "Five minutes, my love," said he, pulling out his watch. "Let five minutes pass without promising to become my wife, and these men shall be ordered away to the place where the faggots are already prepared for their execution."

"Oh, cruel, cruel man! Have mercy, have mercy!" she exclaimed. Her eyes seemed to be wondrously dilated, her lips quivered and grew pale, her limbs tottered under her, and she fell backward upon the floor.

"God of heaven, I have killed her!" cried De-Villiers, thoroughly alarmed. Then lifting her in his arms he placed her upon the bed and loudly called for assistance. The attending squaw made her appearance, and applied some stimulants to Marie's temples, and in a short time she began to show signs of returning consciousness. At length she opened her eyes, which were closed, and looked wildly about her, while she brokenly exclaimed:

"Oh, tell—me—they have not—surely—sent them—to the flames? The governor—cannot—be so barbarous. Let them be saved—let them be saved. Alas, I cannot—bear to have them burned!"

DeVilliers now made a signal out of the window

for the troops and prisoners to withdraw, then retiring to Marie's bedside he watched over her with
great anxiety, until he saw her mind restored to its
normal condition. His desire to work upon her
feelings, so as to extort from her a promise to
marry him, returned with her recovery; and in answer to her inquiry of what had been done with the
unfortunate prisoners, he replied:

"They are respited until to-morrow at noon, my
love, in order that you may have time to decide
upon their fate and mine. And oh, may I entreat
you, Miss Frasier, to resolve on saying the word
which will save them from destruction and me from
despair. I shall now leave you, that you may enjoy repose. Give your commands to the squaw,
who waits on you and she will supply you with
whatever the garrison can afford to make you comfortable."

The shock the fair girl had received had thrown
her into a high fever, and a certain wildness in her
manner alarmed the squaw Halmanna, who was
ordered to attend her, so much so that she was on
the point of recalling DeVilliers, when the prophet
Tonnawingo appeared, greatly to the squaw's relief, who thought if anybody had power to do her
charge any good it was the prophet, and upon his

asking to see the young lady she readily admitted him. Tonnawingo bade her remain below and not come near, unless called. In a few minutes the prophet was in the presence of the troubled maiden and was assuring her by his calm voice and manner to bare bravely with the trials that surrounded her. His very appearance produced a powerful effect upon the excited mind of this child of the forest and she listened to his words.

"My daughter, hear me! My words are comfort and they are truth. Thou hast this day been greatly imposed upon by the wicked governor of this fortress. The prisoners who were before thee are not condemned to suffer, nor are there any now under condemnation.

"Alas! those who were condemned—twelve gallant soldiers, my heart still bleeds for them, were meanly given up by the governor ere I could interpose in their behalf, and in spite of all my exertions were carried across the Allegheny river at noon this day, and committed to the flames. Their sufferings are now over and on this occasion the tribes will require no more victims.

"Hear me, my daughter. Those who were sentenced to die returned not back from the council meeting this morning, but a band of Ottawas went with them to the place of death.   Hear me further.

"I was among the English prisoners that were left after the Indians had withdrawn, and was assuring them of safety, when the governor came among them.   He ordered twelve of them to be separated from the rest.   He promised them permission to return to their countrymen under Colouel Dunbar, if they would advance into the middle of the parade ground and there kneel uncovered, before a young lady who would appear at her window, and in that humble posture obtain her consent to their release.

"He informed them, that while making their supplications, they should not speak, as the lady did not understand English, but that he himself should convey to her the purport of their request, and report the lady's answer.   You see, my daughter, his whole scheme has been a falsehood.

"Therefore, my daughter, hear my advice.   Persevere in your refusal to become this man's wife.   Powerful as he is, the Great Spirit is more powerful than he, and will frustrate all his designs against you.   Before many days I trust Maneto will raise up a deliverer for you, and disappoint that bad man in his designs.   My daughter, treasure this advice in your heart, and fear neither the cunning nor the force of the tempter.

"My child, the military parade that the Governor is attending will soon be over. He will then, no doubt, return to you. I must therefore withdraw. May the great Being on whom you depend protect you, and keep you firm."

He now departed—but before leaving the house he laid upon Halmanna, the squaw, his commands that she should inform no one of his visit to the sick lady.

"Far be it from me," replied Halmanna, trembling, "to disobey the prophet of Maneto."

"Then may Maneto bless thee," said Tonnawingo, and waving his awful wand over her head, he quickly passed out of her sight.

CHAPTER XXVI.

A VILLAIN DEFEATED

IN about half an hour after the prophet withdrew, DeVilliers visited Marie. He expressed great satisfaction to find that she was so much better than he had expected. Seeing the maiden was in need of rest and quiet, he made his visit short, all the while exhorting her to a decision favorable to his happiness and the lives of the unfortunate prisoners.

The next morning, wishing to gain in her esteem, by a conciliating demeanor towards her he admitted her plea of indisposition, and did not insist on joining her at breakfast. Shortly afterwards, however, he entered her apartment. She appeared tranquil and resigned, because the suggestion of hope had given her consolation, and inspired her with fortitude.

"Miss Frasier," said he, "I need scarcely express my happiness at seeing your serenity and contentment so much restored that I think you could in time bring yourself to live comfortably with me.

This circumstance affords me some hope that my application for your hand may not be altogether in vain."

"Sir," she replied, "I have been thinking of that affair; but it is really one of too much importance to be decided without more deliberation than I have yet given it."

"Ah! Miss Frasier," said he, "surely you cannot hesitate to interpose a single word between twelve fellow-beings and destruction; and you know the hour speedily approaches, which, without that interposition, shall consign them to their fate."

"Monsieur DeVilliers," said she, "I have never yet asked a favor from you for myself, and when I first entered these walls I felt that I never would. I have now changed my mind so far as to make a request, which I hope you will not refuse to grant."

"Ask it, my sweet one," said DeVilliers; "anything but parting with you, I pledge my honor shall not be denied."

"My request," said the maiden, "is within your power to grant. It is only that I may be indulged with a few days longer time to deliberate on this matter."

He paced the room for some time in silent meditation. At length he said:

"You will never find me unreasonable, my be-witching girl. You shall have a few days; but, oh, let them be few—for my heart longs exceedingly to call you my own."

"Give me one week," said she; "alas! I fear even that will be too short for my purpose."

"My fairest love!" cried he, "must I postpone my bliss so long? But I will indulge thee. I will show thee that by so doing, I value thy comfort and thy wishes, more than my own. I will now hasten to inform the unfortunate Englishmen that they have obtained from thee at least one week's re-prieve from their awful sentence, and oh! may they at last obtain from thee their final deliverance."

She made no reply to him, for her soul despised his deception. She even feared to look at him, lest the indignation in her eyes should betray that she was aware of his falsehood. He, however, did not tarry long ,and very much to her satisfaction he bade her good morning, and retired.

The next day happened to be a gala day among the French, possibly on account of its being the birthday of some saint. Arrangements had been made for celebrating it by a grand fete in which the greater part of the soldiers were to engage.

It was planned that about two hundred and fifty

should proceed at mid-day to a rising ground, for years since called Grant's Hill, nearly half a mile to the eastward of the fort, where they should march and countermarch, fire artillery and musketry, eat a hearty dinner, get drunk, sing, swear and dance, until they were tired out, when they should return to the fort in the evening, tumble into their couches, and snore off their debauch like gay fellows.

Accordingly, about twelve o'clock nearly the entire garrison was put in readiness to march away to the scene of revelry.

Marie had just stationed herself at her window, to view the scene, when she beheld Tonnawingo entering the fortress-gate accompanied by an Indian chief, of a tall and majestic figure. DeVilliers had, at this moment, entered upon the parade-ground for the purpose of issuing orders. He halted as he perceived the prophet and the chief advancing toward him. After conversing a few minutes with the former, he made an obeisance to the latter, and calling a soldier, gave him some instructions, when the soldier led the way, followed by Tonnawingo and his companion, to the Governor's house.

In a short time the soldier returned to the ranks,

and in less than fifteen minutes more the drums and fife struck up a quick march, and the whole party proceeded to Grant's Hill.

Soon afterward Marie perceived the prophet alone, crossing the area before her window, going towards the gate. He suddenly looked back, and at a time when he was not noticed by any one in the yard, hastily saluted her, and continued on his way out of the fort.

She had rather expected a visit from the counselor of her youth, and her thoughts were dwelling upon his apparent sudden departure from the fort when Halmanna entered her room, and informed her that she had been commanded by the Mingo prophet to conduct a chief of the Piantia tribe into her apartments, but she was not to reveal his visit to any other person in the garrison.

"What can the chief want with me?" thought Marie. "But he can want nothing but good, since he comes by advice of Tonnawingo." She therefore bade the squaw to admit him. Her heart beat wildly as she heard his steps advancing. She rose to meet him, at the same time beckoning Halmanna, who was entering before him, to retire.

He was dressed in an elk-skin robe, the long skirts of which reached almost to his feet. This robe was closely wrapped around his figure to enable one to see the symmetry of his form and was secured at the waist by a broad belt handsomely ornamented. His cap was made of beaver skin, with a high plume formed of feathers of different dyes, which Marie had noticed as they glittered in the sun when he was crossing the parade ground in company with Tonnawingo. Tassels made of bright feathers hung down from each side of his cap over his cheeks, partially concealing his features. His feet and legs were covered with moccasins and leggins, in the usual fashion of the Indians.

. This chief, so majestic in his person and so splendid in his apparel, on entering the chamber of Marie, approached her evidently with much emotion, and to her great astonishment addressed her in English.

"How sorry I am, Miss Frasier," said he, "to find you a captive in such a place, and in the hands of such a man! But I forgot—you do not know me in this disguise. Alas! has the form of him, who loves you with an ardor beyond what man has ever felt for woman, so quickly faded from your mind, that the mere changing of the hue of his countenance has prevented you from recalling him?"

Marie still stood gazing upon the stately chieftain before her with a look of bewilderment.

"Must I name to you the man who loves you with a tenderness and devotion which he can feel for no other? Alas, must I name to you George Washington?"

"Oh, my friend!" cried she, alarmed for his safety, "friend of the oppressed! Hero of thy country! How is it that you have ventured upon this dangerous ground? I tremble lest you be discovered. The Indians would have no mercy upon you, and the French who possess this place are scarcely less barbarous."

"To rescue you, dear one," he replied, "I would not hesitate to enter here or elsewhere. What would I not venture for such a purpose? But, fear not, Miss Frasier, I come strong in the confidence of doing a good deed, and if I should fail doing my duty in the attempt to serve the fairest and most injured of my country's daughters, it shall be a fall just as glorious and honorable as in defense of my country's flag and honor."

"But, dear sir," said she, "was it not rash to risk that life on which, perhaps, the salvation of a nation depends, for the safety of a poor individual like me?"

."It is never rash to perform our duty," replied the hero; "no matter what may be the risk. Thou wert in distress. I was informed of it. That information was a call from heaven to hasten to thy rescue, and fear not but what that same high power will assist me in accomplishing it."

"But, sir, were you not afar off when I was seized? By what strange means could you hear of it, and by what miracle are you here, in the midst of terrors of Fort DuQuesne so soon, and uninjured?"

"I shall inform you," said he. "It was two evenings ago. I had just returned from the burial of General Braddock, when your brother Paddy entered my tent, and acquainted me in a few words, but though few, they were words that cut me to the heart.

"How to rescue you, was the absorbing thought of my mind. To think of force was in vain. The remnant of Virginians left by the late battle was too few to be thought of, and Dunbar is commander of the regulars. Personal efforts seemed the most feasible, and I resolved to try them. The prophet had desired me to meet him in his cavern with as little delay as possible. Therefore, furnishing Paddy with a horse, we set out, he leading the way.

"We arrived at the place of the Prophet's concealment last night. I at once approved of the plan he had formed, and as he had already provided all that was necessary for its execution, we set out from his cavern about two hours since, and thank Providence have thus far succeeded. The rest remains for the night to accomplish. All that I require of you is, that you will be courageous and brave in the part you will have to act.

"Tonnawingo provided a disguise for you as well as for me, and as soon as the people of the garrison have gone to rest, if we can only make our way out of the fort, he will be in waiting at no great distance, with horses ready to carry us to safety. This is the dress you are to assume." Here he drew forth from under his robe, the habiliments of a squaw.

"When the proper time arrives, you will throw these over your other garments, and thus disguised you will act as my interpreter with the sentinel, and solicit permission for me to pass out of the fort to worship, according to the custom of the chiefs of the Piantia tribe, beneath the red oak tree to which you are to guide me."

"Ah, but," said she, "if the sentinel refuses we shall be detected, and then—oh, sir, your destruction will be inevitable. It is better not to attempt it—it is, indeed, too dangerous. Why should you suffer along with me? Let me bear my own misfortunes alone!"

"Fear nothing, dearest Marie!" replied Washington. "If the sentinel should refuse, I shall have a remedy at hand."

"But, dear sir," said the trembling girl, "the govcruor may come and discover you here, and then you will be undone."

"He knows me only," said Washington, "as a chief of the Piantia tribe, come here by order of his nation, to form a treaty of alliance with the French. Tonnawingo is my interpreter, and the governor has agreed to give us an audience to-morrow morning after breakfast. In the meantime he has given orders that I shall be entertained in this house with all proper respect. The squaw Halmanna has received particular instructions from the prophet, which you no doubt are aware she will not be easily induced to disobey. As to the Governor finding me here, he will, you may be assured, return with too much noise and bustle, to take me by surprise. And cannot I readily resume the apartment allotted to me before he reaches the house? So, on the whole, Miss Frasier, I do not see that I stand in much danger of being detected."

"I shall pray to our Heavenly Father that you may not be detected," said she, "and I shall do all in my power to assist you."

After a few more words, Washington bade her adieu for a short while, and to lull suspicion as much as possible, and also with the view to learn as much as he could of the different parts of the fortification, so as to be serviceable in any future expedition against it, he walked openly and unmolested around the grounds during the afternoon, inspecting the entire defences of the fort.

Towards evening the revelers on Grant's Hill returned to the fort, as Washington predicted, with a great deal of noise and hilarity, many of them being almost overcome with intoxication. On their approach, Washington retired to his apartment, where he anxiously awaited the hour when he might again visit his beloved and conduct her to safety.

The governor had imbibed freely, yet not to such an extent as to benumb his senses. He longed to betake himself to the presence of his captive and there gloat upon her loveliness, but he had yet clearness of mind to know his present condition might militate against the favorable answer he was expecting from the maiden; therefore he resolved to plunge deeper into dissipation, in order to bury deep in the gulf of inebriation all remembrance of her charms, and after a lengthy snooze to hasten to her side and enjoy them. So far as the Piantia chief and the arrangements for the morrow were concerned, DeVilliers had entirely forgotten them, or, if he had not, he was in such a condition of mind as not to care for them.

Washington's apartment adjoined that in which the French officers now quaffed their wine, and roared and sung and swore, until the whole house rung with the noise. At length at a very late hour, he had the satisfaction to perceive, by the clamor growing less, that the potent effects of the grape were telling upon them. At length a dead silence succeeded the riotous and unbounded noise, and Washington justly concluded that the revelers had sunk into a drunken stupor akin to insensibility.

*

It was long past the hour of twelve o'clock. Everything in the governor's house was still and silent as death; even the squaw had retired to rest, and, excepting Washington and Marie, there was probably not a wakeful eye under its roof. Washington stole cautiously out of doors, in order to learn how matters stood in other parts of the garrison. All was as motionless and silent as his heart could wish. The measured tramp of the sentinel at the fortress-gate was all that could be heard. The clouds in the sky were heavy and the face of all nature was enveloped in a thick mantle of darkness.

Having learned that all things were favorable, the young hero hastened to the chamber of Marie. He found her waiting with impatience for his appearance.

"Miss Frasier," said he, "thank heaven, the hour is favorable. Haste, lovely maiden, throw on your ·disguise. Be of good courage, and let us leave this abode of wickedness and brutality. God will assuredly open the way for us."

A minute or two sufficed to make her ready. She caught Washington's arm. They descended the stairs slowly and without noise, and boldly walked across the area towards the gate.

"Hello, who comes there?" shouted the sentinel. ("You are my interpreter, remember," whispered Washington to Marie, "as I do not speak French.")

"We are friends," replied Marie, imitating as well as she could, the pronunciation and tone of a squaw.

"And where are you going, my friends, at this

hour?" asked the soldier. "Why does your companion remain dumb?"

"This is the Indian chief that came here to-day with the Mingo prophet," she replied. "He cannot speak your language, and on that account requested me to solicit your permission for him to pass out to worship the Great Spirit beneath the branches of the red oak, as all the chiefs of his tribe have been accustomed to do at this hour of the night, twice every moon, once in the full and once in the wane."

"And pray, Mrs. Squaw, what is your business with this chief? Let him go and worship where he pleases and as long as he pleases, but for you, my dame, I would advise you to go and get some sleep. He can worship devoutly enough without you, I dare say. Turn back, mistress, if you please." Here the sentinel rudely pushed her back from him, while she replied, in some affright:

"Ah, sir, my good soldier! I must indeed go with this chief. He is a stranger, and does not know where to find a red oak tree—I must guide him."

"Let him take the first tree he meets," said the sentinel. "It will answer the same purpose

whether it be oak or hickory.   But as for you, Mrs.
Squaw, I say you shall not pass here to-night."

"Sir," returned Marie, her agitation having so
much increased, that she forgot her assumed character of squaw, and to the surprise of the soldier,
addressed him in good French, "sir, this chief declares he will not go without me.   Oh! pray, do
now, my good friend, permit us both to pass, and
heaven will bless you!"

"Hello! who are you?" cried the sentinel.   "You
seem to be rather too christianized to be a squaw.
I believe there is something wrong about this.
The governor has a lady in his keeping.   I think I
must keep you both within the walls till we see who
you are.   It would cost a bullet in my heart, if I allowed that lady to escape.   Back to your quarters
this moment, or by St. Dennis, I shall call the
guard."

At this instant the sentinel seized Marie rudely
by the arm, and endeavored to separate her from
the chief, calling out loudly at the same time for the
assistance of the guard; but there was one French
soldier destined that night, to nevermore return to
the vine-clad hills of his native land, for he fell with
a dagger plunged to the hilt in his heart, by the
whole of Washington's tremendous force.

The brave man seized the trembling girl in his arms, for terror had rendered her unable to support herself, and hurried with his burden out of the fort to the spot where Tonnawingo, attended by Paddy Frasier, was waiting with horses. Marie was in a moment placed upon one of them, and her strength being sufficiently recovered to enable her to retain her seat, they hastily left the place, Tonnawingo leading the way and Washington and Paddy bringing up the rear.

The numerous shots they heard fired from different directions round the fort, soon told them that the garrison was alarmed, and that the next day there would in all probability be a hot pursuit made after the fair fugitive, who had thus escaped from the clutches of a tyrant.

About an hour and a half brought them to Tonnawingo's cavern, from whence Paddy removed the horses to a secluded dell at some distance, for the purpose of pasturage and concealment.

After entering the cavern and receiving some refreshments, Marie began to feel her equanimity of mind returning, and with this comfortable feeling came a realization of what the gallant Washington had done for her.

"Ah! Colonel Washington," said she, "to you I

owe more obligation and gratitude than I can ever express."

"Miss Frasier," he replied, "I am happy in the thought that a kind Providence has made me the humble instrument of preserving you from such misery. I have told you with what ardor and sincerity I love you, and how much my happiness depends upon a union with you, and although you have not thought proper to encourage my passion by one single whisper of its approval, yet I have persisted in loving you, and even looked forward with a fond hope to the day when you might show me some return."

"My brave, my generous protector!" cried she, "how can I answer you! Would that I could recompense your kindness, that I could show my gratitude, that I could prove to you how much I esteem your excellent qualities, and admire your noble character! But you ask what is not in my power to give." Here she checked herself for a moment, and then resumed: "Yes, I will entrust thee with the secret of my heart. I owe it to thee, alas, what do I not owe thee? But thou shalt have my confidence. Perhaps I have withheld it too long, and thereby encouraged thee to entertain hopes which I feel sorry to say must end in disappointment. My heart, dear, kind friend, is an-other's."

"Another's!" exclaimed Washington, stagger-ing back, and for a moment turning pale; but soon the violence of the shock, severe as it was, yielded to the energy of his heroic soul. A moment's strug-gle took place, then he recovered his composure, although not ease of mind.

"I am to blame, sir," she continued, "for not re-vealing this to you sooner; but I was too timid, or rather I feared the result of a rivalry between you and the youth who had gained my affections before I saw you; for, believe me, even when you first sought my heart it was not mine to give."

"Then Marie," said Washington, with great calmness, "I know my fate. It is to go through this life with my heart's fondest hopes blasted. But I shall try to be resigned, for I believe it is the will of Providence. My soul, I know, shall never sink under any calamity, since it does not now sink under this, which is the severest I can ever exper-ience. But, Miss Frasier, although I am denied the dearest wish of my heart, I still have a solici-tude and anxiety for your welfare, and the welfare of all your friends, for be it remembered that, from this date, neither you nor your friends will be longer safe in this locality. There should be a removal to Virginia or some more thickly settled region."

She was about to make reply, when the sound of footsteps hastily advancing along the dark passages of the cavern arrested their attention. In a moment Doctor Killbreath appeared, and without ceremony addressed Tonnawingo.

"Your petition has been granted, father; but it only prolongs Captain Addison's life till Monday at noon."

"Pray, what of Captain Addison!" exclaimed Marie. "Where is he? Oh, tell me—tell me! for heaven's sake, what is to become of my Charles!"

At the prophet's request, the doctor replied that he was a prisoner in the hands of the Indians, and that he had been respited from the flames till Monday. "But," continued the Doctor unwisely, "I fear his death will be inevitable, for it was with great reluctance they granted him the reprieve. The faggots were already—"

He said no more, for at that moment Marie fell lifeless to the floor. Washington hastened to her side and lifted her in his arms. She breathed not; she was deathly pale, and the only sign of animation was a slight quivering of the lips. Washington carried her to a couch to which **Tonnawingo** conducted him. The soul of the hero, as he bent over her and beheld the hand of death thus apparently upon her, felt the most acute sorrow he was ever doomed to experience.

The most judicious means within reach were applied for her recovery. At last, after a considerable time, she began to show signs of returning vitality, then suddenly she appeared to again relapse into a state of insensibility.

Doctor Killbreath now proposed to extract some blood from her arm, which was accordingly done, and shortly after, to their great relief, she regained the power of her suspended faculties.

Washington was now aware of the one who was the object of her affection. He had never dreamed of it before. "Captain Addison," thought he; "she loves him. Her happiness depends upon his welfare. Oh, that he may be saved from the cruel doom which now hangs over him, and she spared the heart's anguish which would come with the loss of his precious life."

He took Doctor Killbreath apart and conversed with him for some minutes, then returning to Marie, addressed her: "I must leave you hastily, Miss Frasier," said he. "I am glad to see that you

The Rose of the Wilderness

are recovering. Support your trial with fortitude; and may the God of heaven restore you to happiness. Farewell; my duty calls me elsewhere."

"Farewell, generous, noble Washington!" said she, holding out her hand to him. He could not refrain from pressing it, for the first time he had ever taken the liberty, to his lips, while she repeated, "Farewell, noble-hearted young man! I shall never forget thy kindness."

Washington took one look at her beautiful countenance. He dared not trust himself with a second, but hastened from the cavern in great agitation, followed by Doctor Killbreath.

CHAPTER XXVII.

OUT OF THE JAWS OF DEATH

THE reader will recollect that in the battle of July 9th, when Braddock's proud army was crushed, we made mention of Captain Addison slaying a savage in the act of leveling his rifle at Washington, only a few feet distant. That savage happened to be a hero of great repute in his tribe. Several of his brethren perceiving the fall of their favorite gave a blood curdling war whoop and rushed upon Addison, resolved to make him a prisoner at all hazards, in which they succeeded, as the attention of the British was at that time entirely taken up in protecting the body of their fallen General.

When the battle was over the Connewago chiefs, into whose hands he had fallen, held a short council; and fearing that if taken with the other captives to the fort, there might be a probability of the French by some means or other depriving them of their prisoner, they at once set out with Addison and another prisoner, a Virginian by name of Bartley, who also had slain a chief, and proceeded towards the head waters of Chartiers Creek, where they intended to hold a council, in order to condemn their victims to the flames in the regular manner.

During the march these two men were stripped almost naked and with their hands tied behind them they were driven along, being subjected all the while to the most barbarous treatment, sometimes being whipped with rods, and at other times goaded with sharp pointed sticks, until the blood trickled down their sides and backs.

At nightfall they halted upon the banks of a small stream, at least ten miles from the field of battle. Here they tied Addison and his fellow prisoner back to back, and then danced around them in a wild and frantic manner, each participant trying to inflict some species of torture upon the poor men lying helpless on the ground.

After thoroughly exhausting themselves they proceeded to prepare their supper, which consisted of a deer they had killed upon the way. They threw to Addison and his companion several large slices, but both men were too much overpowered with a sense of their situation to be anxious for food. We are unable to record the anguish that filled their hearts and minds that night as they lay stiffened and sore, thinking of their fate on the coming morrow. Charles Addison especially bemoaned his fate when he thought of his loved one, whom he had fondly anticipated meeting after the engagement.

Early the next morning the unhappy men were compelled to resume their journey for about ten miles further, when the Indians again halted at a place where five or six wigwams, inhabited by some squaws and children, were located.

Here a feast was again prepared for the party, and the prisoners were again offered nourishment, of which they partook but sparingly. When the feast was over, Taksuma assembled the warriors in council to condemn the prisoners, who were placed on the ground before them.

Captain Addison's sentence was the first to be passed, but previous to this Taksuma addressed the braves, extolling the virtues of the slain warrior, ending with the words: "Brothers, he has gone to Maneto. But we must avenge his death. Are ye for kindling the flames?"

The council signified its assent by a terrific yell that caused the prisoners to start and look wildly about them. Immediately six warriors were ordered to prepare wood for the occasion, which was to take place in three hours. The other prisoner was soon condemned, and both were to be bound to the same stake and to endure the flames together.

While the preparations were going on for the burning, the savages raised an exultant cry, for it seemed as if a third victim was rushing forward to satiate their vengeance. A white man was seen running in great haste, and as he drew nearer Addison shuddered when he recognized in the approaching stranger his former companion, Dr. Killbreath.

The Doctor, however, advanced fearlessly, and holding out the wampum of Tonnawingo, he informed the Indians that he was a messenger from the prophet, and was immediately received with a shout of welcome. He then advanced to the sachem Taksuma, who was pointed out to him, and delivered to him the Prophet's petition according to instructions.

Taksuma immediately called upon the warriors to be attentive.

"Listen, brothers," said he, "to the desire of Tonnawingo, the holy prophet of Maneto. The prisoner Addison is not prepared to die. Maneto will be offended if we deprive him of this man's

soul, which is not now fit to go into his presence.
Brothers, Tonnawingo the Prophet, who declares
the will of Maneto, asks that this man's life be
spared for a quarter of a moon longer, that his spirit

the Great Father who made it.   Brothers, I think
we dare not refuse, for the Prophet's words are the
words of the Great Maneto."

The greater number assented with a voice of applause, but there was a chief, brother to him who
was slain by Addison, who strongly objected to the
extension of time, but was finally over-ruled by
Taksuma.

Doctor Killbreath had now a short conversation
with Addison, and took the opportunity to inform
him of the state of affairs at the Frasier's.   Addison was overcome when he learned the fate of
Marie and sweat great drops of agony as he real-

heart stood so much in need of his services.

One of the chiefs now informed Taksuma that
the hour had come for the execution of the other
prisoner.   Orders were therefore given to have
him led forth to the stake.   This unfortunate man
took a last farewell of Addison.

"I go before you to an awful doom," said he.

"But this is, perhaps, a privilege, as my sufferings will be the sooner ended."

"Farewell, Bartley," said Addison.   His heart wrung with a grief and anguish unknown to his doomed companion.   "Your fate is indeed preferable to mine; seven days of such mental torture as I shall endure is of no trifling consideration.   May a kind Providence take you."

They then shook hands and Bartley moved toward the stake.   When within a few yards of his place of doom, he stopped suddenly, and beckoned to Doctor Killbreath.

"You are a stranger to me, sir," said the victim, "but you are a Christian and a Briton, and your face indicates that you have a feeling heart.   I think, therefore, you will not refuse to grant an easily performed request of a dying man."

"If in my power, I will assuredly grant it," replied the doctor, who felt much moved over Bartley's coming fate.

"You carry a rifle," observed Bartley, looking at that on which the doctor leaned.

"Yes, sir," returned the doctor.

"It is charged, I suppose," said the victim.

"It is, sir," was the reply.

"My heart would be thankful for its contents ere

these savages commence torturing me," observed Bartley.

The doctor mused for a moment on the propriety of granting this request, at length looking into the prisoner's entreating eyes, he could withstand the workings of compassion no longer and he resolved to gratify him let the consequences be what it would.

"You shall have them," said he.

"May heaven bless you," replied Bartley. "Farewell! I hope we shall meet there," pointing upward, and he marched to the place of execution with a firmness and a look upon his face that astonished his savage tormentors.

The victim was tied to the stake, the red-hot irons and flaming brands were prepared for torturing him, and a half-dozen savages waving these terrible implements in the air, were rushing forward to drive them into his flesh, when the report of a gun was heard.

Bartley's head fell forward on his breast and his body slipped down and hung limp by the bands that bound him.

Outraged at being thus disappointed in the gratification of their barbarous revenge, pursuit was made of the doctor, who had taken to flight. Killbreath was making a gallant dash for freedom, when unfortunately for him one of the Indian children, who had been playing around, appeared in his course, too late for him to turn aside. The result was, that the doctor in trying to avoid the child plouted forward and fell in a heap, with several of his pursuers, who were close by in the race, on top of him.

Great was the clamor, and they would have instantaneously inflicted upon him all the tortures they had intended for Bartley had not Taksuma interfered.

"Brothers," said he, "let us be cautious in this matter. This man is the messenger of Tonnawingo, the prophet of Maneto, and he bears the sacred wampum. True, he has deprived you of your victim and dared profanely to interfere with the customs of your fathers. But we can wait. I will send a swift messenger to the prophet. Brothers, Tonnawingo himself will condemn his action. Let us detain him as prisoner, until we hear from the prophet."

This was accordingly done. A messenger was dispatched to hunt up Tonnawingo, and our worthy friend, the Doctor, was placed in one of the wigwams under guard of one warrior, while on the

Out of the Jaws of Death

other side of the encampment three braves kept watch over Captain Addison.

The messenger sent in search of Tonnawingo, learning that he was likely to be found at Fort Du-Quesne, directed his course thither, and arrived at Grant's Hill at the time the French soldiers were holding their revels. Having no objections to partake of the good cheer that was politely offered him, and applying himself with vigor to the wines which were handed him profusely by the merry Frenchmen, who wished to amuse themselves with his antics, he soon forgot all about his errand, Doctor Killbreath, Taksuma, Tonnawingo and everything else, but the enjoyment of his drunken frolic, consequently failed entirely in performing his mission.

The Indians being short of provisions at the camp, formed into small bodies and went off in search of game, leaving none behind but squaws and those guarding Addison and the Doctor. On account of being able to speak Indian, the Doctor soon ingratiated himself into the good graces of the squaw who brought him food. He, by offering her little trinkets as presents, and saying sweet things to her, which was not averse to even an Indian squaw, who perhaps had never taken her first

lesson in the deceit of the world, won her confidence. She soon grew very fond of him, and on
the evening of the second day of his confinement
the Indian that watched over him growing drowsy,
requested the squaw to keep guard over the prisoner while he would enjoy a short sleep.

This was the Doctor's golden opportunity, and
he soon prevailed upon this tender-hearted female
to elope with him, promising her all sorts of fine
things, among others to make her his wife as soon
as they would reach a place of safety, assuring her at
the same time that his master Tonnawingo would
not fail to bless her and procure for her the forgiveness of her friends. This was listened to by this
simple child of nature, and believed, for she had
learned the lesson of love.

The Doctor's hands were accordingly loosened
and they set off through the forest, the Doctor taking care to carry with him the sentinel's rifle, and
without saying good-bye; consequently they were
not missed for hours after.

The Doctor and his dusky companion first
walked along arm in arm, then the desire to increase the distance from the camp induced the
Doctor to break into a run, the squaw for a while
keeping at his side. But the reader must remem-

ber that the Doctor was very anxious to reach home, and accordingly increased his speed, so much so that ere long he out-ran the squaw, and forgetting all his fair promises, and protestations of love, and regardless of her cries, her tears, and her upbraidings, he cruelly left her, all wearied and forlorn, amidst the clouds of night, in a dense forest, either to follow him at her leisure or retrace her way back to her wigwam a weary but wiser woman.

*   *   *   *   *

The last day of Charles Addison's reprieve from his impending doom had at length arrived, and any faint hopes that he might have harbored of a final deliverance were now scattered to the winds.

The brother of the slain chieftain and other Indians who had gone on a hunting excursion now returned to enjoy the burning of their prisoner.

Addison was tied to the fatal stake with such barbarous ferocity that the bands cut his flesh down to the bone. A blazing mass of pine knots had been lighted on one side, to apply to different parts of the fagots around him. He gazed up at the clear blue sky that he knew would soon be obscured by the blinding clouds of smoke, and as he did so he breathed a silent prayer for strength to bear his tortures like a man. Taksuma stood ready to give the order for applying the fire, when a loud huzza burst from the crest of the hill on the right, and a troop of cavalry thundered down the decline while a volley of musketry rung out on the air, which leveled to the earth six of the Indians, their chief Taksuma being among the number, while the rest scarcely waiting to see the extent of the slaughter fled in panic through the woods pursued by the troopers.

In a moment the sword of Washington had cut the bands of Addison and the hapless victim was rescued from the fire of savage vengeance, ere a single particle of it had touched his body.

"Ah, it is thou, matchless Washington!" cried Addison, embracing him as soon as his arms were loosened, "that hast restored me to liberty and life."

"My friend," replied Washington, "I shall do more; I shall restore you to happiness."

"What dost thou know, wonderful man," exclaimed Addison, "that can make me happy?"

"I do know," said Washington, "that if anything on earth should tend to make a man happy it would be the heart and hand of a lovely, pure and true woman, like Marie Frasier."

"Thou hast truly spoken, most noble Washington," cried Addison, with a wild mixture of hope, joy and surprise, "but where—oh, where is she? Has she been delivered out of the clutches of that monster?"

"Thanks be to a kind Providence," said Washington, "she is at present safe from all danger, and you are now safe also, and may you both long continue so."

"And it is to you, Colonel, that they both owe it," said Doctor Killbreath, coming forward and shaking Addison warmly by the hand; "I wish you joy from my soul, Captain, both for a long life and much enjoyment. You may thank Colonel Washington for both. He plunged into the heart of Fort DuQuesne, and rescued my sister-in-law, taking her out of the Governor's house apparently under their very noses. But, gentlemen, had we not better look into these wigwams for something to eat, for after such a long and rapid ride I confess I feel as though a venison steak would not taste bad."

"I propose first," observed Washington, "that we find some clothing for Mr. Addison; then we can look about us for some food."

"My portmanteau," said the Doctor, "will furnish him as good a captain's uniform as is in the army. I knew the captain would be sadly in need

of a suit, so while you were assembling the men at
Great Meadows, I provided for him the necessary
wearing apparel."

So saying, the Doctor led forward his horse, un-
strapped his portmanteau, and produced a captain's
uniform of the provincial service, complete in all
its parts, which, although it did not fit Addison in
every particular, answered for present purposes,
and by the forethought of Washington an extra
charger had been brought along so that when they
were ready to travel, a good horse was at his command.

On exploring the wigwams not a man, woman
or child was to be found; but they found what was
more to be desired, namely, a nice lot of venison,
the result of the hunt indulged in by the Indians
within the past few days, and in addition to this
they found a preparation of Indian corn called
hominy.

The troopers, after scouring the woods for miles,
and putting to death all unfortunate braves who fell
in their way, but sparing the squaws and children,
had by this time all returned.

After caring for their horses they secured some
refreshments for themselves and rested for an hour
or so, for they had ridden long and hard. They then

prepared for the return journey, which in due time brought them in the neighborhood of Frasier's, some hours after darkness had set in.   Dr. Kill-breath conducted Washington's party to a secluded dell where they were safe from observation, while Washington and Captain Addison made their way to the residence of Gilbert Frasier.   It is unnecessary to say they met with a hearty reception.

Addison was informed that Marie had been under the protection of Tonnawingo ever since her rescue from Fort DuQuesne, as it was not deemed wise to have her return to her home for some time, as in all probability the French would visit the house repeatedly.   They had already paid several visits, and a thorough search had been made, but without securing the coveted prize.   It was also deemed best for neither Addison nor Washington to run the risk of capture by the French, which might happen if they tarried long at Gilbert Frasier's residence, but the hour was late and although Addison was wild to see his beloved Marie, he was forced to pass the night under Gilbert Frasier's roof.   He, being worn and jaded from the loss of so much sleep, for since the day of the battle his eyes had known scarcely a moment's slumber, quickly sank into a deep refreshing sleep, which lasted until morning.

With the coming of a new day he was anxious to be off for Tonnawingo's cavern, but he was doomed to bear a half hour's provoking delay, for Dame Frasier would by no means permit her esteemed guests to leave without their breakfast, and in this Washington seemed willing to indulge her.

At length all obstacles being removed, Washington and Addison set out for the cavern. Marie Frasier had suffered much anxiety in regard to the fate of her lover, but Tonnawingo had informed her that he had learned through Paddy that Washington had passed that way with an armed body of men to try to effect his rescue.

The prophet did not feel positive that the rescuing party might arrive in time, though he did not communicate his fears to the maiden, but rather sought to cheer and console her, bidding her to have hope and trust in the Great Father bringing her lover back to her unharmed.

They were occupied at breakfast, conversing about the misfortunes of Charles Addison, when they heard the sound of persons entering the cavern.

"My child, I have a presentiment that there is good news approaching," said Tonnawingo.

"Heaven grant it!" she replied, "but I am so ac-

Oh, joy! joy! it is so!" and the next moment her head was on Addison's bosom, with his arms thrown lovingly around her.

"My dearest Marie!" he exclaimed, "we have at last met, and I trust that never, never again while we live shall we part!"

Washington and the prophet wisely withdrew to the entrance of the cavern to talk over matters, and we will also do the same, leaving the two happy, re-united lovers to uninterrupted enjoyment. After some lapse of time the prophet and Washington returned. As they drew near, Marie, holding the hand of her lover, advanced toward Washington. Her eyes were liquid with tears, and her bosom rose and fell, showing deep emotion. The young hero met her gaze calmly. Suddenly she addressed him. "My deliverer, and thine!" she exclaimed, looking for a moment at Charles. Then gazing up into his calm face, she burst forth: "Oh, Washington, Washington! thou incomparable man! What can I say? What can we both say, to express the gratitude we feel toward thee? How can we ever thank thee for the great interest thou hast shown in our behalf?"

To say that Washington stood before this, the one woman of all the world to him, unmoved, would be to charge him with stoicism. Far from it; he was moved, but he had a soul superior to his feelings, and capable of controlling every impulse that stood in the way of duty.

His voice was calm, and his eyes full of admiration as they always were when they looked upon this beautiful "Rose of the Wilderness." He took the hand extended to him, saying: "Miss Frasier, no thanks are needed; the witnessing of your joy on this occasion is ample recompense for all my exertions.

"But let me say that it will recompense me still more to witness the confirmation of your felicity. Captain Addison," said he, "give me your hand." Here for a moment he appeared much affected, and a sudden paleness passed over his face. It continued, however, but an instant; the cloud passed swiftly away and all the firmness, nobleness and dignity of America's pride shone full and bright from his countenance.

"My friend," said he to Charles, "the lady by your side, I have loved as I shall never love another. But you possessed her heart before she possessed mine. You have become necessary to her happiness, in competition with which I value my own as nothing; and I know well that she is necessary to yours. Take her, my friend; make her your own, and may you long be happy together."

"My best of friends!" cried Addison, his voice full of tremor, with the force of his admiration for his deliverer's magnanimity. "You, you alone of all men could be capable of this. I shall not attempt to express my gratitude. But a heart like yours can easily imagine it. You say you loved my Marie. I once for a moment suspected it, but I was secure in her fidelity, and cast all suspicion from me, as it was an injustice to her. I estimate highly the sacrifice you have made, of hopes which must have accompanied a love for her, and highly should I appreciate myself, could I imitate you in the magnanimous sacrifice of such hopes at the shrine of friendship and duty."

Then turning to Marie, he bowed low, saying, "Fairest of all Eve's daughters, your Charles acknowledges his inferiority to this man."

"And well may you acknowledge it," replied Marie, proud of her lover's admiration of the hero, and she rejoiced that he did not hesitate to acknowledge him his superior in virtue and greatness of mind.

Washington now again addressed Marie. "Miss Frasier," said he, "there is yet one thing remaining to set my mind at ease respecting you, that is your removal from this region, where you are now beset with innumerable perils. I entreat you to leave it with the man of your choice. Give him a legal right to protect you in the midst of society. I shall then be assured of your safety."

"Sir," she replied, "Captain Addison is aware of my only objection to his wishes. If it were removed I should not advance any other."

"She refers to the consent of my father," explained Addison, turning to Washington.

"Marie," said her lover, "surely you would not put an objection like this in the balance against your safety and my happiness? Believe me, my father is not so mercenary that he would expect his son's bride to bring with her a dower of gold. He has too much liberality as a man, and tenderness as a father for that."

"But his consent, at all events, should first be procured," returned Marie. "You are his only son; he has no doubt been an indulgent father; and it would be giving him ground for offence if you should take such an important and irretrievable step without his approbation, nay without his knowledge."

"Miss Frasier," said Washington, addressing her, "I have heard what you have said, and such sentiments become you; they are just such as I would expect from one of your delicacy of feeling and strong sense of propriety. I am glad that there are no other obstacles in the way of a union of hearts and hands, and I am happy indeed to be able to remove a part of them at least. You know me too well not to suppose that I shall be the obliged one, if you accept the offer I am about to make. It has pleased a kind Providence to bestow upon me a fortune amounting to more than the average man's share. A portion of this I can easily, and shall gladly, devote to the promotion of a purpose so dear to my heart as your welfare and safety; and I must beg leave to make over to you deeds of such possession as shall reconcile your future father-in-law to your alliance with his family. I trust—"

Here Tonnawingo, who had been a silent listener, hastily interrupted Washington. "Stay, my son; where will thy generosity end? Permit me to speak. You have plunged into the midst of her enemies and snatched her from ruin. You have relinquished in favor of a rival the most fondly cherished wishes of your soul to promote her happiness, and now you would bestow your fortune upon her.

"But hear me, glorious man! and believe me, she does not require this last instance of your generosity. Marie is rich—as rich in worldly goods as the father of any man, whom she may take as her husband, should wish her to be. She is my heiress. She is my daughter! my only child." Then turning to the maiden, he cried: "Oh, Marie, Marie! I am no Indian—I am a son of Europe. Oh, embrace me, for I am thy father!"

The subtle mesmerism of the heart and mind act quickly. "My father! Can it be?" she exclaimed, as she threw her arms around him and rested her head on his bosom. "My father! Oh, joy, joy! How long I have felt it so, yet knew it not. For I never have felt forlorn in thy presence. Heaven has indeed been kind to me this day, in restoring to me both a lover and a father. But why did you not reveal your identity sooner?"

"Hear me, my daughter," replied Tonnawingo, again clasping her to his heart. "In your infancy I saw you happy and safe and I was content. It

was the same until within a few days.   I would not,
therefore, disturb the serenity of your life, for I
could see nothing gained by doing so.   I had acquired an influence for good over the children of
the forest, in the character of a prophet among
them, and which I believed in an emergency might
be useful to you and your friends.   But I perceive
that my sphere of usefulness must, for the good of
yourself and others, be changed.

"We must leave this wilderness, for the repose
and safety which once blessed it has fled.   We
must mix in the ranks of society, my daughter.   It
may be new to you and perhaps irksome to me.
But it will afford you safety and an opportunity of
performing duties both useful to yourself and
others, which cannot be performed here.

"My friends," said he, to Washington and Addison, "I perceive that you are surprised at this dis-
covery, and no doubt feel a curiosity, since you find
I am not an Indian, to know what I really am.
You shall be satisfied, but at present I shall be able
to give you but a brief sketch of my history.   At
a more convenient season I may, perhaps, enter
more minutely into its details."

CHAPTER XXVIII.

STORY OF THE PROPHET

I AM," said Tonnawingo, "by birth a Scotch-
man, and a Highlander. My European
name is Mackintosh, a name in which my
zeal for an unfortunate cause has been given
a place in the history of Britain. At the death of
Queen Anne, the friends of the house of Stuart,
among whom I was the most zealous, for I was then
young, enthusiastic and rash, resolved to re-estab-
lish their exiled representative upon the throne of
his ancestor.

"The Earl of Mar was the first to raise the stand-
ard of insurrection in the Highlands, and I was the
first to join him with the whole strength of my clan,
consisting of nearly a thousand men, as brave as
ever wore tartan. We soon heard that the Earl of
Derwentwater, and some others, had raised forces in
England to support the same cause, and were on
the way to join us in the Lowlands of Scotland. I
was detached at the head of twenty-five hundred
men to meet them in the Lothians. We crossed the

Firth of Forth and I immediately invested Leith, which surrendered; but, the Duke of Argyle hastily throwing himself into Edinburg with a large body of men, I did not enter the capital.

"I proceeded without delay to join our English confederates who waited for us at Kelso. Being now nearly six thousand strong, we resolved to push boldly into England, and strike a sudden blow at the Hanoverian government. Fortune smiled upon us until we reached Preston, when she ceased forever to encourage our cause. We were besieged by a powerful army and compelled to surrender. All who were in authority were carried to London and imprisoned in Newgate. About this time, the Earl of Mar was defeated in the Highlands, and the friends of the Stuarts gave up the contest.

"We had made an heroic attempt to place our monarch in power, but paid dear for it. Almost every week brought the intelligence of the execution of some of my confederates. I who had been much more active than many who had suffered, had therefore no reason to expect any mercy. For several months there was no word of my trial. But finally I was notified that it would take place in a few days. Several of my fellow prisoners, also under charge of high treason, were to be tried at the same time. The evening previous to the sitting of the court, six of us planned an escape. We soon overpowered the jailor and his assistants, and in a moment were lost in the crowds that daily throng the streets of London.

"My Scottish property was now lost to me, for I was declared an outlaw. I was soon in beggary, but making my way to France, the interests of the Stuarts was sufficient to produce me a captain's commission in the French army. In a few years I was sent as lieutenant-colonel of a regiment to Canada. My superior, disliking the climate, soon returned to Europe and I was made colonel. In this capacity I was stationed for a number of years at a fort near the Falls of Niagara. Here I had an opportunity of becoming thoroughly acquainted with the manners and customs of the Indians, and learning much of their language.

"I also found opportunity to improve my fortune by purchasing their furs and sending them to Quebec for sale, where I formed connections with mercantile houses for that purpose. I had never yet thought of entering upon the marriage state, but upon one of my visits to Quebec I beheld one to whose graces, accomplishments and virtues I felt delighted to pay homage. She was the daughter of the commander of the Quebec garrison, and only, a few years from France.

"I became entirely captivated with her charms, and although I was then thirty-seven and she but twenty-two, and while she had refused a score of suitors, I had the happiness to win her heart and the promise of her hand. Her father at first objected to consenting to our union, for he was both' wealthy and proud, but at last yielded.

"We were somewhat more than a year married, when by Monsieur d' Anville (my father-in-law) interceding in my behalf, I was appointed to command the garrison at New Orleans. I was instructed to proceed there by way of the Ohio river, to take notes of the most eligible situations for a chain of forts the French government contemplated erecting from the St. Lawrence to the Gulf of Mexico. I set out with my wife, who was attended by, one female servant. We were accompanied by six officers who had also received appointments at New Orleans.

We advanced on our journey, receiving assurances of friendship from the different tribes on our route, and without meeting with any accident until we reached the mouth of French Creek, when unfortunately our servant girl sickened and died, and

my wife was left without any female attendant.
We felt this accident all the more acutely as Marie,
which was my wife's name, was then in delicate
health, expecting soon to possess maternal felicity.

"We were in quite a dilemma, for there was no
possibility of replacing our deceased servant with
another from Canada before the expected event.
By mere accident we heard of an Indian Queen residing on the banks of the Monongahela not far
from our intended route, whose society, it was
thought, would be the most suitable the country
could afford to my wife under present circumstances. We accordingly hastened hither and Alliquippa received us with great friendship and kindness.

"My wife, however, still felt so uncomfortable
over the prospect before her, with only savage
women to attend her, that it was with great joy we
learned of some white women being in the vicinity,
who had been carried off by a party of Indians from
the English settlements in Pennsylvania. I hastened to the Catanyan village, where the captives
were to be found, and had the good fortune to prevent our friend Gilbert Frasier and his family from
being sent to Canada.

"Gilbert, assisted by the Indians, soon erected a

commodious habitation, to which my wife, Marie, was conveyed. During her illness Mrs. Frasier waited upon her with the tenderness of a mother. But, alas! the termination was a death-blow to my happiness. My child, she whom I now clasp to my bosom as my only offspring, came into this life as her mother, my wife, the joy of my heart, departed it—she was dead.

"I can scarcely bear yet to think of the agony I felt when informed of my misfortune. I shall not try to recall it. My senses became bewildered. I have at this day a vague remembrance of having fled from the fatal spot, with a view of hastening to Canada, and from thence to Europe. Here comes a blank, for my reason had become suspended.

"Months later I found myself among a band of Iroquois Indians, almost upon the borders of the Mississippi river. As my intellect became restored, I was seized with an intense desire to see my child, to revisit the spot where I had in my frenzy left her. The Iroquois had found me almost naked, and being astonished at the wildness of my manner, they had thought proper to preserve my life under the impression that the hand of Maneto was upon me.

"As this opinion of the savages had probably

saved my life, I believed it best, when I recovered, not to have them think differently. At length my desire to inquire after my child became so strong that I seized an opportunity to leave the Iroquois with that in view. I had traveled eastward as far as the Scioto river when a party of the Mingoes seized me. I, however, understood their language and could converse with them. My appearance was that of an Indian, for I had in order to avoid danger used the dyes of the Iroquois in coloring my skin. I also had resolved that if I fell in with any tribes on my way to pass off as a favored one of Maneto. I therefore represented myself to the Mingoes as originally belonging to a remote nation of Canadian Indians, and that I frequently had visions that instructed me to go towards the Ohio in order to teach the tribes there the will of the Great Father.

They received my statement and besought me tc be adopted into their tribe, that they might have favor with Maneto in their battles with the Ottawas. I accepted and became by adoption the son of their great sachem, Fallakamsha, who had lost a son in the late fight with the Ottawas, and therefore received me, with all the usual formalities, in his stead. I continued the spiritual adviser of affairs in the Mingo tribe for some time and was looked upon with great reverence, and my fame as the prophet of Maneto spread to other tribes.

"My desire to learn of my child still urged me to proceed eastward. I informed Fallakamsha that a vision had ordered me to this section and requested his consent to my journey. He at once gave it, saying a sachem of the Mingoes should never oppose the revelations of the Great Spirit.

"I came to Frasier's. Neither he nor his family knew me. I saw my child, I kissed it and pronounced a blessing on its head. I returned to the Mingoes for the purpose of extending my influence among the Indian nations. I have succeeded to my entire gratification. In a few months I again visited my daughter, and in order to be near her and watch over her I sought and found this retreat. I became her instructor, and I felt happier than ever I thought I could be.

"I was useful in the preservation of life for I held a power over the savages, and ofttimes saved lives that otherwise would have perished in the flames. In order to maintain my hold upon the Indians, I was obliged to perform apparent miracles. In this I was greatly assisted by the shrewdness and sagacity of Paddy Frasier, who alone was in the secret of my being a European, although he knew nothing further of my history.

"Paddy's ability to pass as an Indian, enabled me to learn of their doings, which seemed a mystery to them. It was by his management that the eagle which was sacrificed instead of Doctor Killbreath at Fort Le-Boeuf, was found so opportunely wedged between the rocks at Lake Erie, and numberless other instances."

At this juncture Tonnawingo, or rather the Laird of Mackintosh, was interrupted by a sudden entrance of Paddy Frasier, with the information that a party of French soldiers, commanded by DeVilliers himself, had just surrounded his father's house, threatening to burn it, and carry the whole family prisoners to Fort DuQuesne, in order to compel them by torture to reveal the place of Marie's concealment.

CHAPTER XXIX.

CONCLUSION

A NEW trial had come to Marie, and one which would have overpowered her, had not the strong, assuring voice of Washington at once fell on her ears. "Fear not for your friends, Miss Frasier. I have at hand a force sufficient to rescue them from these miscreants. My life for their safety. Father, sustain and comfort thy daughter until we return. And, now, Captain Addison, you and Paddy Frasier follow me."

They hastened to the dingle where his troops were encamped. Their gallant horses swept the ground at full speed, and in a few minutes the French party were attacked almost by surprise. The greater number of them fled at the first onset, and those who stood to give battle only stood to be slain or captured.

DeVilliers, who was a good soldier, did all in his power to form his men, and prevent their flight. He mounted his horse, and galloped from place to place after his flying soldiers.   His exertions were however, soon ended, for Paddy Frasier having pointed him out to Captain Addison, who had never to his knowledge seen the man, now snatched a broad sword from a trooper he rode hastily upon the Frenchman.   So intense was the bitterness of his rage against him, that as he came upon his enemy unawares, his first impulse was to strike him to the earth, but he checked his blow.

"Turn, execrable villain!" shouted he, "and defend thyself."

"Who the devil are you?" cried DeVilliers, as he turned towards his antagonist.

"I am the sworn avenger of Marie Frasier's wrongs," said Addison.

"By heaven, then, you are no doubt her lover, I suppose, and the destroyer of my bliss!   Have at thee, then!"

He hastily fired his pistol at Addison's breast, but the horse of the latter at that moment throwing up his head received the bullet in his brain, and fell to the earth, while Addison's sword plunged into the neck of DeVillier's horse, which fell at the same time.

In another instant the combatants were on their feet with their drawn swords in their hands, frowning terribly at each other in all the desperation of deadly rage. They spoke not, but sprung at once to the attack. The sparks flew from their weapons, the motions of which were so rapid as to be scarcely discernible to the eye. The sound of their clashing blades rung loudly on the air. By a sudden stroke Addison dashed his opponent's sword aside as he was coming with a violent thrust toward him, and the next instant ran his own through DeVillier's neck, who fell to the earth groaning and pouring forth a torrent of blood which soon terminated his life.

"So perish all the foes to virtue and the oppressors of innocence!" cried Addison. "Marie is avenged; I at length have done something to deserve her."

By this time the French had either all fled or surrendered. Gilbert and Denny Frasier, as well as Doctor Killbreath, having refused to divulge the whereabouts of Marie, had been bound, for the purpose of being carried prisoners to the fort, were now set at liberty, and Nora and her mother soon recovered from the fright into which such violent proceedings had thrown them.

The family now hailed Washington as their deliverer; and the ardor with which Gilbert and his wife expressed their gratitude to God and to him as God's instrument for their preservation, sunk deeply into his heart; and he resolved if possible to persuade them to at once leave a region where they could no longer enjoy safety, and make their residence in the future within the pale of civilization and law.

Gilbert assented, saying, "Ye hae wi' the blessing o' God, delivered us frae the house o' bondage, an' wherefore should we no submit to be guided by you to the land o' safety? For I trow we canna bide langer here; let us gang whar' we can, unless we want to fa' into the pit o' destruction."

Washington wished to proceed without more delay to the Great Meadows, lest the French should come out with their whole force from Fort Du-Quesne to attack him. Addison hastened to the cavern to inform Marie and her father of their victory, and the consent with which all their friends had given to accompany the troops to the inhabited country, and that the whole party would soon be in readiness to set out for Dunbar's camp.

When Gilbert was informed that Tonnawingo was the father of Marie, he manifested great joy.

"Noo, Nellie, wife," said he, "did I no tell ye

mony a time that the prophet could na' be an Indian?

"He had aye owre muckle sense, an' gifts sae like a Christian, that he could na' ha' talked better on what was richt an' wrang, an' what was true religion, gin he had been born at Maughrygowan."

"An' I aye had a notion," replied Nellie, "that the French officer, wha was sae affectionate to his wife, wad yin day or ither come back to look after his dochter."

With the help of Washington's men, Gilbert made his arrangements for his departure, and soon had his horses equipped for transporting his family and effects from the home where he had enjoyed so many years of peace and comfort, but which could not now be assured to him by remaining.

The Laird of Mackintosh, or, if the reader please, Tonnawingo, soon arrived with his lovely daughter at Frasier's, and the whole party immediately set off for the camp at the Great Meadows, where they arrived in less than two days. The day following, Dunbar struck his tents, and the army, accompanied by our friends, proceeded by easy stages to the Fort at Wills Creek. It was agreed upon by our party that they should remain here until a messenger, who was at once dispatched from Addison to his father, acquainting him with the state of affairs, his prospects, and his wishes, could return with an answer.

Although the army proceeded to move onward after a few days' rest, Washington gratified his friends by remaining with them, until he could witness the ceremony that would secure them to each other forever.

To keep the readers no longer in suspense as to the fate of these two faithful lovers, we hasten to relate that as soon as old Mr. Addison received his son's letter, he set off at once for Wills Creek, in order that he might behold the charmer of the wilderness, who had so entirely captivated his boy's heart as to cause him to reject some of the most desirable alliances in Philadelphia. The first sight of Marie removed his surprise at his son's preference, and the first conversation with her so delighted him that he took an early opportunity to remark to Charles:

"It is no wonder, my son, that you became enamored of this sweet blossom of the forest, and felt such an ardent desire to plant her in your bosom, and carry her to more congenial air. I really give you credit for waiting with so much patience, during the slow process of obtaining my consent."

"I deserve no credit on that account," replied Charles. "Whatever is due to my forbearance in not making her prematurely my own, and depending on your indulgence afterwards for pardon, is altogether owing to her. Even at this moment her consent to make me happy depends upon yours."

"Then mine you shall have without another moment's delay," said his father. "Secure her as speedily as you can, my son, for I really believe she is a prize, and may heaven make you long happy together."

The son was filled with delight on hearing the words of his father, and in his exuberance of joy could not avoid kissing the old gentleman's hand with rapture.

"I shall sign and seal articles as to money matters with the Laird this very night," remarked the elder Addison.

"As you please for that, father," returned Charles with indifference, for he at that moment cared not a farthing for money matters.

In a few days the great object of all the desires of Charles Addison was obtained. His Marie was made his own, and the great heart of Washington took comfort in beholding safety and happiness secured to her for whose fate he had long felt such a warm and tender solicitude. The next day he bade the bridal pair an affectionate farewell and returned to Mount Vernon.

Addison and his bride, together with his father and the rest of their friends, made their way to Philadelphia. His mother was delighted with her daughter-in-law.

This sweet "Rose of the Wilderness" was soon introduced into the first society in her country's capital, which she continued long to adorn. Her father resided, cheerful and happy, under the same roof with her, enjoying, amidst the luxury of ease and literary recreation, the satisfaction of her presence, as well as that of her children. He remained an honored partaker of all their joys for about twelve years, when he took his departure to join his long-lamented wife in the regions of immortality.

With respect to Gilbert Frasier, the kindly intentions of Washington to bestow upon him a comfortable home in Virginia met with disappointment.

"I thank you, Colonel," said he, when the illustrious protector of himself and family, before he left them at Wills Creek, made a most generous proposal to Gilbert. "I thank you frae the bottom o' my heart, for your kindness to me and mine, baith for what ye hae done, an' what ye noo offer to do. But I canna gang to bide in Virginia, whar' there are sae mony blacks, the very sicht of whom wad mak' my flesh creep to look at. But I'm as thankfu' as gin I took your offer, an' I'll no forget, while my soul an' body hang thegither, to pray for blessings on your gude heart, as aften an' sincerely as I'll pray for my own bairns."

Charles soon discovered that Gilbert's wishes were inclined towards his former residence on the Juniata. He purchased it for him, and the kind-hearted protectors of Marie's infancy removed to one of the most attractive spots along the banks of that picturesque stream, where their declining years were spent in as much contentment of mind as they would have enjoyed at Maughrygowan itself.

Their son Denny married shortly after their moving to this place, which he continued to culti-vate for his father until the death of the old people. It is said that he then sold this farm (Paddy having relinquished all claim to it), and returned to the old home in the wilderness. He remained there until the days of the Revolution, when he was stricken down in some marauding attack of the Indians.

The place at Turtle Creek has long been known

as "Frasier's Field," though many changes hav̱ taken place, and the then wild forest has become the site of populous cities.

The future fortunes of Doctor Killbreath afford nothing worth relating. He settled down to the practice of his profession in some locality near his father-in-law's residence, where it is probable some of his descendants may be found in the same profession at this day.

No doubt the reader has observed that our friend Peter McFall has not figured on the scene since the attack on his master at the battle of Fort Necessity. The irrepressible Peter after his return to Philadelphia, fell in with the captain of a sailing vessel and, with the assistance of a few friendly glasses of grog, he was induced to take a trip across the Atlantic. Peter accordingly set sail for a port on the other side, but had no sooner landed than he was picked up and hurried on board one of the king's ships, without his consent being asked. At length Peter obtained a release from the king's service and made his way back to Philadelphia, and was taken again into his master's service, when one day while hurrying down Market street, who should he run across but the fair Esther Gist. We have not time to relate the courtship, although it was brief, but, as Peter himself expressed it afterwards, he put the question so nately that the fair Esther could not say no, and they were soon "swately" married and lived very comfortably together to a good old age, remaining all the while in the service of Charles Addison.

As to Paddy Frasier, about the time that his father returned to the farm upon the Juniata, he established himself as a merchant in the town of Carlisle. He continued in this business very prosperously, until the winter of 1776 when, hearing of the distress under which the army of his favorite Washington labored, he abandoned his merchandise business, collected a goodly company of gallant spirits like himself, well skilled in the use of the rifle, and putting himself at their head, he joined the hero of his country, about three days before the daring attack upon Trenton, which turned the scale of war in favor of the friends of freedom. He continued with Washington, taking part in all the successes and reverses that followed, many times receiving the kindest words of praise from his beloved commander for his valiant services.

He finally fell, bravely performing his duty, at the very close of the great struggle. It was at the battle of Yorktown. He was leading his men in the storming of a British redoubt. A ball struck him in the breast. He staggered and fell. His men would have stopped to carry him off the field, but waving his hand, he cried:

"Never mind me, my lads! Push on! You know your duty." When the redoubt was taken they found him dead, with the captured colors of a Hessian regiment tightly grasped in his hands.

The commander he so much loved stood by his grave, when after the battle they gave him a soldier's burial, and passed upon the inanimate remains of the companion of other days that had endured with him the cold and hardships of that journey from Le-Boeuf, this eulogium: "There never was a braver man nor a truer friend."

Charles Addison, although he loved his Marie dearly, yet he loved the cause of freedom also, and she, brave woman as she was, girded her husband's sword upon him and bade him go and fight for the liberties of the oppressed, assuring him that her prayers would follow him.

He proved, throughout the long eight years of struggle, a faithful officer under the command of his beloved general, and when the close of the confliet came, he returned with honor and renown to the bosom of his family and was spared to enjoy their companionship for many years.

Lightning Source UK Ltd.
Milton Keynes UK
UKHW021932180219
337529UK00011B/853/P